MW01100581

How would You Choose To go?

The Killing Farm

Jay Newman

09/10/2023

FriesenPress

One Printers Way
Altona, MB R0G 0B0
Canada

www.friesenpress.com

Copyright © 2022 by Jay Newman
First Edition — 2022

The novel, Cold Vengeance and the character Agent Aloysius X.L. Pendergast appear courtesy of Douglas Preston and Lincoln Child. It was released on August 2, 2011, by Grand Central Publishing.

The Killing farm is a work of fiction. Names, characters, places, and incidents either are the product of the author's imagination or are used fictitiously. Any resemblance to actual persons, living or dead, events, or locales is entirely coincidental.

Eye image courtesy of Lynette Newman

ISBN
978-1-03-916311-9 (Hardcover)
978-1-03-916310-2 (Paperback)
978-1-03-916312-6 (eBook)

1. FICTION, THRILLERS, MEDICAL

Distributed to the trade by The Ingram Book Company

AUTHOR'S NOTE

Back in December of 2000, two directors sat back stage of the Pumphouse Theatre in Calgary discussing the pros and cons of legalization, and thus The Killing Farm was born. What began as a rough outline for a comedic stage play, eventually evolved into the first draft of a psychological thriller. For many years the manuscript was left untouched but not forgotten, until an epiphany brought the story back to life.

The author would like to thank George Smith for his counterpoint in the conversation that inspired the theme of the novel. Jessica Legacy for reading the earlier drafts and offering her valuable, professional advice that helped form the finished product. His brother, Cory Newman, his father, Bill Newman and his mother, Diane LeBlanc for supporting and believing in him all these years. Douglas Preston and Lincoln Child for creating such a complex and brilliant character as Agent A.X.L. Pendergast, as mentioned in the story. Most importantly, he could not have succeeded without the love and support from his wife, Lynette and children, Malia and Liam.

THANK YOU

PROLOGUE

It had been three hours since the sun had set, which left a slight chill in the night air. The only illumination in the area, to break the monotony of darkness, came from a series of flood light standards placed at thirty-metre intervals along the deserted roadway. With the nearest light source obstructed by a two-story brick-and-mortar building, the contractor, dressed head to toe in black, had a clear view of the North Star, located at the end of the Little Dipper's handle. Crouched between a green recycling dumpster and the cool brick wall of the building, he turned away from the night sky and opened a large blue duffel bag, which rested at his feet. Within the main compartment of the bag, he found a M40A3 bolt-action sniper's rifle. An old weapon, but it was in fine condition as its owner took immaculate care of it. He then pulled a high magnitude, laser-assisted scope from a side compartment of the same bag and slid it across the rails on top of the rifle. A faint click indicated the scope was in place. Next, he reached into an inside pocket of his jacket, removed a long black cylinder and screwed the well-oiled threads of the suppressor on to the end of the barrel. Finally, he pulled an object from his deep jacket pocket and loaded the single 7.62mm round into the chamber. He snapped the bolt closed with a distinct click.

The contractor concealed the empty duffel bag under the dumpster, slung the strap of the firearm over his shoulder and crept out of hiding. He was unlikely to encounter anyone walking about at this time of night, but he remained cautious. Crouched low in the shadows, he crept around to the back of the building. An iron rung fire escape ladder, affixed to the brick, reached upwards to the rooftop, with an opening on to a grated metal landing at the second story.

He stepped out of the shadow and began his climb up the cold rungs of the ladder. He paused at the second floor long enough to peer through a window that faced the fire escape. A red glow from two exit signs within revealed an unoccupied floor space, devoid of any furnishings. He continued his ascent to the top, threw his legs over the raised ledge, and landed upon the gravel-covered roof. Crouched low, protected by the short stub walls surrounding the rooftop, he moved toward the southeast corner of the building. Each step crunched on the loose gravel. Nevertheless, with the floor below unoccupied, he was unconcerned that his noisy movements would draw any unwanted attention.

He pulled a photograph from his jacket pocket and studied it. The subject was a white male with short-cropped brown hair and a hooked nose. He sat alone at table in a crowded restaurant. Judging by the candid nature of the setting, the subject likely had no knowledge of the photographer's presence. On the back of the photo the words, "*Stuart Dawson, level two, fourth window from the left.*" were written in neat block letters. He returned the photo to his pocket and turned his attention across a courtyard to the two-story building a hundred and twenty yards in the distance. On the second floor, the fourth window from the left flickered with a dim blue light.

He pulled the M40 off his shoulder and unfolded the eight-inch swivel type bipod attached to its bottom. He swept away a small area of the gravel, knelt down on the rooftop and placed the bipod's feet on the raised ledge. With the buttstock rested between his shoulder and cheek, he peered through the scope in search of the window in question.

As the sight panned across the building, it passed three darkened windows before the target's apartment came into view. It was dark within the apartment, but for the television set that flickered with images of a groundskeeper on a putting green, filling a gopher hole with plastic explosives. A large sofa, illuminated by the glow of the screen, faced the television. Though the occupant wasn't visible from the contractor's current vantage point, just a smooth two-foot slide to the right, brought a head and shoulders into view. He adjusted the focus on the scope and centered the cross hairs on the back of the target's head. Without a clear identification of the man in his sights, he moved the cross hairs to the wall on the target's right. With a flick of his finger on a button on top of the scope, a beam of laser light briefly placed a small red dot on the wall. The mark turned to see what he had caught in his periphery, and with that, the contractor had a clear view of the target's profile. He was a perfect match to the photograph he had in his pocket.

The target's attention returned to *Caddyshack*, and the cross hairs once again found the sweet spot on the back of his head. The contractor relaxed and took slow deep breaths. By the third breath, he held it, and remained still. The cross hairs never wavered as his finger tightened on the trigger.

"Bang", he whispered through clenched teeth.

There was no shot. No flash from the muzzle, or recoil from the rifle. He hadn't even bothered to take off the safety catch. It was too soon; the contract was for the following day. The last time he completed a contract ahead of schedule there were consequences. He was reprimanded by his employer, who threatened to turn him over to the authorities should it occur again. As it was, he had lost privileges, which had cost him a number of lucrative contracts.

He lined up the shot once more for good measure, this time he placed a tiny red dot on the base of the target's skull. With a crestfallen sigh, he snapped the shutter down on the scope, ejected the round from the chamber and slid the cartridge into his pocket. He looked down at the cold metal firearm in his hands then back at the target's window. A fiendish grin began to form upon his lips. A mere twenty-four hour wait, and he would be back in that very spot, with the target once again in his sights. Twenty-four hours is an insignificant amount of time in the grand scheme of things.

Sweeping the disturbed gravel back over the bald spot, the contractor re-slung the rifle over his shoulder then made his way back to the ladder, where he would descend from the rooftop and return to the reality of his daily routine.

CHAPTER ONE

The early-morning sun hung just above the horizon, casting its light upon the endless fields of yellow canola. As far as the eye could see, the yellow blossoms stretched out across the central Saskatchewan prairie. Their long stalks bent over in the breeze, as a rusty blue pick-up truck sped down the long gravel road that bisected two of the fields.

Behind the wheel, Captain Travis Hawkins steered the old truck through familiar territory as he had done every month for the past two years. Having finished his week off in Regina; he was enroute to his posting at a government run facility, commonly known as the Farm. Due to the nature of the facility, General Roger McGovern, the Chief of Defence Staff, handpicked Hawkins to run the facility as a military operation. The authorities had decided that military presence was necessary since the compound housed some of the most dangerous, as well as the most desperate people in the country.

Hawkins winced in pain as a wheel hit a pothole in the road. The sudden jolt had sent his back into spasm, the result of a condition called Degenerative Disk Disease. A condition that altered the course of his career and landed him in his current post.

Travis had been an army brat all his life. His father was career army, so he had grown up on Canadian Forces Bases. When Travis was sixteen, the Hawkins family was stationed in Halifax and his father volunteered to go overseas to Vietnam to join forces with the US troops against the Vietcong. Canada held an antiwar policy in the matter of South Asia, but that didn't stop more than thirty-thousand Canadians from volunteering. He never returned home.

At eighteen, Travis himself enlisted. He worked hard; he trained even harder to become the best soldier he could possibly be. Everything appeared to come so easy for the then Private Hawkins. In the beginning, he was one of the fastest on the training courses, and most accurate on the shooting ranges. In the trades, he worked hard to receive his Journeyman Mechanic Certificate. By this time, he was in command of his own platoon, training the new generations of soldiers to use their strengths and excel in their fields. Hawkins regularly commanded some of the strongest troops in the country. He was an officer that every C.O. dreamed of, and he never once left the borders of Canada to join the overseas conflicts. His own body had betrayed him.

He received his diagnosis at the Sunnybrook Veteran's Hospital in Toronto, where his superiors offered him an alternative to a full medical discharge. Just a few days after his release from the hospital, he accepted his new assignment from General McGovern, one that came with a rank promotion. Captain Hawkins was to spend the remainder of his military career pushing papers at a secluded compound in the back roads of the prairies, fifteen kilometres east of the nearest hamlet of Penzance.

Hawkins shouted out another profanity as the front wheel of his pick-up struck another pothole. Fortunately, for him, he wouldn't have to endure the pain and torture for much longer. As the truck crested a small hill, the seventy-acre fenced compound stretched out in the distance before him. A few buildings were visible from that point on the road, and one could clearly make out a large, wooded area on the far side of the compound, a racetrack in its foreground, and a massive water tower high above the trees. Watch posts were located on each of the four corners of the fence-line, and a short driveway broke off from the main road, which lead up to the front gate.

Hawkins drove the old Ford up towards the gate where a security guard, Sergeant Walter Morgan, stepped out from the small Guardhouse. He brought the rusted pickup to a stop before the automatic gate, and Sergeant Morgan stepped up to the truck with the salute. Hawkins rolled down his window and handed him his security pass. Morgan reached for the pass and pulled a small hand scanner from his belt. The device chimed, indicating an approved barcode and the gate began to move to the side with a clatter of metal upon metal.

Good morning, sir." Morgan said. "I trust you had an enjoyable week."

"Walter," Hawkins smiled, "there are a total of fourteen military personnel assigned to this compound, and the other twenty-six are civilians. We have been working together nearly two years now, I think it would be safe for you to ignore protocol occasionally and call me Travis."

"Sir, yes sir," Came the stern reply.

Hawkins chuckled while he returned the pass to his jacket pocket, "Carry on Sargent. Have a good day."

Thumb to palm, Morgan then snapped his flat hand sharp to his temple with a smile. "Catch ya later, Travis."

"Atta boy." Hawkins laughed. He waved as he accelerated the truck through the front gate.

**

The entrance foyer of the administration building was comfortable and inviting. The walls were painted neutral beige, and a large bay window allowed an abundance of natural light to fill the space. Several comfortable brown leather chairs occupied the room. Some skirted the perimeter, while others formed a cluster at one end, surrounding a small coffee table. Above these chairs, a large landscape painting spanned most of the length of the wall. A reception window filled the wall directly across from the entrance, with a door on either side. Beyond the window was a small room, large enough for a single desk complete with a computer and security monitors, a chair and two large filing cabinets.

Captain Hawkins pulled his pass-card out of his jacket and swiped it in the small card reader to the left of the further most door. He heard a faint click as the indicator LED on the reader turned green. He pulled the door open and stepped through, into the corridor beyond, before the door swung closed behind him. More nature themed paintings filled the spaces between the six doors that lined this stretch of hallway. Hawkins passed by the first door on his left, that lead to a storage closet, and entered the door on the right, across from a co-ed washroom. The door opened into a small kitchenette where the delicious aroma of fresh coffee filled the room. Aside from the pot of steaming coffee on the counter, the room appeared to be uninhabited. The kitchenette was modest, with only a small fridge and a counter, equipped with a coffee maker, a toaster, and a sink. A small microwave filled a cubbyhole in the upper cabinets. A single round table surrounded by four chairs occupied the centre of the room, and an empty coat rack stood next to the door. Since they served all the meals in the cafeteria, located in the residence building next door, they utilized this room mostly for coffee breaks.

Hawkins pulled his personal coffee mug from the cupboard, poured himself a cup of coffee, and dropped three cubes of sugar in after it. Without bothering to stir, he picked up his mug, exited the break room, and continued down to the end of the hall. The farthest wall of the corridor contained a heavy metal door, behind which was a small holding cell. Lastly, there was a door on either side of the corridor next to the holding cell, Valerie's office on the left, his own on the right.

As he reached for the door to his office, he glanced back towards the opposing office. His posture stiffened as he turned to knock upon Valerie's door, but he stopped before his knuckles struck wood. He wasn't sure what stopped him from knocking. They had been stationed together at the Farm since the beginning. In fact, she was the one who had debriefed him in the hospital.

He found himself drawn to her instantly, not only by her natural beauty, but also by the evident compassion that she radiated the moment she entered the examination room. She immediately took an interest in his condition, and his thoughts regarding his future in the Armed Forces. Valerie was so patient and understanding that, in the beginning, Travis mistakenly thought that she was there to assess his own mental state. Instead, he soon learned that she was only there as a formality to meet her new colleague and to update him on the nature of his next assignment. Since that day, their relationship continued to grow stronger. He cherished every moment he spent with her, and was under the impression that she felt the same.

Still, he hesitated. He would speak with Valerie soon enough, however insecurities toward his feelings for his colleague outweighed his instinct to check in with her at that moment. Captain Hawkins pulled his hand away from the doctor's office door and turned back to his own. With a capitulating sigh, he exited the corridor into the familiar comfort of his office.

The office of Captain Travis Hawkins was the picture of neatness. A clean modular desk, which housed his personal computer, occupied a third of the room. Next to the monitor was an office telephone and a large blotter, which covered the surface of the desk. Aside from that, not a single sheet of paper, or so much as a pencil or paper clip was visible. He kept everything else hidden away in drawers or in the large filing cabinet next to the window. On the wall above the desk, he displayed three framed commendations, one for excellence in sharpshooting, his journeyman mechanic certificate, and one for duty, above and beyond. A photo of his brother's family also hung on the wall next to his awards. His brother Chris, a former NHL player for the Winnipeg Jets, looked a lot like Travis—save his nose that was broken too many times to count. His wife Angela was a lovely woman, a schoolteacher, and together they had two handsome boys, who currently attended The University of Toronto.

Hawkins moved around his desk and placed his coffee mug on a rubber coaster that he pulled from his top drawer. He booted up his computer and leaned back, sipping his hot beverage while he waited. Upon entering his password, a cheerful electronic chime indicated that he had received e-mail. He grabbed hold of the mouse, clicked on the mail icon, and opened the program on the screen. There were fifteen new messages. The first thing he did was delete all the annoying social media notifications. That left seven. Three messages were from insurance companies of past clients, one from his physiotherapist, and two from his mother. The most recent message was from Valerie, with the subject line, "Re: New Clients- files attached."

The clients came from referrals from other psychiatrists and physicians around the country. Referrals to the Farm occurred only after they had tried and failed all other avenues.

Hawkins opened the file and read its contents.

Subject-Ian McDonald- male- age 47
Lethbridge, Alberta
Impetus-Terminal cancer

Subject-Catherine Dean- female- age 24
Toronto, Ontario
Impetus-Depression/Anxiety

Both subjects due to arrive tomorrow, evaluation to
commence Wednesday a.m.
From the office of Dr. Valerie Lough

The remainder of the document gave a brief background of each of the two subjects, complete with photographs and their psychiatric evaluations. Hawkins read each report thoroughly before he selected the print icon and clicked okay. The muffled sound of the printer emanated from one of the cabinets below his desk. He pulled open the door that concealed the device and slid out a hard copy of the document. Pulling a gel ink pen from his drawer, he wrote a name beside the first of the two subjects, Kevin Richards. He paused and considered the second client. He minimized the email program and selected an icon labeled Personnel, then clicked on the name *Carlisle, S.* He scanned through the file that contained a series of notes and several photographs. A grin formed upon his face, and he jotted down the name Stephen Carlisle next to the second subject before he replaced the pen in the drawer. Hawkins then picked up the telephone receiver, dialed a five-digit number and waited to hear the voice of Dr. Lough.

"Good morning, Travis. How was your week off?"

CHAPTER TWO

Something was wrong. The contractor dressed head to toe in black, muttered profanities under his breath while he peered through his scope at the target's window. He took his eyes off the sight long enough to check his watch, 11:09PM.

"Shit."

He continued to scan the room under ten time's magnification. The TV flickered, casting a soft glow in the room, as it did the previous evening. This time however, the couch before it remained vacant. The contractor panned to the right until the next window came into view. Light glowed within; however, with the aluminum blinds drawn he was unable to see what was happening inside.

"Come on ya bastard," he grumbled to himself, "what the hell are you doing?"

No sooner than he asked the question, did the bathroom light go black. He returned his view to the sitting room just in time to see his quarry return and sit down in front of a commercial where a shirtless, well-toned black man peddled men's deodorant.

With relief, he brought the cross hairs around to find his mark. At that distance, with virtually no wind, the shot would be an easy one. He saw no need for the laser sight as he felt it would take away from the challenge. With a deep breath, he released the safety catch and slowly let the air from his lungs. As he expelled the last of his air, he held it. He was so still, there wasn't so much as a twitch. There was no movement but for his right forefinger as it tightened around the trigger. He timed his moment between two heartbeats and squeezed. He simultaneously felt the recoil of the rifle along with the muffled sound of exploding gunpowder. Through the scope, he watched as the bullet penetrated the glass and entered the back of the target's head, which sent a crimson spray out the front. The inertia of the shot forced the body forward and the target slumped down out of sight before the sofa. A heavy coating of blood and matter obscured any images displayed on the television set at that moment.

The contractor lowered the rifle and gazed upon the target's perforated window. He shook his head in disappointment.

"Nothing." he muttered under his breath.

Despite his best efforts, he simply could not recreate the thrill and gratification of his first kill. Two years' worth of contracts, dozens of methods. Men, women; it didn't seem to matter. Nothing could compare to the first time that he watched the life drain from her eyes. He had to be patient. It had to happen eventually. All it would take is the right contract.

His shoulders slouched forward while he returned the catch to the safety position, ejected the shell casing, and dropped it into his pocket. He was just in the process of removing the suppressor from the end of the rifle when the sound of crunching gravel behind him took him by surprise. The contractor spun around and raised the unloaded rifle, to find a single figure that stood on the rooftop between him and the escape ladder. It was none other than the man who had hired him.

"Did your shot hit its mark?" The new arrival asked. His face gave no indication of his feelings on the matter.

"Of course," the contractor replied. "It was a clean shot through the back of his skull. He is quite dead."

"Very good. I trust you will clean my rifle before you return it to me in the morning."

"No problem."

With a nod, Captain Hawkins went to leave, but stopped and turned back at the last moment. "Oh yes, one more thing Mr. Carlisle. We have two new clients due to arrive in the morning; I have assigned one of them, a woman, to you. That will give you a week to prepare."

Another contract? Already? He had never received two contracts back-to-back. It was unheard of. Still, an opportunity like this, there had to be a reason for it, and a woman to boot. Who was he to turn it down?

"Thank you, Captain." His posture straightened significantly." I'll be ready.

"Excellent. I will brief you in full once you've met with Dr. Lough." With nothing left to say on the subject, Captain Hawkins gave a subtle nod, returned to the ladder, disappeared over the ledge, and left the contractor, Stephen Carlisle, alone with his thoughts.

**

Captain Travis Hawkins entered the suite ahead of the Medical Examiner, Dr. Elaine Wall, as he did on every such occasion. An eerie glow flickered in the living area of the otherwise darkened apartment, and a conversation between two unseen men could be heard from the same location. Before he turned on the light, Hawkins drew his sidearm and moved deeper into the room toward the source of the glow. He discovered the television remained on; the flickering images obscured by a generous coat of dried blood. The distinctive voice of Jimmy Fallon, one of the voices he had heard upon entering, confirmed that Hawkins was indeed alone in the apartment.

"All clear," he called out behind him, and with a subtle click, the single fixture bathed the room in artificial light.

It took but a moment for Hawkins to confirm what Mr. Carlisle had told him. The room itself was in quite a state. Red spatter stained the television and wall opposite the sofa, and the body of his latest client, Mr. Dawson, laid out on the floor; face down in a pool of his own blood. A small red hole entered the back of his head. Hawkins rolled his former client on to his back, to reveal a significant exit wound from his forehead.

Hawkins looked up at the window beyond the sofa. A small hole penetrated the centre of the glass. He moved closer to get a better look. His reflection in the window put the small calibre hole at the centre of his chest, a web of fine cracks fanned out from the void. He closed one eye and peered outside through the hole. Across the courtyard, in the darkness beyond, he was able to make out the shape of the building where he had left Mr. Carlisle just minutes earlier.

By the time he had completed his survey, the Medical Examiner had completed her own initial assessment of the late Mr. Dawson.

"Liver temp suggests that he has been dead less than thirty minutes, consistent with your report," the ME explained. "Cause of death, as you've likely guessed, is a GSW to the head, rear entry, through and through."

Hawkins turned his attention back to the bloodstained wall. Under closer examination, he discovered the projectile lodged in the drywall. He reached into his pocket and removed two objects, a pocketknife and a small brown envelope. He held the open envelope below the intrusion, used the pocketknife to dig out the bullet and allowed gravity to drop it down into the pouch. He then sealed the evidence and slipped both it and the knife back into his jacket.

"Seems pretty cut and dry to me," Dr. Wall concluded as she retrieved a stretcher from the corridor. "Give me a hand with this, would you?"

Captain Hawkins helped the doctor lift the body onto the stretcher and left her to her task as he exited the client's apartment. He crossed the hall, went down the stairs and into the front foyer where the business centre was located. The three desks, each topped with a personal computer and printer were all vacant.

He sat at the desk furthest from the door and switched on the computer. It took a painfully long time to load, but eventually a login screen appeared. He typed in his username, twhawkins, followed by his eight-character password, which appeared as a row of asterisks. Following the Government of Canada welcome screen, came his profile page. There, he selected the email icon on the top right and began drafting a letter to d.richaud@guardianinsurance.ca, with a carbon copy to V. Lough. In the subject line, he typed ECE-80096.

Ethical Controlled Euthanasia for client ECE-80096,
Mr. Stuart L. Dawson of Brandon Manitoba, has been
approved by Dr. Valerie Lough and carried out by contract under the supervision of Captain Travis Hawkins of
the Federal Assisted Release Measure. Mr. Dawson has
met all requirements under Article 86, thereby granting
us beneficiary status.

From the offices of
Captain Travis Hawkins CO
F.A.R.M.

CHAPTER THREE

Day One

"We are live in three, two, one..."

"Good evening. I am currently standing before the front gates of the infamous facility known as *the Farm*, the final instalment of Prime Minister Ron Alexander's three-part Canadian Diversification Strategy. During his campaign, the Prime Minister stood firm on a platform stating that Canada needed to grow with the times, and was quoted as saying, "How can any nation flourish in the twenty first century with early twentieth century ideals?

Alexander's plan for socio-economic growth, that began nearly six years ago with the legalization of marijuana and other recreational drugs, soon moved on to include government operated brothels. With the enormous success of the first two instalments, Canada's leaders implemented the most controversial policy to date: the legalization of compassionate euthanasia.

Then, three years ago, on June thirteenth, the act became law. The act addressed a number of concerns raised by the decision, that included the extension of the criminal law protection to both physician and non-physician health care providers involved in the lawful provision of assisted euthanasia. The act also introduced important safeguards for those patients, who may be vulnerable; that are reflected in the government policy.

Now, two years after the inaugural contract, the Killing Farm is once again in the news. Shortly after eleven PM last evening, an act of compassionate euthanasia was carried out within this facility in respect to their most recent client, a man we all know as the former Premier of Manitoba, Stuart Dawson.

Dawson's name monopolized the headlines a number of years back when he contracted AIDS while on vacation in South Africa. Little is known regarding the circumstances that lead to his exposure but since the diagnosis, he had led a public battle against the disease. Last night he lost that battle.

We will have the full story on the life of Manitoba's former Premier this evening at six.

This is Laura Bentley with CBC news in Penzance, Saskatchewan."

**

Hawkins lost count of how many times he had yawned, since returning to his office just ten minutes earlier. He took another sip of his hot coffee and massaged the sleep from his tired eyes. He'd been up late the previous evening putting the final touches on the paperwork for Stuart Dawson's contract, and now, with the early morning sun just beginning to shine through his small office window, he sat before his desk to prepare himself for the arrival of the two new clients. He had a pair of file folders laid out upon his desk before him. A green folder, labelled *ECE-80097 – Ian Montgomery*, and another, a light blue folder read *ECE–80098 – Catherine Dean*. He completed his perusal of the first and slid the folder behind the other, when there was a knock at his door.

"Come." He called out to the unseen visitor.

The door swung open, and Hawkins straightened as his colleague Dr. Valerie Lough stood there, framed in the doorway. She looked lovely, with her dark curly hair pulled up off her neck, and her light green, almond shaped eyes, which sparkled in the light when she smiled in greeting. Hawkins' cheeks began to flush, and as he averted his gaze from the beautiful doctor, he invited her in.

"Good morning, Val, please sit down."

Despite the fact their offices were opposite one another, they had seen little of each other the previous day. Dr. Lough was busy for most of the day in final evaluations with Mr. Dawson, and Hawkins himself was neck deep in bureaucratic paperwork in preparation for the final act. This was more or less the first time they had an opportunity to sit down together since his return to the compound.

Valerie wore a white button up shirt and a black knee-length pencil skirt slit partway up the side. As she entered, Hawkins caught a brief glimpse of her thigh as she took long deliberate strides into the office. She carried three folders, one red and two white, in with her. She placed them down on the desk before she sat in the chair across from him.

"Good morning, Travis, how are you doing today?"

Valerie was a kind-hearted woman with a genuine concern for others' well-being. When she asked, "How are you," It wasn't just small talk; she genuinely wanted to know. Perhaps it was an attitude that came with her job, but more than likely it was just the kind of person she was. The two of them continued with small talk for a few moments, to catch up on the past week, before they got down to business. The mood took on a professional tone when Valerie opened the red folder and pulled out a thick stack of papers, stapled together in the upper left corner.

"Okay, so here's your copy of the final document for Mr. Dawson that includes my psychological report and your e-mail to Guardian Insurance." She pulled out a second copy and slid it towards him, "this one is for command. Please sign the flagged pages."

They had gone through the same motions for scores of previous clients; in fact, it often appeared as though they had built the entire facility around protocol. Hawkins signed each page and initialed the appropriate sections next to where Valerie had placed her mark. Once he had completed the document, Valerie slid the papers back into the folder and shuffled it to the back of the pile. She opened the first white file and scanned its contents. "Okay then, we should we begin with Mr. Ian Montgomery. 47 years old from Lethbridge, Alberta. Diagnosed with Chondrosarcoma, a type of bone cancer, seven years ago. Treated at the Tom Baker Cancer Centre in Calgary, with little signs of improvement. Since that time, the cancer has spread to his other organs, and the doctors are not optimistic. He stated that he didn't wish to spend the remainder of his life in pain and was referred to us by his oncologist."

While Dr. Lough read, Hawkins opened the same file on his computer, and followed along with her. "It is no wonder why he's losing his fight.

No children, wife died in the Fort McMurray fires while visiting her sister. This guy has had it rough."

"I have scheduled a meeting with him this afternoon. Hopefully I can get him talking." Valerie flipped the page. You have assigned Kevin Richards. Why?"

"He has already chosen his exit strategy."

She licked her finger and continued to flip through until she found the exit survey and began to read aloud. "I wish to go the same way my wife did."

"He wants to die in a fire."

Her brow furrowed, "How awful. He and I are going to have plenty to talk about. So, what are you suggesting? Douse him with gasoline and light a match?" Her tone was drenched in sarcasm.

"No, that's not how his wife died."

"I haven't had an opportunity to read the official report yet."

"According to the reports, the fire started at the rear of the home where the master bedroom was located. The sister-in-law, the husband and their baby were inside. It appears that Katsumi Montgomery opened the bedroom door from the corridor, which triggered a backdraft. None of the family made it out of the house."

Valerie thought back to the extensive file she had on Kevin Richards back in her office, "And Richards was convicted of murder by arson."

"That's right; however, section C383.8 forbids torture or prolonged agonizing deaths. Slowly burning in a fire would fall under that category. That's where Richards comes in."

"How so?"

Hawkins leaned back in his chair, "Richards was a firefighter back at CFB Halifax. He and his CO had a massive disagreement, after which they busted Richards down from Sergeant to Master Corporal. During the night, Richards broke into the captain's home, and started a fire. Coincidentally enough, it turns out, he had rigged a backdraft, so when the captain opened the door, he was engulfed in flame."

Valerie considered his explanation. "Yes, I know the story, and it's a horrible coincidence. In other words, you want Richards to rig a backdraft for Mr. Montgomery. How do you propose we will accomplish that? We can't set fire to his apartment."

"Oh, gawd no. I figured I would use the two modular trailers we have in storage. We can put them together and build a small apartment inside. All we need are two rooms separated by a door, and Richards can take care of the rest. The trailers are metal, so we shouldn't have much trouble keeping the fire contained, but just to be safe, I will set it up in the centre of the track away from everything else." Hawkins added, "I don't think this one will give us too much trouble."

"All right Travis," she acquiesced, "it fits the parameters, and the *how* is your department, but I want a hazard risk assessment before I sign off on it.

"So noted."

"I, on the other hand, have to try and talk him out of it. Although, because this is a terminal case, the attempt may be moot."

"Do your best Val. You can save me some paperwork." Hawkins then moved on to the next order of business. "Now, what about the other one? Catherine Dean."

Dr. Lough closed the Montgomery file and slid out the third and final folder. She opened the file and read the background report. "Catherine Dean, twenty-four, of Toronto, Ontario. Never completed high school. At the age of seventeen, she got pregnant, and lost the baby. The father's whereabouts are unknown. Catherine jumped from job to job before she was recruited by *The Butterfly Garden*."

Hawkins interrupted, "What's that?"

"Toronto's answer to part two of Prime Minister Alexander's diversification strategy."

Hawkins nodded in understanding before Valerie continued.

"Ms. Dean was employed at the Garden until late last year when she attempted to take her own life. The hospital's resident psychiatrist, Dr. Mansfield, tried for months to break down her walls with little success, and eventually granted her request for a recommendation to the Farm."

She turned to the next page, "And for this you chose Stephen Carlisle again. He just completed a contract last night. I haven't even had a chance to conduct his post-contract evaluation, and you want to toss him another one?"

"Let me show you something." Hawkins returned to his computer, minimized the Catherine Dean file, and clicked open a new one. He then selected a thumbnail that opened a photograph on the screen. Hawkins then turned the monitor so Valerie could see it.

"Is that Lisa Carlisle?" She asked with some uncertainty.

"That's right," Hawkins replied, "Carlisle's ex-wife. His first kill."

"The similarities between her and Ms. Dean are remarkable. They could pass for sisters."

"I checked into it and couldn't find any relation to speak of, but there is most definitely a resemblance. Stephen is one of our best contractors and he often jumps at the opportunity for the more interesting jobs. He has always said that none of the kills since his first has been as gratifying. Who knows, this could be it."

Dr. Lough considered the implications, "I'm not so certain I approve of this idea. The man shows signs of a true misogynist. I see potential for disaster."

"I'm not convinced that he really *hates* women, I think he just gets off on killing them. That said, if you were right about him, then he would have no moral qualms about completing the contract. If you are wrong, however, consider this: Catherine resembles Carlisle's ex-wife, so I would wager that there could be an attraction. Stephen himself is a handsome and charismatic man who could draw her attention as well. If we can lead them in that direction, maybe plant the suggestion, they could hopefully convince each other to leave the Farm alive. This could be an opportunity to save them both."

Valerie furrowed her brow, chewing gently on her tongue, "Seems like quite a stretch to me. How long did it take you to think of that one?"

"I'm trying to appeal to your romantic side." Travis smiled.

"This is your call, but I will tell you right now, this idea has me concerned. I do not want this to turn into an episode. We will introduce them and watch them. If everything goes as smooth as you think it will, you are free to continue, but I hold the veto card here, so first sign of a psychotic break and I pull the plug."

"Sir, yes sir," Hawkins said with playful sarcasm.

"Smart-ass." Valerie continued as she closed the file, "Mr. Montgomery is due to arrive within the hour, and we can greet him together. Ms. Dean's flight is delayed and will arrive this afternoon, but I will be tied up after one o'clock with Mr. Carlisle."

"I'll take care of her. Will you have time for lunch?" he asked, "My treat."

It was Valerie's turn to be playful, "Let me check my schedule and I will get back to you." She finished with a wink, as she rose and moved towards the door.

"I'll give you a shout when Mr. Montgomery arrives," Hawkins called out to her, perhaps a bit too eager.

"Thanks." She stepped out of the room and shut the door behind her.

Hawkins opened his e-mail program once again and started a new message. In the recipient field, he entered scarlisle@thefarm.gv.ca, and then typed the word *meeting* in the subject line. In the body of the email, he wrote:

Carlisle

My office, 1100 hrs.

Hawkins

ECE-80001

Her eyes circled the room, examining each of the faces of her loved ones, as Margaret's eyes were her last remaining body part that she had control over. Soon, she wouldn't have that either. Even though her thoughts, desires and memories remained intact, she could not so much as lift a finger. She thought about it, she tried, but the signal just could not get through.

Amyotrophic Lateral Sclerosis, the doctors had told her. It didn't seem possible; ALS was a man's disease. It didn't affect women. At least that was what she always believed, never giving it a second thought. Of course, she had heard of it, at least by its nickname, Lou Gehrig's disease, but it was something that happened to other people, to men. It certainly couldn't happen to her.

Nevertheless, it did happen to her, and it took hold quickly. She passed it off at first as signs of old age. Weakened joints in her legs and ankles, was common in women in their seventies, so she thought. Her legs got tired when she went for her evening walks through the neigh-bourhood, but there was no pain, so she wasn't terribly concerned. She simply shortened her route. Soon, however, the route couldn't get any shorter. It was a struggle just to stand.

By this point, she had already seen her doctor, who then referred her to a neurologist. She had expected them to tell her that it was some form of arthritis. Something that the doctors could treat with medications. The results were heart wrenching.

It wasn't long before she had completely lost the use of her legs and she had to push herself around in a wheelchair. Soon after that, her husband had to push her chair, as her arms were too weak. The ALS society provided her with an electric wheelchair that she could control by blowing into a tube. Then catheters and colostomy bags violated her body, when she lost control of her basic body functions. For a while, her family had to feed her, until she lost the ability to swallow, and the doctors started her on feeding tubes and intravenous.

Margaret lost all hope the day she lost her voice. The day she could no longer tell her husband and children how much she loved them, how much she appreciated everything they had done for her. She received a pair of glasses with a laser pointer that allowed her to type out messages on a computer screen, but it wasn't the same. She had lost her last remaining ability to contribute to her family.

Two years, three months, and eleven days. That's all it took, from diagnosis to that moment when she lay in an unfamiliar bed in an unfamiliar room on the Farm, looking into the saddened eyes of her husband and children.

Movement in her peripheral brought her focus around to the doctor who was holding her arm, while he inserted a fresh IV port into her vein. Margaret's muscle didn't flinch; in fact, she didn't even feel the pinch of the long needle piercing her skin. It was as if it was someone else's arm.

Captain Hawkins and Dr. Lough had arrived, and the captain was explaining to her the final instructions, and the rest of the bullshit required to cover their asses. She wasn't listening though. All she cared about at that moment was her husband, her daughter, and her son. They tried to keep their expressions strong for her, but she could see the despair in their eyes; their unconditional love for her, and she was comforted with the knowledge that she was still able to convey the same message back to them through her own eyes.

"Margaret Verwey, do you fully understand everything as I have just explained to you?"

One blink for, "yes".

Hawkins began speaking again, but she didn't hear it. Her daughter Maria stepped forward and placed a gentle kiss on her cheek, followed by her son, William. When they stepped back, the face of Arthur, her husband of forty-one years, came into view. He stared lovingly into her eyes before kissing her long and gentle on her lips. Her heart melted in her chest, as she thought she might have actually felt the pressure of his lips against hers.

Another man, Ryan Melville, came into the room. Margaret had met him once previously when he introduced himself as the contractor assigned to fulfil her request. He was abrupt, but courteous when he discussed her condition and how he would administer the injection. On this occasion, he didn't need to speak, his eyes asked the question, to which she responded with a single blink.

She looked back at her family, who all had tears streaming down their cheeks. She hadn't realized until then that they were all holding her hand, one on top of another, her own sandwiched in the middle. She couldn't tell if she was crying too.

Ryan Melville pulled out a syringe, inserted it into the IV port and emptied its contents.

"We will leave you alone with your family, Mrs. Verwey." It was the kind-hearted Dr. Lough. "Pleasant Journey."

The three of them exited and Margaret looked down at the hands that squeezed her own. She couldn't feel them; she wanted them to squeeze harder, and she needed to feel them one last time. There was nothing.

Margaret looked over each of them in turn, attempting a smile. Only they knew if she succeeded, but the loving smiles on each of their lips let her know that they got the message.

Her eyelids were heavy. She fought to keep them open, clinging desperately to her last memories of her family. The room was silent; she was so tired.

"I love you."

She finally closed her eyes.

CHAPTER FOUR

A white Ford Windstar van pulled up to the front gates of the Farm and stopped before the guardhouse. The only visible markings on this otherwise unadorned vehicle, were a single Government of Canada logo located on either side of the van, a few centimetres behind the front signal light. Because the clients don't often leave by their own means, the farm provided a shuttle service to avoid the hassle of abandoned vehicles.

From the backseat, Ian Montgomery watched the routine exchange between his driver and the guard who had just emerged from the small shack, wiping breakfast crumbs from his shirt. The driver handed the guard an identification card, who in turn used a portable scanner to confirm the barcode. The device chimed a cheerful little series of notes, and the gate suddenly jerked and rattled as it began its slow creep open, to allow them room to pass through unimpeded. The guard smiled as he handed the card back through the open window. From there, it was a short jaunt down a smoothed gravel driveway before arriving at a small, single-story building. The van came to a stop in a parking stall next to an old blue pickup. The driver leapt from the front seat and opened the sliding door for Ian to get out.

"You may leave your bag here Mr. Montgomery," The driver said as Ian stepped from the van; "I'll take it up to your room for you."

"Thank you, Alan." He replied.

The driver's name was just about all Ian had learned during the drive from Regina's airport. While Ian sat in the back seat, he made no inquiries as to what may be in store, there was no small talk about their past, nor did Alan press the matter. Instead, they spent most of the drive in relative silence.

Ian, led by Alan up the short set of stairs, was out of breath by the time he entered the front door of the first building. A small sign next to the door read *Administration*. The two men entered the tastefully decorated lobby. "Please have a seat Mr. Montgomery; I will let Captain Hawkins know that you are here." Alan swiped his card and disappeared through one of the two other doors from the lobby.

"Have a seat?" Ian thought as he looked over the large waiting area. Which one? At first, he wondered why they would need so many chairs. Do that many people come here to die? The more he thought about it however, the more it made sense. There are very likely many situations where family would come to see off their loved ones. Sadly, he had no loved ones to see him off, so he had plenty of seating options. Ian selected a chair beneath a large painting on the wall before him. As he eased himself into the comfortable leather chair, he gaped at the depicted landscape. He sat in silence and stared, not realizing that he was no longer alone in the room.

"Good morning Mr. Montgomery." A man's voice pulled him from his daydream. Wiping tears from his cheek, he turned to see a tall man standing over him in an officer's uniform. Next to him was a beautiful and well-dressed woman. Alan was with them, and he showed himself out before the officer continued, "I trust you had a safe ride in."

"Yes, thank you."

The two men shook hands as Hawkins continued, "I am Travis Hawkins, the administrator of the facility, and this is Dr. Valerie Lough. Welcome to the Farm."

Ian let out a brief cough, "Seems a rather strange sentiment considering the nature of your business."

"On the contrary," Hawkins rebutted, "my job is to make your stay with us as comfortable as possible."

"Good luck with that."

Hawkins didn't provoke the confrontation further. Instead, he drew Mr. Montgomery back to the painting. "I noticed you were rather taken by the painting. Do you recognize it?"

"I know the area. That's Logan's pass. I was born and raised in Lethbridge, so my family took several trips through that pass. I think I might even know exactly where the artist had sat to paint it."

Captain Hawkins remained standing, while Dr. Lough sat next to the new Client, lending him a sympathetic ear. "Did you make that trip often?"

"Oh yes. Every summer we would take a trip across the border and through the pass. It was a nice family outing, but I now think, looking back, it was more an excuse for my parents to go shopping."

At the urging of Dr. Lough, Ian continued telling them about his family. He and his twin brother Ron grew up in a tight community where everyone knew everyone else, the kind of neighbourhood where there were community barbecues every summer weekend at one house or another. He did relatively well in school, was consistent in getting above-average grades, and had a few girlfriends, although nothing serious. Overall, he had a typical childhood. After graduating high school, he started working as an apprentice mechanic in his father's garage, while his brother moved to Korea to teach English. While there, Ron met a lovely girl, married her, and hadn't been back since. Ian spent a year working under cars before deciding that it wasn't the job for him. He gave his notice and applied for general studies at the University of Lethbridge.

Partway through his second year, while attending a particularly boring geology lecture, Ian found himself sitting across the aisle from a striking Japanese woman. He caught her eye, and they shared a long glance before she blushed and looked away. There was an instant connection. She accepted his offer to go for coffee after the lecture, and after that, they ended up spending all their free time together.

Though inseparable in their personal life, Ian and Katsumi ended up in different directions at school. While Kat went on into the engineering program, Ian got into business management, graduating just in time for his father's early retirement. Ian took over the operation of the service station, which had since grown to include a convenience store and a Tim Horton's drive through. Within two years of his retirement, Ian's father suffered a fatal heart attack. His mother, who had been dependent on her husband for thirty-five years, deteriorated quickly and soon followed suit. His brother Ron never made it home for either funeral.

Ian and Katsumi were married in a small ceremony with just a few friends and Kat's parents, sister, and brother-in-law. They honeymooned for three weeks in Hawaii, and then it was back to the grindstone. As the years went by, the service station prospered, and Kat worked her way up the ranks at a reputable electrical engineering firm. They were both dedicated in their careers and, although a passionate and loving couple, they never felt they had time for a family.

Then, at the age of thirty-four, Ian began getting sick. At first, it was just minor aches and pains in his joints, but it soon escalated to the point where even sitting was uncomfortable. After a short time, the pain became too much for him to bear. Ian went to his family doctor, who sent him in for a series of tests. The tests came back positive; he had cancer. The disease had started in his bones, and from there it spread to other parts of his body. He was referred an oncologist who started him on radiation treatments and chemotherapy, but unfortunately, for him, he was too far along. He kept getting sicker.

Just a few short months after diagnosis, Ian and Katsumi received some good news. Kat's brother-in-law called to say that her sister had just gone into labour and was heading to the hospital. Kat hated the thought of leaving her sick husband alone for any amount of time, but Ian insisted that she go visit her sister in Fort McMurray for a few days.

Ian was haunted by the memory of that terrible day. The cordless phone gripped in his hand, praying for it to ring. He watched the news program in horror as they displayed images of the fire blazing out of control. Flames destroyed hundreds of homes, evacuated by thousands of residents, and casualties as of then were unknown. Ian trembled, wondering which statistic Kat and her family belonged to, but that call never came. It took seven phone calls to the Red Cross before he learned that there were four bodies discovered at his sister-in-law's address, one man, two women and an infant girl.

Ian Montgomery's entire world came crashing down around him. He stopped fighting the battle against his illness, he no longer cared about the operation of his father's service station, and he distanced himself from all his close friends. As far as he was concerned, his life was over, and he saw only one option.

"There are always options Mr. Montgomery," Dr. Lough intervened, "cancer research becomes more and more promising all the time. Even the slightest chance is better than no chance at all."

"I have already been through all of this before. My chances are up. There is nothing left for me to do but die. It's the only thing left that I have any control over."

"We have a full week together, Mr. Montgomery. Perhaps in that time I can help you find another way of looking at things."

"Yeah, I doubt it." Montgomery hesitated, "About that, does it really have to take the whole week? Could we not speed up the process a bit?"

"I'm afraid we have little choice." Hawkins stepped in, "There are many protocols that we must follow before we are permitted to proceed. In the seven days you're with us, you will have the opportunity to explore our facility to see the many options we have available for your exit strategy. You will also have daily meeting with Dr. Lough, to evaluate your state of mind."

"I'm dying, I'm not crazy." Ian scoffed.

"I completely understand Mr. Montgomery," Hawkins assured him, but ultimately, we must follow protocol. We are required to ascertain your mental state while at the same time, attempt to talk you out of it."

"Talk me out of it?" He began to raise his voice, "I am in a tremendous amount of pain. I need to urinate more often than I care to think about, and not a day goes by when I'm not shitting blood. There is nothing you could say to talk me out of this. I am going to die, and nothing can stop that now. All I'm asking you to do is speed up the process and let me go with dignity. Please!"

He began a coughing fit. Dr. Lough took his hand to calm him while Hawkins handed him a handkerchief. "I am terribly sorry Mr. Montgomery. I fully understand what you are asking, and I am in agreement, but unfortunately my hands are tied."

"But I-" Ian interrupted.

Hawkins cut him off and regained control of the conversation. "Please Mr. Montgomery; give me a chance to explain my situation. Before the Government of Canada can approve your contract, there are certain procedures that I must follow. The truth of the matter is, these procedures are in place to make the process as inconvenient as possible, to deter the majority from making this choice, but nonetheless, I cannot stray from them. It is necessary for you to know *all* your options, including the option of going home alive. Dr. Lough needs to evaluate your mental state and try to help you to choose life. If I do not follow these protocols to the letter, I would be committing murder, and I would be prosecuted to the full extent of the law. I know where you are coming from, but you must understand that my hands are tied."

Ian sat quiet for a moment, processing the information he had just received. He wiped the spittle from his lips with the handkerchief and nodded in defeat. "What am I supposed to do here for a week?"

"Trust me Mr. Montgomery. We will make sure your final week is worthwhile." He looked at his watch. "I'll tell you what. It's a quarter after nine and I don't have another appointment until eleven. It should only take twenty minutes or so for us to do the paperwork and then I will take you on a tour of the compound. I'm quite certain that you will have little trouble keeping occupied for the next seven days."

"And I'll leave you two to your business," the doctor added, "but I will be seeing you again first thing tomorrow morning."

Ian capitulated, and with a polite nod to Dr. Lough, he allowed Captain Hawkins to help him back to his office. Hawkins ran him through the terms and conditions, glossing over the less applicable points. He then indicated a dozen locations that required either a signature or initials. All said and done, they took an hour-long tour of the entire facility on a small golf cart. They had a library, a basketball court, a weight gym and even a swimming pool. Captain Hawkins was right. Ian would have no problem keeping busy until he had completed his final objective.

CHAPTER FIVE

Dr. Valerie Lough sat behind her desk half listening to the contractor, Stephen Carlisle, as he rambled on about the details of the previous evening's contract. While Carlisle spoke, at length about the spray of blood, that escaped Mr. Dawson's forehead, Dr. Lough, lost in thought, stared blankly at his foot. In fact, she hadn't even noticed that he had stopped talking.

"It's him, isn't it?"

Dr. Lough snapped out of her trance with a shake of her head, "I beg your pardon?"

"You were thinking about him, weren't you?"

"I'm not certain whom you are referring to." Her cheeks began to flush.

A coy grin formed upon his lips, "it's okay doctor, you don't have to hide it. It is quite obvious to everyone; everyone but you at least. You like him, he likes you, why continue with the charade?"

"Who?"

"The great Captain Hawkins, of course."

Her expression hardened, "My relationship with Captain Hawkins, platonic or otherwise, is none of your concern Mr. Carlisle."

"I'm sorry Doctor. I am simply expressing my concerns over your unusual disinterest in my account of the incident."

"No," her voice took a softer tone, "it is I who must apologize; you are correct. I was not respecting the value of your time. I promise I will not let it happen again. Please continue."

"There isn't that much more to say, Doc. I mean, you missed the best part," he accentuated the last statement with a wink.

Dr. Lough's cheeks flushed for the second time that session.

Stephen laughed, "Don't worry Doc. I'm just messing with you. I can see that you are quite good at what you do. Whatever the hell that is."

She smiled at the sentiment, "Thank you Mr. Carlisle. I will try to take that as a compliment."

"That reminds me," Stephen leaned back in his chair, "I've been meaning to ask for some time now. With your qualifications, how the hell did you get stuck, in this shithole of a facility? Couldn't you be put to better use in a mental hospital or something?"

"I chose this shithole of a facility Mr. Carlisle."

"But why?" he shook his head with disbelief.

"It's quite simple, Mr. Carlisle. The patients I get here are at the lowest point they have ever been and ever will be in their lives. They have chosen to come here, rather than continue to suffer through the pain. That is my expertise, and if I am able to get through to one person, that makes it even more worthwhile."

"How exactly does one become an expert on the lowest of the low?"

Dr. Lough's eyes looked up and to the right as she considered his question. At the age of eleven, Valerie lost her mother to cancer. Before the tragedy, she had known that her mother was ill, but was kept sheltered from how dire the situation was. After the funeral, things became all too clear for Valerie. She shut herself off from her friends and sought comfort from her father and older brother. To her chagrin, they were far too busy dealing with the loss in their own way. Her father buried himself in work, and her brother joined the Canadian Armed Forces. She had no choice but to deal with her own pain the one way she knew how, silently.

A mere two years later, with her mother's death still heavy on her mind, her father announced that he was to be re-married. Valerie found no comfort in that revelation, and her quiet suffering suddenly became deafening. She fought the authority of her new stepmother and resisted any offers of cooperation. Over the next several years, Valerie was consistently at odds with her family, at the same time remaining silent concerning the true source of her pain. She missed her mother from the deepest reaches of her heart.

Before Valerie turned eighteen, the battle against depression was taking its toll, and she convinced herself that it was time to seek aid from a psychologist. What came as a surprise to her was, the therapist did something that no one else had done previously. She listened. There were no judgements; no accusations, she just listened. Occasionally she would ask follow-up questions, but there was never any pressure to answer, and she would offer suggestions or advice only when appropriate. Each session Valerie grew more and more comfortable in their discussions.

As weeks went by, she learned that her doctor had lost her own father at the age of fifteen. That, she explained, was why she was able to relate to Valerie on a level no one ever had. They talked at great lengths about her situation, helping her to deal with the loss and the pain instead of ignoring it. Every session Valerie's confidence grew stronger, as did her relationships with her family and friends. Valerie looked up to her doctor, not solely as a therapist, but also as a mentor. Her newfound ambition drove her to apply to the University of Manitoba in Winnipeg where, after dedicating four years of her life to her studies, she earned her degree in psychology.

Her career took off. She excelled at her job and her clients respected her for it. She used her own life experience to put herself in their shoes and because she understood personally, what they were going through, she was able to relate to them on a more personal level. Valerie ranked high in her field and became a celebrated expert on Post Traumatic Stress Disorder. She accepted a very lucrative job offer heading up the mental health team at the Sunnybrook Veterans Hospital in Toronto where she was best able to put her experience to use. It was there she first met a certain Lieutenant Travis Hawkins.

"I'm not certain this is the right forum for that conversation Mr. Carlisle. Instead, I would like to talk about your next contract, Ms. Dean. It is highly unorthodox that you would receive another contract so soon after completing a previous one. Why do you suppose Captain Hawkins was so quick to assign this one to you?"

"Are you asking me to guess what is going on inside the good captain's head? I'm afraid telepathy is a bit beyond my abilities."

"I am asking for your opinion, Mr. Carlisle. Why do you think he sees you as the best suited to fulfil this particular contract? There are three other contractors on site right now. Why you?"

Stephen laughed at her persistence, "Okay, I'll bite. If I were to wager a guess, I would say it has to do with her being a woman. Perhaps he thinks that because my first was a woman, another might help me find what I've been searching for."

Dr. Lough leaned back in her chair, crossing her legs, "This is where you typically lose me Mr. Carlisle. This thing you are searching for. You want to duplicate the first experience?"

"Oh no," Stephen leaned in, "not duplicate. I sacrificed the woman I loved to achieve that height. I want nothing more than to experience that incredible rush again."

"So, you are willing to kill for it? Why is it so important to you?"

Stephen leaned back and chuckled. "Let me ask you something Doc. Do you remember your first real orgasm?"

"Mr. Carlisle," her voice suddenly took a stern tone, as if talking to a belligerent child, "that is hardly an appropriate question. I think we'd better move on to a new topic of conversation."

"Don't worry, I'm not asking for details, I'm only asking if you remember it."

Dr. Lough considered what he was saying, "And now you are equating murder to an orgasm?"

"The act itself, no. The feeling I get afterwards; however, that's another thing all together. Nevertheless, you continue to dodge the question. Do you remember?"

"Very well, yes I do."

"And I'm certain that it was exciting and wonderful, and everything you ever hoped it would be."

"Please get to the point Mr. Carlisle."

"Have you ever had one since?"

Valerie's cheeks turned a bright shade of red, "Mr. Carlisle, I- "

"Relax Doc; you don't have to answer that." Stephen backed off, "My point is what if you were never again able to experience that feeling? What if that first amazing orgasm, was also your last? Would you not explore any possibility to get it back? Think about it."

"I guess that's one area where you and I differ. I don't think it's important enough to get that worked up over – most certainly, not important enough to kill."

"Then I'm going to guess that you have little difficulty achieving orgasm. Perhaps even multiples."

Dr. Lough jumped to her feet, sending her chair rolling away. She placed both hands on her desk and stared down her adversary, "Mr. Carlisle, I have been more than lenient with you this session with the hope of getting a better understanding of your motivation, but I will not allow you to continue these personal attacks."

"I'm sorry, was I attacking you?" he asked through a smug grin.

Valerie ignored the question, "I think this might be a good time to put an end to this session. I appreciate you coming in and speaking to me."

While she spoke, Dr. Lough moved around the desk and opened her office door to allow for Stephen's exit. She kept a polite tone to her voice, though the forced smile on her lips and her wrinkled brow demonstrated a certain amount of restraint. Stephen, on the other hand, barred his teeth with a triumphant grin.

"I see that I have struck a chord with you, and I am sorry," Stephen proclaimed as he stood, although there was a definite tone of sarcasm to his voice. "Until next time then?'

"Good day Mr. Carlisle." Valerie watched him as he exited, "I am allowing this contract, for now, but know that I'll be keeping a close eye on both of you for this one."

"I wouldn't expect any less of you," and with that, Stephen Carlisle proceeded down the corridor, and disappeared through the far exit, leaving Valerie alone to sort out what had just transpired. Stephen Carlisle's state of mind weighed heavily on Dr. Lough, but a larger concern for her was how her feelings for Travis were affecting her job.

It should have been easy for her. Since the day she met him, Valerie found him to be hotheaded and impulsive; always so quick to jump to conclusions. At times she found him to be infuriating, yet others—

"I get it," Hawkins had concluded, "You want to send the cripple to babysit the suicidal patients."

"Lieutenant Hawkins, I am surprised at you. I have read your file. You have always pushed your troops to use their strengths, and to learn from their weaknesses. You would never let anyone under your command get away with a statement like that, so I suggest you take a page from your own book and consider this offer."

"Okay, but why me?"

"There are plenty of reasons Lieutenant. First off, due to the delicate nature of the facility, we need a C.O. with strong leadership capabilities, but who also possesses good people skills. Others respect you, because you talk *to* your subordinates, rather than down to them. Secondly, you are a valuable officer, and they would hate to lose you to a medical discharge. This post is unlikely to interfere with your disability."

"So, am I under your command, then?

"Not at all," Valerie leaned forward in her chair. "With this post, comes a promotion to Captain. we would be working closely together as equals."

Dr. Lough recalled clearly how she felt as the Lieutenant's expression changed. A smile formed on his lips, and his eyes remained locked with hers. Whatever switch flipped in his head; he suddenly became more confident. More... sexy. In order to maintain professional integrity, she looked away first and got back to the point.

"So, Lieutenant, how do you feel about this new assignment?"

Hawkins lay back, letting her off the hook, "what would this post entail?"

Dr. Lough straightened in her seat, "you would be overseeing the operation of the facility, delegating responsibilities for all tasks required for service and maintenance. You would also oversee the comfort of the clients, the assignments for the contractors, and the correspondence with command and the insurance companies. I would look after the mental health of both client and contractor."

"Looks like I have the easy job," Hawkins said, rolling his eyes. "So how the hell does this work? How do we finance this operation?"

"It's quite simple, really. There are numerous insurance companies across the country that cover euthanasia, with higher premiums of course. The government has struck a deal with these agents where we take on the onus of death, and the policy pays us fifty percent of the total amount; the other half goes to the estate. The client signs over the policy as payment for our services. The catch is, the clients cannot die by their own hands, otherwise the euthanasia coverage goes entirely to the estate, and we lose the commission. That is why we need a strong C.O. This is where you come in."

"Holy shit, how things have changed." Hawkins shook his head, "civilians used to protest us killing innocents overseas, now we are murdering our own."

Valerie shook a finger at him, "not murder Lieutenant, compassionate euthanasia. There is a huge difference, at least in the eyes of the law. Like any other public facility, we are performing a service. Don't fool yourself though. We will certainly get more than our fair share of protesters. In fact, we have been receiving threatening letters from several different organizations."

"Shit. What the hell are you getting me into?"

"Does this mean you are accepting the post?"

"Do I have another choice?"

"It's this or a medical discharge."

Hawkins turned away, lay back on the examination table and stared up at the ceiling. Valerie stood and placed a gentle hand on his arm. He did not pull away.

"Listen Lieutenant, you joined the military with the intent of serving to protect the quality of life for the citizens of this country. The clients who seek out the Farm, no longer have a good quality of life remaining. If we can no longer protect their lives, we can, at the very least, help protect their dignity."

Hawkins turned back to face her, and again their eyes locked for a moment; before Valerie looked away.

"You present a compelling case. All right," Hawkins said in a steady voice. "I'll do it, but on one condition."

"And what's that?"

"They need to work for it. They need to prove to us that they have no other options; that their lives are not worth saving. I want to have the opportunity to change their minds. If by the end of the week they still want it badly enough, we can let them go."

Valerie smiled with the feeling of great accomplishment, "I do believe that we are on the same page Lieutenant. That is precisely why I will be right there with you."

From that moment on, there was an understanding between them. A mutual respect and admiration. Although at times, it appeared as though their feelings went beyond simple respect. She could see it in his eyes when he looked at her. She felt it herself. If this were to continue, a working relationship or otherwise, she would have to figure out what this thing actually was.

CHAPTER SIX

He stood there unmoving; his breath caught in his throat. His sweaty palms ached, from gripping the iron railing tighter and tighter. It seemed impossible, but there she was, right in front of his eyes. It couldn't be her though, could it? The similarities were remarkable. Her hair was a bit shorter, but the same color brown. Those beautiful blue eyes were the same ones he had stared into so many years before, or were they green? It was all a bit foggy. He swore that her breasts were larger than that, those couldn't be any more than a B cup. Her nose was different too; it came to more of a point. Didn't it? Was it possible? Wasn't she supposed to be dead?

Stephen Carlisle had just spent the last hour with Dr. Lough, forced to share his feelings regarding his most recent contract involving Stuart Dawson. She asked all the usual tiresome questions required of her, while Stephen took great pleasure in toying with her emotions. He had no idea that the whole time he was playing with her, she was playing him as well. He was just returning to his apartment when he spotted the woman down below.

As he stood on the balcony overlooking the atrium, so many questions of his own ran through his head. The woman before him, who he could only assume was the woman Hawkins had told him about, could have easily been mistaken for his deceased wife Lisa. This woman, this imposter, what was her name? Oh yes, Catherine Dean, sat alone with a book, in the cafeteria surrounded by realistic looking silk flowers and plastic trees.

She was surpassingly lovely, and in many ways, very similar to Lisa. His eyes began to well up, overcome with memories. All he could do was stare in silence at a likeness he hadn't seen since—

Well, since the day that changed his life forever.

Stephen and Lisa had been living paycheck to paycheck in a five hundred square-foot, single bedroom apartment in North Vancouver, paying just short of two thousand dollars a month in rent. They were living way beyond their means, but they loved living in a community surrounded by the arts. There was never a shortage of things to do whether it was live bands, art shows or theatre troupes. Just the bills, Stephen worked days as a project coordinator in the construction industry, while Lisa took photographs for a local arts magazine. They always reserved their weekends however, for drinking and live entertainment.

With Canada's diversification strategy in full swing, news reports came in by the dozens that the government would soon be adopting a new, unorthodox policy, and Vancouver would host the first facility. Wouldn't you know it; the club was located only a few blocks from their own neighbourhood. Media and protesters alike, flocked to the grand opening of *The Greenhouse*, a lounge opened to the public that served far more than alcohol, but also a selection of controlled substances such as marijuana, hashish, and psilocybin. The idea behind the Greenhouse was to take these substances off the streets, out of schoolyards, control the purity, and collect the taxes.

Stephen was delighted to discover that Lisa received the contract to photograph the opening event, thereby scoring tickets for the two of them to join in on the festivities. Dressed to the nines and ready for anything, they called a cab to take them the twenty-three blocks to the lounge.

The Greenhouse was a veritable who's who of Canadian culture, actors, musicians, artists and of course the media. One couldn't turn without seeing another recognizable face, although celebrity status came a distant second to the event itself. Second to all, save the media of course, who were more concerned with what Justin Bieber and Ryan Reynolds were smoking.

Not those to pass up an opportunity, Stephen and Lisa sampled a few different menu items starting with pot, joints and water bongs; they then tried the Salvia, which gave them a wild fifteen-minute ride. They finished the evening with dessert, a dry chocolate brownie made with magic mushrooms.

They spent the cab ride home in relative silence. While Lisa sat gazing out the window, mesmerized by the hundreds of lights flying past, Stephen couldn't help but stare at his wife's figure. Her tight black dress clung to her body, showing off her titillating curves, and the lace of her thigh-high stockings stopped below the skirt line, giving him a flash of white skin. As he ogled her, it appeared to him that Lisa's breasts were growing three sizes right before his eyes. His loins burned with a desire unlike anything he had ever felt. If he didn't take his wife soon, he would surely explode. He reached over and placed a hand on her leg, running it up the length of her bare inner thigh. Feeling lace at his fingertips, he pulled her thong underwear to the side exposing her to the open air. She was hot and wet, as he inserted two fingers inside her, and she arched her back pressing her head back into the seat. Lisa's breasts appeared to grow even larger and the bulge in his pants became rock hard. He leaned in and pressed his lips to her warm skin just below her neck while she grabbed hold of his throbbing member. He couldn't stand to wait much longer, he felt as if he could burst at any moment. Fortunately for him, they didn't have long to wait as the cab then pulled to a stop before their apartment building. He paid the driver using a voucher supplied by the event organizers, and they ran up the four flights of stairs to their apartment.

Lisa had immodestly stripped down to her underwear in the time it took Stephen to fumble with the locks and open the door. He barely had enough time to close it again behind them before she slammed her now naked body into him. She leaped up, wrapped her legs around his waist and threw him off balance. The two of them stumbled together over to the sofa where they fell upon the soft cushions. He rolled over on top of her, kicked off his pants, and entered her, thrusting with every bit of energy he possessed. The intensity was nothing like either of them had previously experienced. Each thrust sent pulses through his entire body and her screams of pleasure were piercing.

Stephen didn't want to stop, but her excessive howling was going to wake the entire building. He could remember how angry he felt in that moment. He didn't want to be thinking about his neighbours, he wanted to enjoy the sex. Without missing a beat, he grabbed a throw pillow from under her head and placed it over her face, holding it in place with his own to muffle the loud annoying screams. The passion seemed to increase as she struggled more and more. Her screams grew louder.

"Shut up", he scolded her, pushing the pillow harder into her face.

She fought harder against his thrusts and beat her arms against his back in desperation for her life. The harder she struggled the more empowered he felt, still her screams carried. He adjusted his weight, leaning on the pillow with the full weight of his upper body, all the while continuing his thrusts inside her. When he finally reached orgasm, they both simultaneously went still. He lay there on top of her, taking long deep breaths, more fulfilled than he'd ever been.

He rolled off his wife, tossing the pillow to the floor. Lisa lay unmoving, her eyes wide and bloodshot, her mouth frozen in scream. A glance down at the pillow revealed an outline of her lips eyes and cheeks left behind by her makeup. Something had gone terribly wrong, but at the time, he couldn't think straight, none of it made sense. The woman he loved lay at his feet, yet he felt so powerful at that moment, immortal, and he felt no remorse. He had so many questions, but he couldn't wrap his head around the answers. By the time the adrenaline rush had subsided, he was exhausted. He decided that he would sleep on it and perhaps things would make more sense to him in the morning, so he left Lisa where she was and went to bed.

The following day, dead sober, things had become clearer than he could have ever imagined.

**

Catherine Dean sat alone before a small round table, which supported a single cup of cooling peppermint tea, and a bundle of cutlery wrapped in a white disposable napkin. Open in her hands was a book that displayed a shiny silver dagger and wedding ring upon a white seal depicted on its cover. The title read *Preston & Child- Cold Vengeance*. At first glance, one might find her completely engrossed in her novel. In truth however, her eyes never scanned the words, nor did she ever turn a page. She sat staring at the same spot on the book, focused on a single letter, oblivious to the cacophony of chatter around her.

Catherine had just come out of her initial interview with the administrator Captain Hawkins. She had reluctantly accepted the terms and conditions of her stay, but declined Hawkins' offer of a tour of the compound. She insisted that she couldn't care less, what amenities the Farm had to offer, nor did she have any desire to talk to a shrink. Unfortunately, for the latter anyway, she had little option. The doctor had scheduled a meeting for the following morning.

Left alone in her deep trance, Catherine was unaware of the server who had replaced the cold cup of tea with a steaming one, nor did she notice the man on the balcony leaning on the handrail watching her for several minutes before disappearing down the corridor. She remained in a frozen position, intent on that same word in her novel, until the sound of metal scraping on concrete behind her, startled her out of the trance.

She turned her head to find a man sitting at the table behind her with a small carton of chocolate milk. The stranger sat quietly, his chair turned towards her, opening the mouth of the carton. He took long pull from his milk before setting it down on the table. Without a word, he folded his hands before him and stared at Catherine as if trying to read her like a book.

She returned her attention back to her novel, this time forcing herself to read the words. However, she couldn't concentrate, with the feeling of someone watching. She slowly turned her head, attempting to see him in her periphery. There he sat, hands folded on the table, still watching her with unknown intention.

Catherine turned back to her book, in an attempt to ignore the blatant display she had just witnessed, but she questioned how anyone could possibly concentrate on the words with that insolent jerk sitting right behind her pretending to do absolutely nothing in a brazen disregard for her personal space. Catherine had hoped that if she ignored him, he would eventually get bored and leave. She wondered what he was doing anyway. This clearly wasn't a singles club. Was he hoping to get the attention of the lonely suicidal girl? Fat chance. Catherine had little interest in men anymore; she had no use for them. The Butterfly Garden destroyed any chance she had at love again. She looked back at him, he remained in the exact position he had been in just a moment before.

"Can I help you?" Catherine blurted out with ire.

"I'm sorry?" The man replied, clearly feigning ignorance.

"Is there something you want?" Her irritation increased.

"I'm afraid I don't know what you're talking about," he stated. His calm demeanor was infuriating, "I am just sitting here enjoying my milk."

Her eyes narrowed and the corners of her mouth took a downward turn, "you were staring at me. It was making me uncomfortable."

"Oh that," he chuckled, "I'm terribly sorry to make you uncomfortable, but I can explain. You see, I have been trying to decide how best to approach you, as you happen to be sitting at my regular table. I'm afraid that I tend to be a creature of habit. It's a bit compulsive, really."

Catherine furrowed her brow, trying to assess if he was playing her. She was reluctant to trust his intentions, despite the appearance of sincerity.

"Would you like me to move?" She asked with a facetious undertone.

"Heavens no." He leaned forward in his chair, "not after you've cured me of my disorder. I should offer you a drink in thanks for your well-timed service."

"Not necessary." She tried to return to her novel.

"What's that you're reading?"

She turned to see the man's face peering over her shoulder. Catherine couldn't believe the gall of this asshole. All she wanted to do is sit by herself and read her book in peace. Nevertheless, as hard as she tried to ignore him, she could feel his warm breath on her neck as he read over her shoulder.

"Do you have to read over my shoulder?"

"Not at all." Stephen moved around the table and sat down in the chair across from her, once again folding his hands together on the table in front of him. She tried to ignore him and hide her face behind her book, but she hated having him staring at her from across the table.

"Do you mind?"

"Ah, Preston and Child, I'm enjoying the series as well." He ignored her explosive reaction.

That, on the other hand, got her attention. "You've read it?"

"Of course. Agent Pendergast is a very relatable character."

"Relatable? To you? Well, you certainly do share his persistence."

The stranger laughed at her gibe. "I suppose you're right about that. What I was referring to however is his drive to protect and even avenge his loved ones, no matter the cost. It's his life's work to find justice for those who are wronged, and he's not afraid to cross the line to do so."

Catherine reverted to condescension, "And you can relate to that? Is that what you do, right the injustices of the world?"

"I wouldn't claim to be as honourable as our dear Agent Pendergast, but isn't that in a sense what we are doing here? There are those who have come here because they feel wronged in some way. Whether it's a fatal illness or crippling depression, they have come here to be free of the injustice. The others are here to make sure that happens.

"You make them sound like superheroes."

Again, he laughed at Catherine's sarcasm. "No, most definitely not superheroes. More like vigilantes, classified somewhere in the grey area between hero and villain. More or less, where Pendergast sits, don't you think? The one difference is, I don't believe he gets pleasure from the kill."

Catherine began to pull away again, "Like you?"

"Funny thing, that." He leaned back on the chair and entwined his fingers behind his head. "I've spent the last two years here trying to re-create the experience of my first. I even had one client willing to go through the same motions, but it was to no avail. I have yet to achieve a thrill that comes close to the first."

"And what motions are those?"

"That, my dear, is a story for another time. We have a week to get to know each other."

"So, I was right then? You are assigned to my case?"

The stranger extended his hand toward her, "Stephen Carlisle."

"Forgive my rudeness Mr. Carlisle, but I have no desire to spend the week pretending to be civil to the man who has been hired to kill me."

"Are you so quick to forget that it was you who hired me? This was your idea my dear, it is my job to respect your wishes."

"I came here to die," she stated in a blatant manner he was sure to understand, "not to fraternize with the help."

"The help?"

"Now would you kindly respect *these* wishes and leave me the hell alone."

Stephen stood up and pushed his chair neatly under the table. "You know Cathy; it's going to be a terribly long week for you if you keep your guard up like that. They designed this place so those like you can die by their own terms. Think about whether you want to leave this place alone or if you want to go out in style. It's totally up to you."

"I'm not going to sleep with you." She shouted louder than she had planned.

"What makes you think that I would want to sleep with you? Quite frankly, you are not my type. Too much baggage."

Stephen walked away leaving Catherine unsure of how to respond. All she could think do, was to shout, "Don't call me Cathy."

He never turned around; he simply waved back to her and kept walking. Catherine began to wonder if she was a bit too harsh with him. He was right; she was there on her own accord, but his arrogance and insolence were intolerable, and she hated him for it.

As Catherine turned her attention back to her novel, her mind continued to wander back to the infuriating, yet handsome man who had somehow managed to break down one of her many barriers.

ECE-80023

The roar of nine-hundred and eighty horsepower, the wind on his face, the vibration of the steering wheel in his hand. Niles Buchanan had never driven so fast, had never felt so exhilarated. The powerful 2.4 litre, V8 engine catapulted the retired Ferrari Formula One racer around the 1.5km track. High on adrenaline, he pushed the accelerator to the floor and shot down the straightaway like a rocket. Niles shouted out with joy, forgetting all about the pain and suffering he had to endure over the past five years.

When he was a young man, Niles had little interest in school. It was all too easy. He coasted through high school and still graduated at the top of his class. At the age of nineteen, he continued on to university, majoring in business. Still, he coasted. He spent his days in tedious classes, then after school he would go partying with his friends, drinking, smoking, and hitting on women. This became his routine. Even after he graduated with a master's degree, and got a job with a prosperous trading company, he spent most of his evenings and weekends drinking. He worked his way up the corporate ladder, never considering the possibility that he had a problem.

He passed off the early symptoms as a combination of stress and aging. He attributed the backaches to sitting at a desk all day, and the weight loss didn't bother him since he could have stood to lose a couple dozen pounds anyway. The changes in his skin tone were so gradual, his friends and colleagues never put much thought into it. It wasn't until he ran into an old girlfriend, who pointed out how yellow his skin looked, when he decided to see a doctor.

He must have said the name a thousand times, trying to get the pronunciation right, Pancreatic Adenocarcinoma. He searched dozens of websites, hoping to find another possible ailment that fit the symptoms. Nevertheless, there were no two ways around it. He had pancreatic cancer. The years of drinking and smoking had caught up to him, and he was too far along for successful treatment. As time went on, the pain in his back and abdomen grew stronger, while it became harder and harder to keep food down. He continued to lose weight to a dangerous level. He was merely surviving; there was no quality of life. It was time to put an end to the pain.

The Farm had plenty of options for exit strategies, but none appealed to him. There was only one way he wanted to go. Back home, Niles grew up watching the races with his old man. NASCAR, Indi 500, it didn't matter. Whatever was on at the time, he remained glued to the set. The speed, the competition, the crashes, it was so exciting to watch, and that's how he wanted to die. Money wasn't an issue. He never married and had no kids. He wanted the best.

The best is what he got. Sitting behind the wheel of the Ferrari, approaching three hundred kilometres per hour. He had never truly lived, until he was prepared to die. He throttled back as he rounded the bend, and then punched it as the track straightened out. This was his last chance to see what the car could do. He watched as the needle passed three hundred, three ten, three twenty. He wondered how high he could get it before-

The explosion of rubber as the front left tire separated from its rim was loud enough for Niles to hear over the nine hundred and eighty horsepower engine. As metal hit asphalt, the steering wheel was wrenched from his hands, and he suddenly found himself perpendicular with the track. Fear gripped his heart as the racer flipped, once, twice, the moment seemed to last a lifetime. He looked up in time to see the concrete barrier directly in his path. Niles closed his eyes, braced for impact. All he heard was the grinding of metal on concrete before all went silent.

CHAPTER SEVEN

Day Two

Kevin Richards stepped past the maintenance workers, diligently erecting the dividing wall in the modular trailer, to create a bedroom for the makeshift apartment. As per Richards' instructions, they had sealed all the vents and windows in the outer apartment side to aid in the depletion of oxygen. Still in the early stages of construction, the apartment wasn't yet ready for him to install the ignition mechanism, so he moved on to more pressing matters. Hawkins had ordered a mock-up demonstration so he would know what to expect.

The trailers were set up in the centre of seven acres of blacktop asphalt, skirted by the 1.5 km racetrack. Hawkins built the speedway upon special request for one of the Farm's wealthier clients who wished to die behind the wheel of a high-speed racecar. To remove the onus of death from the client, a well-timed shot to the front wheel sent him out of control and into a concrete barrier. Since then, the track remained unused and was now barren, save the modular trailer and a large metal garbage bin that stood twenty metres off to the side.

Richards exited the trailer and made his way over to the rusted blue dumpster. On the side of the bin, he had previously welded a metal clamp, and drilled a quarter inch hole in the side next to it. Sitting on the ground next to the bin was a compressed gas cylinder, on top of which had a flexible gas line attached to an electronic valve. He picked up the canister and attached it to the side of the bin using the metal clamp, then slid the end of the tube through the hole.

He opened the lid. The bottom of the bin was covered in broken up wood pallets that he had soaked in gasoline. It was a familiar smell. It reminded him of a similar occasion, one that got him into this mess in the first place.

During his post as a fire fighter, Richards had responded to many fires in and around the base. On one particular occasion, a fire broke out in one of the family homes, and his unit was first on the scene. It was a two-story building, and the fire had started in the kitchen on the main floor, which since spread to the stairs, trapping the family upstairs. The officer who lived there was away on duty, leaving his wife and children alone.

While they fought to control the fire, Richards sent in two men to rescue the family. One got out safely with the family, but the second floor collapsed before Private Brady could escape. He wasn't responding on the radio. His superior, Captain Burgess wouldn't risk allowing him to go in after his colleague. They shouted at each other for a while, until Richards decided that Brady's life was more valuable than his own commission. He went into the building against orders and pulled Private Brady out. He had lost consciousness, but he was alive."

After that incident, Sergeant Kevin Richards was busted two ranks, down to Master Corporal. Captain Burgess personally took command of the platoon until he was either able to promote someone to replace Richards or recruit a Sergeant from another platoon. Either way, he didn't seem to be in any sort of hurry. Burgess worked him hard. Harder than any of the newer recruits. It appeared as though he enjoyed making Richards suffer for disobeying him.

Kevin Richards swore he would never blindly follow orders if he thought they would be detrimental to the outcome and, more importantly, he would not be bullied into submission.

One night, while Captain Burgess was out to dinner, Richards broke into his home. The front entryway was carpeted, and had a small side table, which held a small pile of unopened mail, stood in the corner. Two doors led back to the rest of the house. He shut the two doors, and shoved rags into the cracks under them. He then filled the one vent in the room with rags and made certain to shut the window next to the door tight. Finally, he poured a Jerry Can of gasoline on the carpet, struck a match and shut the door on his way out."

Richards' training as a fire fighter taught him that the accelerant would burn very hot and deplete the oxygen quickly. He also knew Captain

Burgess wasn't dumb enough to open a door to a potentially burning building, so he hid between the houses across the street and waited.

The alarms went off and Burgess made it back home before the trucks arrived. Richards watched as he ran to the door, and as he suspected, the experienced captain placed his hand on the door to feel the heat, then turned to vacate the premises. Richards could see the fear in his face as he drew his side arm and shot out the side window. Oxygen filled the entry-way, reigniting the fire. The door blew out, engulfing Burgess in flame. By the time the trucks arrived, it was too late. The house was completely ablaze, and the captain was dead.

Kevin Richards had many regrets over the years. That wasn't one of them. He was tried and convicted of first-degree murder and was sentenced to imprisonment at the Canadian Forces Service Prison, until such time as he was transferred to the federal penitentiary. At least, that's what it said on paper. In fact, they had, transferred Kevin Richards to an entirely different facility.

Ready to give arson another go, Kevin pulled a cigarette lighter and an oil-soaked rag from his pocket. With a flick of his thumb, the lighter came to life, setting the rag aflame. He then dropped the rag in the bin, slammed the lid down and walked away from the dumpster.

Richards walked to the roadway just past the edge of the track, where he returned to a small white golf cart. Sitting behind the wheel, Captain Travis Hawkins watched his approach. He stepped up to the cart and slid into the seat next to the C.O.

"Is it ready?" Hawkins asked.

Richards didn't answer. He reached into his pocket, pulled out a small remote button and handed it over to the captain.

Hawkins hesitated, "you did the work. Don't you want the honors?"

"All yours."

Hawkins took the proffered fob and turned to face the garbage bin in the distance. He raised the fob and held the button for one, two, three. Just as he thought something went wrong, an explosion blew the lid off the dumpster with a blinding flash. Wood and debris began to rain down on the asphalt.

Hawkins watched the spectacle with wide eyes and a hint of a grin, "That was a bit extreme."

"Keep in mind; we pumped pure oxygen into a fire. This wasn't exactly a backdraft, but the concept is," he smiled, "similar. That was just a whole lot more fun. When we do this for real, Montgomery will have to open the bedroom door to introduce the oxygen. There won't be as big of a bang, but it will do the trick."

"How can you be certain he will open the door?"

"He's expecting to die in a fire. I'm sure he will wonder why there is no fire. Or, at the very least, wonder why the whole trailer is on fire except for his room. He'll open the door."

"Most impressive Mr. Richards, you are very thorough. Do you have the supplies you need to rig the apartment?"

"I took everything I need from storage. I'll just need you to get me some more of the accelerant."

"You will have what you require by Sunday. If Dr. Lough gives us the go to proceed; we will complete the contract when he wakes up Tuesday morning."

"Excellent. I will be ready."

Richards climbed out of the golf cart, allowing Hawkins to leave. The captain turned the vehicle around and stopped, "Oh, and Mr. Richards?"

"Yeah?"

"Never rig an explosion like that again without my permission."

Hawkins smiled as he accelerated and sped off, away from the track.

**

It had been twenty minutes since Ian Montgomery had heard the muffled explosion from outside the window of Dr. Lough's office. Though he had assured them that his issues were completely physical and in no way mental, he still had little choice but to sit through excruciatingly boring sessions with the resident shrink. They were in the midst of discussing his high school days, when a blast echoed through the compound.

"What the hell was that?" He asked, indicating the window.

Dr. Lough reminded him that the Farm was still in fact a military compound and one could expect the occasional explosion from time to time.

"It's likely just a simple exercise," she had claimed.

Dr. Lough continued to push on with the session, but Ian was restless. He wanted to know the source of that explosion. By the end of the hour, Dr. Lough had suggested that a good topic of discussion for the next session would be his obsession with explosions.

Ian searched the sky for any signs of smoke, but he was unable to see anything that might indicate where the source would have been. He recalled the tour of the compound that he had taken with Captain Hawkins the previous day. It was a large facility, but he could think of only two places where one could safely set off an explosion like that. The courtyard out front of the guest housing, but that was too close, and the racetrack. That had to be it.

Ian staggered in the direction of the track hoping to, at the very least; get a glimpse of the aftermath. He hadn't made it far across the courtyard before he heard the distinctive whirr of a golf cart. Captain Hawkins appeared from around the corner of the warehouse, behind the wheel of his cart, moving towards him from the very direction he was heading.

"Good morning Mr. Montgomery." Hawkins said as he brought the cart to a stop next to him. "I trust your session with Dr. Lough went well."

"Dandy." The session was the last thing he wanted to discuss right then. "Hey, what was that explosion I heard a little bit ago? It sounded serious."

"I am terribly sorry if we distracted you from your session Mr. Montgomery. It happens from time to time and I'm afraid that it's out of our control. We have the occasional confrontation with a local extremist group."

"Extremist group?"

"They call themselves PALM. People Against Legalized Murder. They started out as your average protestors, but they've since escalated to include violence. They like to toss gifts over the fence from time to time, some of which are quite dangerous, such as dynamite or anthrax. We don't even open them anymore. We detonate them immediately. Considering the size of this last explosion, it looks like this is one of their angrier days."

"How often does this happen?" Ian pressed him for more information.

"Because of the questions of morality surrounding this facility, their group is well-funded by the church. They toss little gifts into the compound quite frequently. However there's no need for concern, Mr. Montgomery, as we have plenty of cameras and a regular watch to keep us appraised of any unauthorized deliveries.

"Why should I be concerned? Whether I die tomorrow or Tuesday, that's the reason I'm here. In fact, they would be doing me a favour if they were to knock some time off my sentence, so to speak."

"True enough." Hawkins agreed, "You seem awfully curious for someone who's given up on the world Mr. Montgomery."

"I have accepted the inevitability of my condition, Captain Hawkins, but I have not given up. You are right about one thing; I've often been told I am rather curious."

"You know what they say about curiosity." Hawkins laughed, "Don't go jumping the gun on your contract."

Ian laughed along, despite the lack of sincerity.

"Don't worry Mr. Montgomery; we will keep you safe for the next few days."

"That's what I was afraid of."

"Can I help you back to your room?"

"No thanks. I can manage."

Hawkins displayed an awkward smile, "Very well. Enjoy your afternoon."

While Hawkins drove off, looking proud of how he handled the situation, Ian stood where he was and pondered what he had just learned. Captain Hawkins' gratuitous disclosure of classified information surprised him. Hawkins had initially struck him as one who would keep such information tight to the chest. He also found it strange that he would joke about something as serious as a contract. Hawkins appeared too disciplined for that. It didn't make sense.

Nonetheless, he grew confident that he may end up getting his wish after all, and after that conversation, he felt quite certain that he would soon be free to complete his journey.

**

As Captain Hawkins pulled away on his cart, he thought back on the interaction, wondering if he was convincing enough. Hawkins had decided not to tell Ian about the backdraft. He was concerned that if the client opened the door knowing the danger, one could consider it as self-imposed. Hawkins always believed that the best lies held a hint of truth. In this case, there was in fact a protest group calling themselves P.A.L.M. that had given them some grief over the years, but they were relatively harmless. They held the occasional march but soon learned that there wasn't enough media traffic to have any effect. The previous fall they did manage to toss a few dozen rotten pumpkins over the fence, though they weren't exactly worth the trouble of detonating.

All that said, it's classified information and what Mr. Montgomery doesn't know won't hurt him. What did it matter if he thought the group was more dangerous than they actually were? It's not as if they would be comparing notes; and after the week is up, it would no longer matter. Hawkins was satisfied that his ruse would successfully hold up as it was intended.

With a cheerful grin on his lips, he turned into the stall before the administration building, pulled the key and went inside to update his beautiful colleague on his progress with Mr. Montgomery and his incendiary contractor.

CHAPTER EIGHT

June 3rd, 2014

The dark clouds, cold wind and distinct smell of ozone did not bode well for the three hundred plus protesters who stood in the grassy courtyard before the giant Peace Tower of Ottawa's Parliament Buildings. Their angry shouts echoed through the streets of the capital while they waved large signs, with phrases written upon them such as "We Have No Need for Weed", and "We Don't Wanna Marijuana". A line of police in full riot gear separated them from the eighteenth-century, gothic revival architecture, and the proceedings held within. The clock high atop the tower informed anyone who was paying attention that the time was approaching two o'clock, the deadline when Parliament would finally reveal their decision to the public.

Among the noisy chanting and inane chatter was another echoing electronic voice emanating from a set of stereo speakers, that were set upon the stone stairway of the Parliament Building. The reporter had previously announced that she stood among a hundred other members of the media, in the entrance hall outside the doors to the House of Commons.

"Energy is high here in the anti-room, as we anxiously await the Press Secretary Martin Wallace to emerge from the proceedings. When he does, he will be announcing a decision two years in the making, a decision on the decriminalization of recreational drugs in a controlled environment. Now, in the final moments of delib-"

A sudden burst of excited shouting cut the reporter's sentence short.

"This is it," the reporter continued in a more urgent tone, *"the doors have opened, and the Members of Parliament are beginning to emerge. It is difficult to tell from their poker-faced expressions any hint of the outcome, but we shouldn't have long to wait. In fact, here's Secretary Wallace now."*

The cacophony of shouts over the radio died down leaving a single voice projecting out across the room, "*Good afternoon. I know you have all been waiting a long time for the decision on Bill 42a, and we thank you for your patience. It was a long and difficult deliberation on a very sensitive subject. With that in mind, it is the decision of the House that Bill 42a is to be passed and implemented in January of next year.*"

The remainder of the secretary's speech was unheard, drowned out by the shouts of the reporters on the radio combined with the hundreds of protesters gathered before the building. What began as rhythmic chanting; quickly escalated to furious screams laced with profanity. Contrary to the raging population of the square, a number of previously quiet voices now called out with cheers of celebration. These new voices stirred the pot, creating frenzy among the crowd. One man shoved another, and a woman took a stray elbow to the face. Soon fists were flying, and the screams became louder. Bloodied faces filled the crowd, and those knocked to the ground found themselves trampled by unruly feet.

Members of the police force pushed in to try to break up the fighting, but the once peaceful protest had become a vicious mob. They pulled batons and cans of pepper-spray from their holsters, as the two groups clashed with fierce determination. While the protestors pushed towards the Parliament building, the police used all the force they could muster to keep them from breaking the front line.

In the surrounding area, windows were broken, shops looted, vehicles smashed, and in some cases flipped over. Trashcans were set on fire. The police arrested hundreds of violent protesters, as the vandals caused hundreds of thousands of dollars in damage.

The media flocked to the area, cameras in hand, excitedly capturing as much of the action as they could without getting trampled themselves. Every news station in the country covered the chaos, and bloggers dubbed it, "Canada's biggest embarrassment since G20".

Despite the angry protests, Bill 42a proceeded as planned, and a popular nightclub in downtown Vancouver became the inaugural test facility. The club was shut down for eight months for renovations and was renamed *The Greenhouse*. Protesters continued to walk the streets around the club, drawing in more numbers with the growing media attention. As the grand opening drew nearer, the numbers increased exponentially.

**

"I wish to call to order, the first meeting of PALM. The People Against Legalized Marijuana."

The roar of applause and cheers from the group of two hundred audience members was deafening in the small Toronto theatre. The middle-aged man at the podium before them raised his hands to quiet them. "Thank you for your support."

"Drugs are a gift from Satan," A woman hollered from the middle of the crowd."

"My son got addicted to the pot and dropped out of school." Another shouted in turn.

The man at the podium could not allow the interruptions to distract him, "Please, ladies and gentlemen. I promise, I will allow you an opportunity to testify towards the end of the program."

The murmurs of the crowd began to die down, allowing him to continue, "My friends, we live in a world where the youth of today are searching for new and creative ways to get high. These children are at an age when they should be learning about responsibility, learning how to be the next generation of doctors and lawyers and politicians. Instead, we are teaching them that it is okay to self-medicate. You cannot handle anxiety. Here, smoke this and you will feel better. Are you feeling socially awkward? Here is a way for you to be the life of the party.

No, my friends, we have a responsibility to our sons and our daughters, our nieces and nephews and our grandchildren, to prevent them from using marijuana as a crutch. Yes, a crutch that will emotionally cripple them for life. For, once they start, they will never be able to cope with what life throws at them, without medicinal aid. Instead, they will become more susceptible to the harder drugs like crack, cocaine and heroin. What happens then? They end up homeless, or in prison, or worse. Is that what we want for the future of our country?"

"No!" A hundred and eighty-seven voices call out in unison.

"Do we want a future of emotionless zombies running our country?"

"No!" The voices grew louder and angrier.

The man at the podium smiled. He knew he had them. At that point, he could have said anything, and those lemmings would follow him to the end of the earth. He went on, at great length, about the exaggerated medical benefits of marijuana, the high potential of abuse, and the lack of safety precautions. He then charged every person in the room with the responsibility to stand up to the federal and local governments to stop the spread of marijuana use and distribution.

"We have a long and difficult road ahead of us, my friends. There are many who support Bill 42a, and they need to be educated. They need to learn that we will not tolerate this sort of legislation, and it is up to us to teach them. It is up to us to take a stand. Take up your signs! Raise your voices! Whatever you need to do to be heard, do it!"

Not once in his speech, did he offer limitations, never did he draw a line, and he was well-aware of that fact. He was counting on the mob mentality, and he knew by the cheers and shouts of profanity that he would get everything out of them he had desired. He did not have to wait long to find out how well.

In the months that followed, the protests were many, and rarely peaceful. They carried out countless acts of violence against Bill 42a supporters in the name of PALM. Vandalism, graffiti, theft, assault, there was no stopping his followers. If the police arrested one, he recruited three more to take their place. Attendance at his meetings grew to five hundred, then a thousand, and more. PALM became a thorn in the side of all levels of government.

His efforts, however, were in vain and the Diversification Strategy continued as planned. Patrons pushed through the lines of protesters to attend the grand opening of the Greenhouse and others like it around the country. The authorities largely ignored their shouts; and arrested many of his more ambitious followers. Worst of all, the success of Bill 42a ushered in the next level of legislation, one more morally vial than the first.

Nevertheless, that was fine. He had plenty of tricks up his sleeves, and an army of followers prepared to do his bidding. To solidify his stance, he decided a name change was in order, a brand that would rile up his followers and bring in more lemmings.

A middle-aged man stood at a podium before a theatre of two thousand angry faces, "I wish to call to order, the first meeting of P.A.L.M, The People Against Lewd Misconduct."

CHAPTER NINE

The soft green colour on the walls, the comfortable high backed leather chairs and the fresh scent of lavender did little to put Catherine at ease in the office of Dr. Valerie Lough. She had dreaded this part. She had been to see shrinks before and never had any use for them. All they ever wanted to do was talk about things that she had tried so hard to forget. She went through it once; she had no desire to relive it again. Sure, they all tell her that it helps to talk about it. Bullshit. The only thing it had accomplished was to bring back painful memories. She had no choice but to sit through these uncomfortable sessions, but no one could force her to talk. She resolved herself to say as little as possible, but just enough to get what she came for. Catherine barely had enough time to sit before Dr. Lough began with the obligatory small talk.

"Good morning, Catherine."

Catherine often wondered why shrinks always began their sessions on a first name basis. Was it a strategy to bring the conversation to a more personal level, to help the patient to better talk freely? Was it easier for patients to relate to a peer rather, than to what they often regarded as a superior? "May I offer you a glass of water before we begin?"

"No thanks."

Valerie didn't press the issue. "Did you sleep well last night? Are your accommodations satisfactory?"

"Just fine."

The truth of the matter was, the apartment was quite comfortable, but she still slept like shit. She couldn't get her encounter with Stephen Carlisle out of her mind. He was so handsome and charismatic, but she found it rather disconcerting how easily he got into her head. She wished he had never introduced himself and at the same time, hoped to run into him again later. Perhaps Dr. Lough was right; maybe she did need a shrink.

"You seem distracted." Valerie continued. "Is there something on your mind? Something you wish to talk about?"

"No, not really."

As Catherine crossed her arms in defiance, her long sleeve slid up her arm revealing a number of healing cut marks. Upon realizing where Dr. Lough was looking, she quickly pulled her sleeves down to her hands and hid them from view.

Valerie crossed her legs and leaned back in her chair, taking a more relaxed pose. "You know Catherine; we will be spending a lot of time together, in fact more and more as the week progresses. I'm not here to judge you, or to assess whether you are fit or unfit for anything. I am here for *you*. It's my job to get to the heart of what's troubling you and see if I can help you come to terms with your demons. I won't push you to talk about anything you don't want to, but two-word answers aren't going to speed up our visits at all. We both have to be here, let's make the best of it."

Dr. Lough's introduction was beginning to make a lot of sense, but Catherine wasn't about to let down her guard for the second time that morning. She sat quietly with her arms folded over her chest.

"So, you tell me then. What would *you* like to talk about?"

Catherine remained silent.

"Very well," the doctor sat up straight in her chair and folded her hands neatly in her lap. "I'll tell you what, I will start. My mother died of cancer when I was 13. The last couple of years leading up to it were very difficult on all of us. There were many changes happening in my life, like any preteen girl, and I needed my mother. As the illness progressed, she got weaker, and she began to struggle with the simplest of tasks. My hair was thick and curly, as it is now, and she used to brush it every night before she got sick. After a while, she was too weak to get through it, so she cut it short. I was so mad at her for chopping my beautiful hair; I hated that this stupid disease was taking everything from me. I knew I was being selfish but dammit, I was just a child. The following day my grandfather drove the two of us down to the offices of the cancer society and we donated my hair to charity, where they would use it to make wigs. Believe it or not, that small act made me feel better. To this day, I wonder if someone is wearing my hair right now."

"Why are you telling me this? What does any of that have to do with me?" Catherine scoffed.

"Absolutely nothing, it has to do with me. I opened myself up to you and shared a painful story from my past, of an event that affected the direction of my life. I'm trying to show you that I'm not some bureaucrat here to evaluate your moral status. I am a fellow woman with my own demons, who has trained to help others cope with theirs. I'm not a monster Catherine; I genuinely care about what happens to you. Talk to me, and let's see what we can accomplish."

Catherine scrutinized Valerie's expression, looking for any sign that she was being manipulated, but as best as she could tell the doctor was speaking with sincerity. "Okay. Not that it's going to change anything, but I'll talk. What do you want me to talk about?"

"Wonderful. Then why don't we start with you telling me a little bit about yourself, and we'll see where it goes from there."

"All right," Catherine acquiesced, "but before I tell you anything, I have just one question."

"Go ahead." Valerie was curious.

"Just who the hell is Stephen Carlisle?"

**

Catherine Elizabeth Dean was born in Mississauga Ontario, a suburb of Toronto with her parents and older brother Matt. Catherine led a relatively normal childhood. She had many friends, did well in school and excelled as a soprano in her school choir. In grade nine, she landed the role of Marian in her school's production of The Music Man.

Things however began to take a turn for Catherine while in High School. Part way through her second semester of grade eleven, she met Patrick Vernon. Patrick was tall, ruggedly handsome, and an all-around bad-boy. He would have been in grade twelve at the time, had he not been expelled and charged with vandalism, for trashing his mathematics teacher's car after an especially difficult exam. That neglected to stop him however from returning to the school every lunch hour to hang out with his friends. They would congregate behind the auto mechanics shop, cigarettes hanging from each of their mouths, kicking around a hacky sack. As tough as these boys portrayed themselves around the school, their focus and determination were evident when the foot-bag was in play.

Catherine and two of her girlfriends would spend the lunch break sitting on a cement-parking barrier, eating their sandwiches and watching the aerial spectacle. The small beanbag rarely touched dirt, as the six boys were in complete control. One would kick it around for a while solo before performing a tricky, behind the back kick, to send it to a friend who continued the dance-like display. Meanwhile the girls would occasionally catch a boy's eye and giggle between themselves.

On one particular occasion, Catherine caught Patrick's attention. A very brief moment was shared from a distance. This was the first time she had witnessed him literally drop the ball. The other boys razzed him about it, but he didn't care because it turned out to be the very icebreaker that he had been looking for to introduce himself.

Catherine and Patrick began seeing each other immediately. It began with just lunch hours and after school when they would make out in the back seat of his rusty Pontiac Sunfire. After a while, she started cutting classes. She would drive off with him to his messy basement apartment in one of his parents' rental properties. Her grades plummeted from a B+ average to a D-, not that she cared about grades anymore. All she was ever interested in doing anymore was hang out with Patrick, get high, drunk or both, and have wild passionate sex. Despite the barrage of threats by her parents, Catherine continued her downward spiral, and eventually stopped going to school altogether. The final blow for her family came when they announced that she was pregnant, and that she and Patrick had decided to keep the baby. That was the last time that she had set foot in her parent's home.

As he wished to prove himself a good father to their unborn child, Patrick went out and secured a job as a laborer for a general contracting company, while Catherine went to work at a local hamburger restaurant. Because Patrick's basement pad was far too small for the two of them plus a baby, they went out and got their own small one-bedroom apartment in one if the city's more undesirable neighborhoods. They spent the next seven months just scraping by to put food on the table.

At thirty-seven weeks, Catherine began having horrible stomach pains, and shortly after that, her water broke. Patrick rushed her to the hospital where she spent the following thirteen hours in excruciating labour. When the time did arrive for Catherine to push, she bit down and gave it everything she had. As the head began to emerge, there was a sudden commotion at the other end of the table as the nurse rushed to grab a tray of shiny tools. Catherine's pleas for information went unanswered while the doctor worked calmly yet swiftly to rectify whatever situation had just arisen.

"Keep pushing Ms. Dean, don't stop now." The doctor had told her.

She did as the doctor instructed, and within the next six minutes, her son was born. However, there were no cries. The medical team took the baby over to a small table with a heat lamp where they made a frantic attempt to revive the infant. As it turned out, the umbilical cord had wrapped itself around the baby's neck as he entered the birth canal, and despite the doctor's efforts, he was unable to save the child.

Catherine fell into a deep depression, closing herself off from those around her, including her boyfriend. Patrick tried to be supportive at first, but it didn't take long before her depression and self-loathing became too much for him to deal with. He left for work one morning, emptied the bank account, and she never heard from him since. Her family offered to take her back in again on the condition that she returns to school, but she refused and remained on her own, trying to support herself. She spent a few years jumping from job to job, serving burgers or waiting tables, living well below the poverty line. She had no time for friends or relationships, so she continued her dejected existence alone, scraping together barely enough money for rent and food. She needed to find a more reliable source of income, and she needed to find it soon.

On one fateful evening, while ignoring the pile of unpaid utility bills, she leaned against the kitchen counter, pushing oil & vinegar-soaked lettuce around her plate with a fork. Open before her was a day-old copy of the Toronto Sun that she had pulled from the garbage bin outside her apartment. Pickings were slim, taking in to account her lack of education. Most of the jobs that piqued her interest required a High School Diploma or better. It appeared that a person needed a grade twelve education just to answer a phone. The situation seemed hopeless.

Resigned to the conclusion that nothing in the crumpled newspaper could raise her spirits, she folded it closed, and returned to her sorry excuse for a salad. She raised her fork and shoved a shriveling leaf of lettuce into her mouth, as her gaze darted back to an image on the front page. Staring her in the face was a way out, an unconventional answer.

What caught her eye was an artist's rendering of a beautiful, yet rather provocative butterfly. The wings were bright and colorful, while the body was shapely and alluring like a woman's body. The headline read, "The Butterfly Garden has Toronto all a flutter. Full story on page 2."

She chewed her bitter greens while she opened to the page. The article began with the huge success after phase one of P.M. Ron Alexander's Diversification Strategy. Lounges like *The Greenhouse* opened all over the country, and all were highly profitable. It went on to describe in detail the safety precautions that they put in place, and the data surrounding taxation. It was quite clear that the decision to legalize recreational drugs was undeniably a popular one.

Bored with statistics and legal jargon, Catherine skimmed down the page until she came to the information she needed.

"In a unanimous decision in Parliament this past June; Bill 42b was approved, thereby changing the law to decriminalize prostitution. Ignoring all the push back from local religious groups, the intent was to open government-approved brothels in every major city, take prostitution off the streets and give the escorts health benefits, thereby making it a safer profession. The business scheduled to open here in Toronto later this month has been named *The Butterfly Garden*."

Catherine finished reading the article set her fork on the plate and walked into her cramped three-piece bathroom. She slid her robe off her shoulders and allowed it to drop to the floor. She stood up straight in front of the mirror, looking over her naked body. She turned to the side and stepped up on her toes to check out her shapely legs and curvy figure. She still held on to a fair bit of her baby weight, but if she applied herself and exercised, she saw no reason why men wouldn't want to fuck her.

Catherine saw this as an opportunity to get herself out of financial desperation. She most definitely had the looks for it. She could sell her body for a couple of years; after all, no one else was using it for the moment. She would rake in the money and reap the benefits. If she enjoyed it, she would continue, if not she could go back to waiting tables.

Unfortunately, it didn't turn out to be as lucrative as she had hoped. She soon found out that this profession required a lot more than good looks and a hot body. She had to learn to disconnect herself from the job itself. She struggled to prevent herself from taking personally all the disgusting and demeaning acts of depravity the clients forced her to do on a daily, occasionally even hourly basis. She looked forward to some of her kinder and gentler clients who came to her, just to feel desirable for a few short minutes. Unfortunately, for her, those occasions were rare. Although The Garden kept their promise of safety and cleanliness, she had to fulfill all her clients' wishes, and the vast majorities were not looking for tenderness.

The career change she thought would pull her from her slump instead pushed her farther into it. She felt defiled and ashamed, and she had brought it all down on herself. She fell deeper into her depression than she ever had. The few luxuries she was now able to afford paled in comparison to the shame and hatred she felt towards herself. The mental anguish was too much to bear.

There was nothing left for her. The Garden had destroyed her body and spirit. She couldn't look for another job. Surely, any manager could see how dirty and disgusting she was. Dating was impossible since the thought of sex appalled her. Besides, she was convinced that she wasn't even good enough to be a whore, never mind a girlfriend. Hundreds of self-defeating thoughts like those, circled through her mind like a skipping record. She could get no peace if she continued this path of destruction.

One night she went to bed with a bottle of dark rum and a full bottle of muscle relaxants. By the time she fell asleep, both were empty. A member of the Garden's security team found her the next morning in a puddle of her own vomit. He had fortunately decided to check on her when she hadn't shown up for work for the third consecutive evening. He rushed her to the hospital where the doctors were able to save her, or at the very least, delay the inevitable.

CHAPTER TEN

"He certainly has piqued her interest, at any rate." Valerie said before putting another bite of breaded veal cutlet into her mouth. "I'm still not convinced that it will be enough to fully draw her in. She has put up some awfully high walls."

Travis swallowed a mouthful of asparagus, "Based on what you're telling me, it sounds as if he has one foot in the door."

"Perhaps, a small toe," she joked.

"Hey, she asked about him. It's a start."

The two of them met up in the small kitchenette, after Hawkins had returned from physiotherapy. Normally they would dine with the rest of the Farm's compliment in the atrium. On occasions such as this however, when it was imperative to keep their conversations distant from prying ears, they preferred to bring their meals back to the private break room where they could talk freely.

Valerie placed another morsel of veal into her mouth. She waited until she had swallowed before continuing. "I'm not so certain that any man will be able to break down her barriers. Her life experience has taught her that men don't respect her, and she resents them all because of it. After three years of selling herself at the Butterfly Garden, sex is nothing more than a job to her. It's true that he took her off guard with his bold approach, but I don't believe that his charm is sufficient enough to keep that door open."

"He has five more days to work his magic, as do you. She hasn't yet chosen her exit strategy, so it's possible that she remains uncertain."

"You have an awful lot of faith in your friend. After talking to her this afternoon I'm not convinced that she's waffling, I think she just doesn't care about a strategy or anything else for that matter. She has severe trust issues. It's going to be terribly difficult for anyone to get her to care again."

"This is unlike you Val. You are giving me the impression you've already given up on her."

"Gawd no, I'm far from giving up, but I'm experienced enough in this to know that it will be an uphill battle all the way. Crippling depression is nothing to scoff at. It is very difficult to treat because a lot of the time the patient is in so deep; they no longer want the help. Before I have any remote chance of helping her, I have to gain her trust."

"I have trust in you Val. If anyone can get through to her, I'm certain you can."

"You flatter me."

Hawkins glanced up at the wall clock, which read 17:22. "Mr. Richards should be coming to my office shortly. I asked him to join us at 5:30 to discuss Mr. Montgomery."

"Okay." Valerie wiped her mouth with her napkin, "I'll have to swing by my office first and grab my notes."

"You say that like it's so far out of your way," Travis teased.

"Hey, if we started having our meetings in my office, we wouldn't have this problem."

"No way, that's your home turf. I'd be worried that you'd spend the entire meeting analyzing my every word."

"Too late, I already do."

**

By the time Kevin Richards entered Captain Hawkins' office, Dr. Lough had already seated herself comfortably in one of the two chairs, opposite the immaculately tidy desk. She sat with a single white folder clutched at her lap while Hawkins searched his computer for a particular file.

"Good evening Mr. Richards," Hawkins began, "please have a seat."

While Richards took the chair next to Dr. Lough, she started in on him with typical psychological small talk about his day. Personally, Richards would've preferred sitting in silence until they were ready to get to the point, but out of respect, he appeased her by answering her inane questions. Not that he had anything to hide. He had spent the day in the workshop tinkering with the device he would use for the up-and-coming spectacle. Nevertheless, he humored the doctor by participating in the obligatory conversational ping-pong. Fortunately, for Kevin, he didn't have to put up with the pleasantries for too long, as Captain Hawkins finally found the elusive file.

Hawkins quickly got to the point, "Okay, here it is, Ian Montgomery. At this point everything we do is merely a formality. The outcome is more or less, set in stone. It is what it is, I'm afraid."

"I would appreciate it if you wouldn't use language like that." Dr. Lough piped in.

"Language like what?" Hawkins asked.

"*It is what it is.* I hate it. I hear it all the time from my patients, it carries with it defeatist connotations. What you're basically saying is; we can't do anything about it, so why bother trying?" She then added with a distinct tone of sarcasm, "C'est la vie."

"It was just a figure of speech, Val. It doesn't matter how you word it," Hawkins argued, "in this case, like so many others we get here, there is absolutely nothing we can do to affect the outcome. Either he dies here on his own terms, or he sits at home and waits for the disease to kill him. Either way nothing changes."

Dr. Lough began to raise her voice. "I'm not talking about this case; I simply stated that I don't like the statement. If you-"

"Do you know where it came from?"

Both Hawkins and Dr. Lough stopped, taken off guard by Mr. Richards' question that came calmly out of left field.

"Where what came from?" Hawkins asked.

"That statement. It is what it is."

The tension in Hawkins' shoulders relaxed along with the tension in the room. He gave Richards the floor. "I'm all ears."

Richards smiled, "When Apple computers first released their brand-new operating system, completely independent from Microsoft's Windows, the technical support team was bombarded with complaints regarding compatibility issues. In response, Steve Jobs told his techs to reply by stating that it is an independent operating system, and *it is what it is.*"

"Is that true?" Dr. Lough asked.

"I don't know, I read it somewhere."

Hawkins laughed, "All right, it would appear we got a bit off topic. Thanks for that though, Mr. Richards. Let's get back to Mr. Montgomery."

Dr. Lough nodded her head in agreement.

"Okay then. I had an encounter with him this morning after Mr. Richards' effective display. It appears as though Mr. Montgomery took great interest in what was transpiring. I had to dodge his questions to avoid him finding out about the backdraft."

"You make it sound like a trap,"

"It's the loophole we must go through in order to remain within the guidelines of the contract. He can't knowingly die by his own hands."

"Give me some credit Travis," Valerie argued, "I know how this works. I'm only saying that your statement makes it seem underhanded."

"You two argue like an old married couple."

Travis and Valerie both blushed with embarrassment. They caught each other's eye for just a moment, and then poised themselves to continue. Hawkins went on to describe his encounter with Ian and got them up to speed on his fabrication regarding the PALM organization. Dr. Lough listened with professional courtesy, jotting down the odd note to ensure she could effectively back up her colleague's story. Richards remained silent, sporting a smug grin, until Hawkins had finished his report.

"And he bought it?"

"He appeared to. I exaggerated the threat, but I don't think I said anything too unreasonable to believe. Besides, we are finished our testing, and Mr. Richards has finished playing. Isn't that right?" He looked towards Richards with stern expression.

"Of course."

"There you go. Mr. Montgomery will have no further reason to concern himself with PALM." He turned to his computer and opened an email, changing the subject, "Now, according to maintenance, they plan on having the construction complete by tomorrow afternoon. I would like you to have your system in place soon after, but before we furnish it. I want to be able to hide your installation."

Richards leaned forward, "You don't need to worry about my installation. He won't know it's there. I have two small gas lines entering the common room between the baseboard and the floor. Once the carpet is in, you won't see it. I will be able to pump the gas in and saturate the carpet without even entering the apartment. The igniter can go anywhere under the carpet. I'll just drill a hole underneath for the wires. After that, all he needs to do is open the door."

"And if he has a last-minute change of heart?" Valerie asked, "What then?"

"Forever the optimist," Travis teased, "he will have an emergency exit, as well as a phone with a direct line to me. If he changes his mind, I will be the first to know, Mr. Richards will be the second. He is very good at starting fires, but he is also well trained to put them out."

CHAPTER ELEVEN

Good morning and welcome to the Talk 860. It's 7:05 and I'm Joe Foster. It is looking to be a fine Tuesday, with a high of twenty-two and only a five percent chance of showers later in the day. No issues so far on the drive in, but if you see anything on the roads, feel free to give us a shout at 555-TALK

The big news of the day, and I'm sure many of you have been chatting about it, is the big announcement from Parliament late yesterday afternoon. In case you've been hiding under a rock the past four years, yes, I am referring to the final decision on Prime Minister Alexander's Diversification Strategy, the legalization of assisted euthanasia. Judging by the number of calls coming in, it appears as though the decision has struck a chord. So, the question for today is, "Are you for or against the decision?"

"Let's take a call. Good morning, you're on Talk 860."

"Good morning, Joe. I love your show. I listen every day."

"Thank you for listening. What's your name?"

"I'm Deborah."

"Hi Deborah, so how do you feel about Parliament's decision to legalize assisted euthanasia?"

"Oh, I'm all for it, Joe. I just wish they had done it sooner. My husband suffered for an awful long time before he finally passed away last summer. This could have saved him a whole lot of pain. He had asked the doctors so many times to help end the pain, but all they could offer him was more drugs to make him numb. It was so hard on everyone to watch him suffer like that. He would have been very happy with this decision."

"Thank you for sharing with us, Deborah. I am sorry for your loss."

"Thanks, Joe."

"Next caller, welcome to Talk 860. Who am I talking to?"

"This is Steve West."

"Good morning, Steve. What do you think of the decision?"

"Well Joe, I think those hippy-dippy socialists need to get off their collective liberal asses, and do something that will actually benefit the country, instead of worrying about legalizing shit that no one gives a rat's ass about."

"Those are some strong words, Steve. There are many who believe that this strategy is the first step towards making the country stronger. They believe that decriminalization will take some of the stress off our legal system so they can worry about the bigger issues."

"We never had to worry about that crap when the Conservatives were in power. If those fuc-"

"I'm sorry Steve, but our sensors had to cut you off. Everyone is entitled to their opinion folks, but we ask that you keep it clean while you are on the air. Thank you. Who's our next caller?"

"My name's Grant."

"Hey Grant, what's your opinion on today's issue?"

"Thank you, Joe, for providing an outlet where people like me can share their opinions on subjects that matter."

"That's why we're here Grant. What's on your mind?"

"Ecclesiastes 7:17 says, "Do not be overly wicked, and do not be foolish. Why die before your time?" There are many in the world who make the same mistake. They presume that their body is their own to do with what they please. That, Joe, couldn't be further from the truth. God created man; therefore, your body belongs to God. Those who don't take care of their body defile His creation."

Here comes the honourable Ron Alexander with his new laws, suggesting that it is okay going against God's will, to destroy what He created. You fill His lungs with marijuana, and His veins with crack. Then you sell His body to sexual deviants for their pleasure. Now, with this new law, you can end the very life He created, well before His chosen time."

This new legislation has given man control over his own body, but what are the consequences? You have stolen that body out of the hands of our Lord, and for that, those who defy God will surely perish for eternity in hell. God has given you a gift. He has allowed you to use that body for an entire lifetime, and it is up to you to take care of that body, not defile it with your bad judgements."

I implore each and every one of you to not give in to Alexander's evil plan. Don't allow him to rob you of the gift given to you by God. Protect His body by protecting your own. Don't jab it with needles or allow strange men to penetrate it, but most of all; don't rob Him of the life He created for you. Your body is a Temple, and Temples are meant to be worshiped."

"Alright, thank you for your, uhm, insight Grant. You have given us a lot to think about. Wow. Okay, I suppose now would be as good a time as any to hear from our sponsors, and we'll be back with more Talk 860."

**

The small receiver crackled with static. Though the words were difficult to make out, he was still able to understand enough of the conversation to know exactly what was going on. The three individuals he was eavesdropping on were completely oblivious to the small black disc he had stuck to the underside of Captain Hawkins' desk during his initial interview. Ian Montgomery was pleased with his own ingenuity.

Unimpeded by any form of ailment, he stood up from his chair without effort and walked to the counter to pour himself another cup of coffee. He took a sip while the voices continued behind him.

The conversation was intriguing to say the least, once they had made it past the mundane small talk. "It is what it is." That's what Hawkins had said. The idea was laughable. Ian listened with amusement as the captain described their conversation with a misplaced sense of pride. He had no idea that *it* wasn't necessarily what it seemed to be.

The best lies contain an element of truth.

After his wife Katsumi died in the fires, Ian began to lose his battle against cancer. That was true. As far as he was concerned, his life was over. He had lost his wife; he lost his health and he saw only one option.

He turned to God.

Every bit of strength he had left went into his faith. He went to church several times each week to pray. If there were no services, he would sit in the quiet church in private worship. Ian grew strength from his prayer and met a young couple who invited him into a support group with fellow congregation members suffering with terminal illness. Ian grew even more strength from the group.

The next time Ian returned to the oncologist for the next series of treatments, the MRI scans miraculously revealed that the tumors that had once spelled certain death had since shrunk down to a size that gave him a fighting chance for survival.

Convinced that God had answered his prayers, despite the doctor's assurance that the treatments were what had saved him, Ian kept up his part of the bargain. He devoted himself heart and soul to the church. He took control of his support group to teach them that survival was possible if they gave themselves to the Lord. He even began to preach to the congregation.

The following examination with his oncologist revealed unexpected results; the cancer had gone into remission. Ian found a new lease on life, and the only thing that outshone his faith was his arrogance. He had beat cancer. He was now more certain than ever that God had other plans for him. Now he needed a cause, something he could unite the church against and lead them to victory. The answer was obvious. He would fight against those who embraced the sins of the bible.

Ian founded a group and named it PALM. He recruited followers from churches across the whole country and brought them together in unity against a common enemy, the Diversification Strategy. They took a stand in Vancouver when the government decriminalized drugs, and they marched in Toronto when they legalized prostitution, but by opening the Farm and condoning euthanasia they were spitting in the face of God. Taking control of life itself from the very one who created it. This was an abomination and it had to stop.

He created an alias to protect his name from any illegal wrongdoings and organized protest rallies at the site. He started a website where he posted weekly slanderous blogs and wrote hate mail to high-ranking government officials, all from the comfort of his own home office. Despite the fact that he organized the events himself through the PALM social networking account, he never attended his own rallies. As the cause grew momentum, he didn't even have to do that much anymore. The flock organized themselves. All the years he sat at the head of the table; not once did he hold face-to-face interviews for the media. Nobody knew the identity of the man behind the mission.

Ian's frustrations grew as more and more of his writings and protests fell by the wayside. The press showed up to the first couple of marches, but since no more than a half dozen people crossed the main gates on any given week, they found the rallies too ineffective to be newsworthy. Within hours, his website plummeted from over eighty thousand daily hits to less than two hundred. His message was getting lost in the corruption that the country had embraced. He couldn't allow these atrocities to continue. He had to find out exactly what went on behind the gates of the Farm. Now he had to find a way in. Fortunately, for him, his Oncologist was also a devout member of the PALM Organization.

The best lies contain an element of truth.

"No one is going to believe that; it needs to look legitimate. Can't you just change the date of an earlier scan?" Ian Montgomery recalled the conversation with his Oncologist and PALM subordinate, Dr. Jason Simpson, who sat at his office computer doctoring reports.

"Altering medical documents is highly unethical, Mr. Montgomery, not to mention incredibly illegal."

"Do you honestly believe that changing a couple of dates on a sheet of paper is more unethical than the atrocities they are committing at the Farm?"

"No, but-"

"We cannot allow them to spit in the face of our Lord, and if that means taking a few risks and breaking a few rules, the so be it."

"Yes, I know. I get it. But I could lose my practice, or worse, go to prison."

Ian had placed a reassuring hand on the doctor's shoulder. "Don't worry my friend. No one is going to prison today."

Dr. Simpson nodded in silence, turned back to his computer, and continued clicking through documents, while his boss read over his shoulder.

"There, that one," Ian shouted, pointing at the screen, "January 17th. That's when you believed my condition was hopeless. Change that one to today's date."

"Okay, but it won't be enough. One document does not make a case for euthanasia."

"Then I guess you have some writing to do. Come on Jason, you've been doing this for twenty-eight years. You know what terminal looks like. Get creative; add a few paragraphs about pain management and quality of life. Hell, take a chapter from someone else's file. Surely you have a couple patients on that box who would have been good candidates for the Farm."

"Holy shit, Ian." His hands were trembling. "What you are asking me to do-" He couldn't find the words to continue.

Ian Montgomery placed his hands on the armrests on either side of the doctor's chair, brought his face close and whispered directly into his ear. "This is not up for debate, Doctor. You will do this, and you will make it unbreakable. I want to be on the Farm inside of a month and if you can't make that happen, I will make your life and the lives of your family, a living hell. Do I make myself clear?"

A bead of sweat formed on Dr. Simpson's temple, dripped down his cheek and onto his lab coat. Without another word, he turned back to his computer, minimized the Montgomery file, and opened another labelled, *Connor Ward- Deceased.*

According to this new fabricated version of the truth, the cancer returned with a vengeance, inoperable. There was no stopping the spread of the disease. Pain management became decreasingly effective, and he no longer possessed the will to fight. Ian Montgomery received a referral to the Farm as a viable alternative.

Through his research into the Farm's activities, he was very aware of their one-week policy to try to talk the client out of the contract. Ian was quite happy with that arrangement, as it gave him ample time to identify their weaknesses without having to worry about falling victim to his own ruse.

So, there he sat before a cheap radio receiver listening in to what the targets had assumed to be a private conversation. This one he found to be of great interest, as they were discussing him. In a delightful display of irony, Hawkins unknowingly used Ian's own organization as a scapegoat for his little scheme. Ian didn't immediately understand why Hawkins was lying through his teeth during their conversation in the courtyard, but now he knew precisely what the truth entailed.

A backdraft, very clever.

His research had paid off. He needed another scandal and there it was. Kevin Richards, an arsonist, working as a contractor at the Farm instead of living out a life sentence in prison for premeditated murder. It couldn't have worked out better if he had planned it.

"*Give me the timeline,*" came the voice of the lovely Dr. Lough.

"*It'll start after dark,*" said the voice of the man named Mr. Richards, who apparently held his contract.

"Let's say *Twenty-three hundred hours,*" Captain Hawkins added.

"*Okay, lights out; he goes to bed in the trailer,*" Dr. Lough again.

"*That's right,*" Hawkins continued. "*Though we are calling it a satellite apartment. Monday evening, I will have you prescribe Mr. Montgomery something to help him relax. We can't knock him out, but we want him to be able to sleep.*"

"*Diphenhydramine will make him drowsy, but he'll still be aware.*"

With that final important tidbit of information, Ian heard all he needed to learn of the conversation in Hawkins' office. He would begin preparations immediately to turn the contract around and throw it back in the face of that heathen, Captain Hawkins. He knew their plan, now he just needed his own. He would not be taking any sleep aids, nor would he be spending any more time in the burning trailer than he absolutely had to. Getting out would be the easy part. Turning the tables would take a little more effort.

Ian turned on his laptop and opened the browser. If he were going to pull this off, he would need some help. He knew exactly where he was going to get it.

**

Byron Daniels held a can of condensed tomato soup and squinted to read the ingredients. Ever since the doctor diagnosed him with high blood pressure, he had to watch his sodium intake and this particular brand contained far too much for his liking. He placed the can back on the shelf and selected another. That one was even worse. It was starting to look like soup wasn't in his future.

Dinners had been so much easier before his wife left. She'd prepared all his meals, and never from a can. She always had complete control over what went into his food. Three meals a day, seven days a week, and delicious food at that. She truly was a fantastic cook.

Nevertheless, she left him, claiming she felt underappreciated and overwhelmed. What the fuck was that supposed to mean?

Byron could never understand why she was complaining. For 27 years, he had gone to work five days a week in a distribution warehouse doing manual labour while his wife stayed home. Her only job was cooking, cleaning, and taking care of the kids. Now that their four children had moved out, she didn't even have that task anymore. Yet, she accused *him* of being ungrateful. Byron didn't care though; he didn't need her. He was doing just fine on his own. He picked up the first can of soup again and tossed it into his shopping cart.

A bit further, down the aisle he began eyeing a box of macaroni and cheese when the sound of croaking frogs came from his jacket pocket. He reached in and pulled out his smart phone. A notification informed him of an incoming message from a popular social networking site. Using the touch screen, he opened the application to find a general message for all members of the PALM group.

Protest rally at the Killing Farm this Thursday at 8 AM sharp.
Bring everyone!

The message came as a surprise to Byron. They hadn't marched in months. In fact, he hadn't heard from his friend Ian in several weeks. What exactly was he up to?

The phone croaked a second time. This time however, it was an instant message directed to him only.

Byron, I need you to bring a few things. Shopping list to follow.
Ian.

Just like old times. Ian always seemed to have two messages: one for the flock, and another for his ears only. It had been like that since the beginning, at the First Baptist Church of Lethbridge. Once the last of the patrons had left, Byron Daniels would sit alone in the Pastor's office, awaiting the arrival of the man who had invited him there. He remembered too clearly, how quiet it was in the church the last time he saw his friend. He recalled clearly, hearing the raindrops as they tapped gently on the roof above, and the slosh of the cars, driving on the wet road outside.

Then a break in the silence. Hard soled shoes tapping on the wood church floor; soft at first, and gradually got louder. Then the click of the latch on the office door, and the creak of the hinges, as his friend appeared before him.

"Hello Byron, thank you for meeting with me."

Byron stood to greet him, and they shook hands. "Hey, Ian. So, what's going on? Why all the secrecy?"

"Please, have a seat."

Byron returned to his chair, while Ian reclined back in the Pastor's comfortable office chair. "Have you been following the news the past week?"

"I don't pay much attention to the news. Just the shit the guys at work talk about at lunchtime."

"But you've heard about the Farm?"

"Of course. Damned pussies taking the coward's way out. It ain't natural."

"I knew we'd be on the same page, my friend." Ian leaned forward. "So, what are we going to do about it?"

"Shit, I don't know. We could shoot everyone who tries to go in."

Ian scoffed, "I don't think that would be the smartest idea. We would be giving them exactly what they want and committing murder in the process."

"I wasn't serious."

"Well, I am being serious." Ian began to raise his voice. "I need you to be serious too. We have a real problem here. Those Godless hypocrites think they can defy the word of our Lord, and they must be stopped. It is up to us to carry out God's will."

"Geeze, Ian. I only meant that I don't have any ideas. You're the educated one. Tell me what you want to do, and I'll help you."

Ian relaxed, "I don't know yet. Who do we have, loyal to our cause?"

"Well, you got me. Randy, and Sheldon for sure, probably Larry too. And there are another twenty or so who will follow us if we march."

"No, we aren't going to march, at least, not yet. We need something else, something that will get their attention. Something they can't ignore."

"And what's that?"

Ian swiveled around in his chair and stared at the artist's rendering of Jesus on the back wall. "I'm still working that out, my friend." He turned back and placed his hands, palms down, on the desk. "But now that I know who our players are, I have a few ideas."

Byron leaned in closer. "And are you going to share those ideas?"

Ian leaned back, which put some space between them. "All in good time, my friend. All in good time."

Now, it would seem as though that time had come. Ian was clearly up to something. But where was he? He said *bring* a few things. Would Ian be attending this one? That would be a first for the books. Nevertheless, he now had preparations to make. He would have to pull the signs from storage and round up all the usual suspects. Then it was just a matter of fulfilling Ian's wish list.

In the meantime, he had dinner to consider. He stared down at all the cans and packages of easy to prepare meals in his cart with disgust.

Screw it.

Byron abandoned his cart in the aisle and made his way to the front of the store where the fast-food franchise beckoned him to grab himself a cheeseburger.

ECE-80035

This was nothing like the first-person shooter games he played on the Xbox. There were no power-ups or first aid kits. There was no hiding behind a garbage bin, waiting for his pursuers to lose interest. They were looking for him, and when they found him, they were going to shoot him. There would be no respawning. When they shot him; game over.

Bruce's lungs burned in his chest, and his eyes stung from the sweat and dirt that dripped from his forehead. He thought it would be an exciting way to go, but he'd never been so scared in his life. He wasn't afraid of dying; he had already come to terms with that inevitability. The inoperable tumour that seized a large portion of his brain had already insured that. No, he was terrified of the two hunters with assault rifles, chasing him through the woods until they found him and shot him. What if it wasn't a clean shot? What would happen if they only wounded him, and he died a slow agonizing death? How long would he have to suffer before they finished him off? He had heard somewhere that a belly wound is the worst pain imaginable.

He gave up trying to run. There were too many roots to trip over and the low hanging branches scratched his face all to hell. He decided to try hiding in a bush for a while, clinging to the small rifle they had issued him. The woods weren't very large, but he still had no clue where the hunters were. He listened for twigs snapping under footsteps or the rustle of leaves, but he heard nothing. All he could hear was his own heavy breathing. What was he thinking when he signed up for this?

Hawkins had told him to come up with a safe word. Something for him to shout out if he changed his mind and the hunt would be over. *Riders* was his safe word. Seemed like a great word at the time. They were the best team in the league, and they had just defeated the Bombers the evening Hawkins asked him to make the choice. Now, he realized, running through the woods, chased by men with guns, was a ridiculous time to be cheering for the Roughriders.

He heard a whisper coming from his left. Bruce brought his rifle around and blindly pulled the trigger. Red paint splattered upon a nearby tree.

"Over there," he heard the whisper.

Shit.

He bolted from his hiding place and sprinted in the opposite direction. A shot rang out behind him, and a section of bark exploded from a tree next to him. He was so tired and scared; he thought he would throw up. If ever there was a time to shout out the safe word, that was it.

Nevertheless, he didn't. If he threw in the towel, that would be the end of the contract. There would be nothing left for him to do but go home and wait for the tumour to destroy his brain. That was unacceptable.

He stopped again and hid behind a large tree with his back against the rough bark. He remembered a time when he could have run like that without issue, but the tumour had taken its toll and changed everything.

Again, he had no clue where his predators were at that moment. He craned his neck to peek around the tree behind him. There was no one in sight.

Without warning, he suddenly felt cold hard steel press up against the back of his head and heard an unmistakable click. He knew exactly what that meant, and everything was finally okay. Bruce had already taken the time to say goodbye to everyone he needed to before he left Regina, just a week earlier. Those closest to him knew where he was going, while the others would find out soon enough. Fortunately, he didn't have a girlfriend at the time, which only left his parents. He couldn't imagine what they were going through. Outliving one's children goes against the natural order of things. Even so, they had supported him through the rough times, and were sympathetic with his decision to go to the Farm. He wondered though, how they would feel about the fact that, at that very moment, he had the muzzle of an assault rifle firmly pressed into the back of his head.

They may have been able to take comfort in knowing, it took only a moment, and he barely heard the shot.

CHAPTER TWELVE

Day Three

It was busier than it had been in the last couple of days. It seemed, as though the vast majority of the Farm's staff were all sitting down in the atrium for breakfast at the same time. Fortunately, for Catherine, she had snagged a small table to herself that only had one chair. She hoped the lack of additional seating at her table would reduce her chances of being disturbed. So far, she had been successful.

With a plate of half eaten toast and marmalade cooling before her, she tried with great difficulty to read her book, but she found herself rereading the same passage repeatedly. Why couldn't she stop thinking about Stephen Carlisle? How could she be so foolish to allow him to get inside her head like that? Why did she let her guard down?

Again, she attempted to push the thought of him away, but the harder she tried to forget, the more she thought of him, the things she should have said and the arguments she could have made. To make matters worse, she found herself wondering where he was at that moment. As it turned out, she didn't have long to wait for the answer.

Catherine looked up to the familiar sound of metal dragging on stone to find the presumptuous bastard pulling a chair across the floor towards her table. Without so much as the simple courtesy of asking, Stephen plunked himself down in the chair across the table from her.

Ignoring her dumbfounded expression, he broke the silence between them, "So how is our Special Agent fairing on this fine morning?"

Uncertain of how to respond to his approach, she replied with disdain in her voice, "I'm not sure yet. You haven't given me enough time to get back into it."

"What have you been doing then? Your toast his half eaten, your water glass is empty, and you've been staring at the same page for the last twenty minutes."

Catherine blushed, "Have you been-"

"Relax, I'm not stalking you. I was eating my own breakfast over there." He indicated a recently vacated table in the corner. "I saw you staring blindly at your book, looking troubled and I thought you might like a distraction."

She eyed him suspiciously. She didn't recall seeing him in the room previously. "That really isn't necessary," she replied clutching the book tight to her chest, "I'm not in the mood for idle chitchat."

"Why not? Everyone on this compound, whether they have met you are not, knows exactly why you're here. It's no big secret, there's absolutely nothing to hide. You're facing the end with open arms but you're closing yourself off to those around you. Think about it for a second. You've given yourself a death sentence and you have five days to live. What are you going to do with those days? Are you going to sit by yourself and struggle to concentrate on your book, or do you want to have some fun in your final days?"

"What I want is for you to leave me the hell alone. Just who do you think you are? You don't know me. You don't know how I want to spend my last days. Have you once considered that I might want to relax and enjoy a book by my favorite authors without constant interruption? Are you too arrogant to think that whatever I do with my time here, I might not want to spend it with you?" Her voice began to carry, and others started to take notice. "I have asked you more than once and I don't want to ask again. Please, leave me the hell alone."

She could see by his expression that Stephen likely considered her request for only a moment, but clearly decided that it wasn't in either of their best interest for him to leave her alone. He instead tried a more direct approach. "So, have you put any more thought into your process of elimination?"

"Excuse me?" Stephen took Catherine completely off guard with his complete lack of tact.

"Have you chosen how you want to die?"

She found it impossible to hide her disdain for this man, "I really don't care. It's not that important and quite frankly I don't want to have this discussion with you."

"Not important? Are you kidding me? You have a wealth of opportunities at your disposal. Or should I say, *for* your disposal?" Stephen laughed. "You came here to die. At some point you must have considered how."

"I told you-"

"Come on; think about it for a moment. Do you want it quick and painless, or slow and agonizing? Will it be neat and tidy, or will you leave a big mess? Your options here are virtually endless."

"You're disgusting."

"Am I? You're sitting here before me with your nose in your book, trying desperately to kill the time as quickly as possible until Hawkins grants your request. You are at the Farm. You are not here for a week of R&R by the pool, which incidentally we have next door if you're interested."

"You're despicable."

"Again, with the insults. Have I once done anything to provoke your hatred? I am telling it as it is. Like it or not, for the next five days we're living under the same roof. Now, you have two choices, you can sit on your ass all day, be antisocial and watch the clock, or you can utilize what this facility has to offer and perhaps even enjoy your final week on Earth."

"Why is it so important to you how I spend my time here? Why do you even care?"

"Because I believe that if you're going to die anyway, you might as well go in style. Once you've resigned yourself to be here, there is no longer anything left to worry about. Can you think of a more fitting time and place to live freely with no regrets? I hate to see anyone waste such a glorious opportunity."

"You certainly have a strange outlook on life."

"The position I've been given isn't exactly the most orthodox of stations. It gives me a rather unique perspective."

"I can't argue with that," Catherine finally relented.

"So, what do you say? Put Agent Pendergast down for a couple of hours and walk with me. Let me show you around the compound. Who knows, maybe you'll find something else more exciting to occupy your time."

"Fine," she said with contempt, "I'll go on your little tour, but I'm telling you this. Once we are done, that's it. No more intrusions. I don't want to talk to you; I don't want to see you. After this, we are finished. Do you understand?"

At that moment, Catherine felt as though there were a hundred eyes upon her. She glanced around the room and realized she must have been speaking louder than she had intended. She began to feel like the entire room was watching her and she needed to get away from those judgmental glares. She cowered in her chair and closed her eyes, hoping they would all look away.

"Very well, Catherine. If after the tour you still feel the same, I'll leave you alone."

"Oh yes; I assure you, I will feel the same. Now, can we please get this over with?"

While Catherine tucked her book away in her shoulder bag, Stephen stood and patiently waited for her to finish. Satisfied with the outcome, the remainder of the diners had returned to their breakfasts and carried on their individual conversations. Catherine stood; cheeks red hot partially out of anger, part embarrassment, and followed Stephen across the atrium and out the front door.

**

"May I ask you a question?"

"Certainly."

"What do you know about PALM?"

Dr. Lough considered Ian's question, trying to recall her discussion with Captain Hawkins the previous evening. "I don't think that's an appropriate topic of conversation for our sessions. I don't see how my knowledge of an extremist group would benefit us right now."

"Come on, I've been a pretty good sport about this so far. I have answered all your questions, I've told you most of my life story already. All we have left to discuss is my horoscope and my favorite colour, and we still have five days to go. It's burgundy, by the way. There you have it. I just freed up some more time. What's wrong with the occasional bout of irrelevant banter?"

Dr. Lough smiled. The fact of the matter was, she was expecting this topic to come up and had prepared for it. She was concerned however, if she would be able to back up Hawkins' ruse. "Very well, but I know little about their daily operation. I do however know that they are an extremist group with strong ties to the church and an equally strong stance against euthanasia. They accuse us of disobeying God's master plan, that we are no better than hired assassins."

Ian shifted in his chair with a show of discomfort, careful not to break his cover, "If I may play devil's advocate for a moment, couldn't you say in a sense, that this is in fact the case? Are we not right now conspiring to defy God's will?"

"I think that if you truly believed that we wouldn't be having this conversation right now, but I believe that we are respecting the wishes of the client. It is he or she who needs to decide what they believe is right or wrong. The truth is we don't want to euthanize anyone. We want our clients to leave here on their own two feet. That's why I'm here, to try and talk you out of it."

"Well, we both know that's not going to happen."

"Then I'm not certain I understand why we're having this conversation?"

"Just curiosity really. Captain Hawkins told me about the group who is a threat to the compound. I'm curious as to what kind of people would direct so much anger towards a single target. Who are they?

"To be honest, I don't know that much about them. I know a few names that I got from conversations on their webpage forum, but they've never mentioned a specific church. Whoever orchestrates the whole thing never shows up to any of the demonstrations. They send all of their communications anonymously on PALM letterhead, and aside from reciting the odd Bible verse, they haven't given us any indication of who they are or where they come from."

"And do you see this as cowardly?"

"I never said that, nor would I ever suggest it. I'm sure they have their reasons for wanting to keep anonymity. It has however compromised their credibility."

"Why would you say that?"

"No one has ever followed through on their warnings. For all appearances, PALM seems to be an empty threat."

Valerie suddenly realized that she had made a mistake and she hoped that her face didn't betray the disappointment in herself. She was unaccustomed to deceiving her clients, and had inadvertently downplayed the group that Hawkins had already played up. Not wishing to linger on the subject any longer, she attempted to steer the conversation away from the topic.

"So, if we have satisfied your curiosity for the time being, may I continue with our scheduled session?"

Ian's eyes narrowed, as if in contemplation. Had he clued into her blunder? Had she just undone everything Travis had started? If he caught them in a lie, she would never be able to regain his trust and it would greatly affect their future sessions. She hated lying to him, so much, and she was so relieved when he relented.

"By all means. What you wish to discuss now?"

Finally, having returned to her comfort zone, Dr. Lough leaned back in her chair, crossing one leg over the other, "Why don't you tell me about how you met your wife."

**

Byron Daniels stepped into Al's hardware just as the owner turned on the red neon OPEN sign. Byron never understood why they called it Al's, since as far back as he could remember, a long-time family friend, Randy Barker, owned it. He and Randy both attended the same church, and it was Byron, who convinced Randy to join the PALM organization. As a hardware store owner, with easy access to any material and tools they might require, Randy was a valuable asset to their group. In addition, Byron was aware of Randy's strong ties to a militant group of the Aryan Nations, which, now more than ever, would be most beneficial to their cause.

Byron first walked up and down the aisles, selecting numerous items from Ian's list. He grabbed a canvas backpack, coil of rope, electricians' pliers and a ten-in-one screwdriver before making his way to the back of the store where Randy stood behind the counter.

"Mornin' Byron," Randy said at his approach, "Fine mornin', isn't it?"

"Fine enough. How's business?"

"Can't complain."

Not wishing to risk customers walking in on their conversation, Byron decided to get straight to the point, "You get the call out last night?"

"Yup, sure did. My nephew is going to mind the store while I'm out."

"Perfect. Now listen. There was a second message that came directly to me. I'm going to need a few items."

"Sure thing, whatever you need. Help yourself to anything in the store."

"Already did that." Byron indicated the pile of goods on the counter. "You don't tend to keep the rest of the stuff on your shelves. If you know what I mean."

The shopkeeper nodded, "Let me see your shopping list."

Byron slid a folded sheet of paper across the counter and left it for Randy to pick up. His brow furrowed as he read the contents of the hand-written wish list.

"The electronic devices aren't a problem; I've got most of what you need in the back. The rest though is a pretty tall order."

"How tall?"

"You need it for tomorrow's demonstration?"

"Yup."

Randy took a moment to consider, "Five grand."

Byron clenched his jaw to appear more shocked than he was. It wasn't common knowledge that the church funded group brought in a hell of a lot more money than it doled out, and the coffers held a substantial balance. Five grand was a drop in the bucket, but Byron didn't want the shopkeeper to know that Ian had given him full access to the P.A.L.M accounts, as he feared that Randy's price would reflect that knowledge.

"That's pretty steep."

"You're not giving me much notice."

Byron feigned reluctance, "All right. You'll have the cash by closing tonight."

"I'll make some calls."

"Good." Byron began filling the backpack with the remaining hardware items. "I trust our deal covers these few items."

"Just make sure I have the cash in hand by the end of the day."

The two men shook hands. Byron collected his things, and, on his way out the door, snatched a roll of grey duct tape off the shelf. With the chime of the door and a grateful wave behind him, he was gone.

ECE-80041 *REDACTED*

The dissonant clatter of plates and cutlery, mixed with a clamoring of voices, echoed throughout the dining room during the busy lunch period. The servers rushed from table to table, bringing out steaming hot dishes, and clearing away the empty plates. At times, the room became so noisy; one couldn't even hear himself think.

At least that's what went through the mind of Aaron Land, as he sat alone at the small table, head bowed, concentrating on his plate of cooling meat loaf and green beans. Slouched over the table before him, he tried to bite down and ignore the obnoxious clatter. He squeezed his eyelids tight, took several deep breaths and tried to direct his thoughts to the meeting he had that morning with Captain Hawkins.

A new contract. What was his name? Derrick something. McNeill, no, McLain. Yes, that was it, Derrick McLain. Just arrived that morning. AIDS, that's what Hawkins said. He was dying of AIDS. Thank gawd! There'll be one less faggot in the world. Gonna need to wear gloves for this one. Don't wanna get no AIDS on my hands. Unless he wanted to be shot. That'll work. Don't have to be close for that.

Movement in his peripheral notified him of someone standing next to him. It was likely one of those pretty servers wanting to refill his coffee.

He looked up, "No thank you, I've- "

It wasn't a server, nor was the man standing next to him pretty. He was the exact opposite, in fact. He was tall and slim with gaunt features. His eyes lacked colour and were sunken in, with dark heavy bags hanging below them. His tongue darted out of his mouth in a failed attempt to moisten his pale, cracked lips.

The stranger's mouth formed a grotesque smile as he spoke, "Are you Arron Land?"

Arron suddenly realized who the man before him must have been, "Why? Who are you?"

The pestilent man extended his hand in greeting, "I'm Derrick McLaren."

"Okay, so?"

"I'm your next target." He blatantly stated.

"You aren't supposed to have that information. What makes you think-?"

Derrick interrupted, "Relax, I watch the news, Mr. Land. I know exactly who you are."

"Could you get to the point already?" Arron was becoming irritated, "Why are you disturbing my lunch?"

"I need your help."

"My help? What the fuck makes you think I would want to help you?"

Derrick sat in the chair across from him and leaned into whisper, "I don't want to be stuck here for a week. I want you to kill me sooner than that, like this afternoon."

Arron pushed his chair back, putting some distance between him and the intruder, "Are you out of your fucking mind? Do you seriously think I would go to prison for you?"

"Keep your voice down, my friend. You'll draw attention."

"I am not your friend, you fucking homo."

Derrick smiled, stood, strolled around the table and stopped behind Arron's chair. "What's the matter Arron? Don't you like me?" He began massaging the contractor's shoulders.

Aaron jumped up from his chair, knocking it over and pushed Derick away from him, "Don't touch me, faggot!"

Looking around, Derrick realized they had the attention of the entire room. Smiling, he took a step forward, backing the angry bigot into the wall. "Come on, Aaron. I want to go out with a bang. And you look like you would be an excellent bang." He kissed his finger and touched it to Aaron's lips.

Land lunged forward and grabbed Derrick's wrist, twisting it behind his back. He pushed him forward, slamming his face down onto the tabletop.

Derrick looked up from the table, blood trickling from his nose, "Yeah, that's it. I like it rough. I'm in the perfect position now. Come on Mr. Land, fuck me in the ass."

Arron Land roared in anger as he shoved his adversary away from him, sending him tumbling over the table, and crashing to the floor. The room now echoed with shouts for him to stop, while others pulled out radios to call for security. He ignored the shouts and knelt on Derrick's chest. "Shut up! Shut up now!"

Derrick's lips managed to form one final grin and he spoke between his struggling breaths, "you know you're beautiful, when you are angry?"

Two security guards arrived just a few moments later to pull the contractor off his target, but it was too late. Blood covered Derrick's face, along with Aaron's fists. As the guards fought to hold him between them, Aaron continued to scream bigoted obscenities at the man who had bled to death by his own hands. By the time they had his wrists cuffed behind his back, all the fight had drained out of him. Shirt and pants covered in Derrick McLaren's blood, he stumbled back to the Administration building where he spent the next twelve hours in the holding cell.

The following morning, a secure transport arrived at the compound to escort the prisoner to the Saskatchewan Federal Penitentiary.

CHAPTER THIRTEEN

"When you offer a dying man, or woman for that matter, an opportunity to decide how they want to die, you tend to get some rather unusual requests."

"Yeah? Like what?"

The mid-morning sun reflected hot off the black asphalt of the large courtyard and warmed the air. Catherine walked alongside her acting tour guide across the expanse, while keeping close enough to talk but also at a distance enough for her own peace of mind. She still didn't trust Stephen and felt certain that she would be long dead before she ever did.

Stephen stopped in the middle of the courtyard. "Right here is a perfect example. We have had a number of contracts fulfilled on this very court-yard, three of which were public executions. The first was a man from New Brunswick who wanted a traditional beheading. He was a big fan of the Elizabethan-era movies. The second was a hanging. We built gallows on a stage right here in the centre. We drew straws to determine who got to pull the trapdoor lever."

"Was it you?"

"Unfortunately, not. It was a contractor named Aaron Land. That was one of his last assignments. He's back in prison for killing outside of the contract."

"Why would he do that? It seems as though you guys have a lot of freedom here."

"Well," Stephen stated with a wink, "not everyone here is as stable as I am. There are very strict guidelines we need to follow here; otherwise, we are exactly the psychotic murderers the protesters think we are. We cannot complete a contract until the scheduled time."

"Or it's back to Federal Prison?"

"Generally speaking, yes. However, Hawkins can be reasonable. I jumped the gun once by eight hours. For sniper contracts, I like to line up my shot ahead of time, so I learn their routines. Every night leading up to the contract, I do a practice run. Well, on one occasion, I had accidentally clicked off the safety, and ended him early. Though Hawkins had grounds for imprisonment, he had already signed and approved the contract, so he was lenient. I was confined to my quarters for three weeks and denied contracts for sixty days. That was my one and only free pass. There won't be a next time."

Catherine nodded in understanding, "So, who was the third?"

"Third what?"

"The third execution." She brought him back from his digression.

"Oh, right. The third you may have heard about in the news. A man named Andrew Chan was facing six life sentences for his involvement in an organized crime family. They offered him a swift execution in exchange for his testimony. He stood against that wall in front of a firing squad."

"We don't have capital punishment in Canada, how could they justify that?"

"Quite simple; money. It costs the taxpayers an awful lot to keep a twenty-eight-year-old man in prison for the rest of his life. This method only cost the government the price of six bullets."

"Sounds corrupt to me."

"How so?"

"This sets a horrible precedent. It tells the criminals that they don't have to do hard time. They have the option of ending it quickly, or better yet, they can get themselves a job as a government assassin at the Farm."

Now Stephen's guard came up. "Let them set the precedent, if it takes some of the burden off the prison system. As for the jobs, do you know what the inmates do while they're in prison?"

"Rot?"

He ignored the sarcasm. "They work. They all have jobs doing laundry or mopping floors, cleaning up highways or working in the kitchen and workshops. There are no free rides, but they do get wages for it. More of the taxpayer's money."

"Okay, so?" She wondered where he was going with this.

"Have you ever thought about why this compound has such high fences laced with concertina wire; or why there is a guardhouse, and twenty-four/seven security personnel?"

"Not really, no."

"It's for us, the contractors. I can't leave. I'm still in prison. I'm doing the job that they assigned to me. The difference is, I don't get a wage. It is a mutual agreement. They provide me with a mechanism for my addiction and I provide them with a service."

"You don't get paid? I thought you were hired as a contractor."

"Naw, that's a title they made up. It sounds more honest than assassin."

"So why you? Why were you chosen for this special treatment?"

He chuckled at the very thought, "There are a couple reasons. The official reason is I'm determined to recreate my first, which makes me a high risk. I'm likely to do it again, so they might as well put me to good use. Off the record, it was a political move. I killed my wife after getting wasted at one of Alexander's facilities. They wanted to keep that as quiet as possible, so they hid me here where they can keep me from talking. Everyone here is in the same boat. Aaron got off on killing a prostitute at one of the brothels during some asphyxiation erotica. Ryan went on a legal acid trip and began performing open-heart surgery on his father-in-law. He isn't a doctor. The authorities don't want the public to know that these facilities aren't as pristine as they make them out to be, so they hide us. Conrad wasn't involved in drugs or hookers, but he's a real Hannibal Lecter kind of guy. He remains in maximum security and they bring him in for those occasions that require more moral separation than the rest of us possess. That beheading, for example. He's normally not that violent, but he's not right in the head either. The last guy is Richards, but he's military. They likely just wanted him here for his expertise."

"Which is?"

"He usually handles the thrill kills. They call him when people want to leave a big mess behind."

"I can't believe I'm having this conversation with you. This whole thing is surreal."

"Why would you say that?"

"This has got to be the most morbid walking tour in history. I went on a midnight ghost tour of Victoria once. That wasn't half as creepy as this place."

"Don't worry, you won't find any hauntings here. Everyone here dies happy. I don't know if I would go as far as to call it morbid though. After all, we are trying to put an end to others' pain and suffering. While we're at it, they get to have one last thrill. Who are we to deny them that?"

"You're a saint."

Stephen laughed, "Come on, we have lots more to see."

"The anticipation is killing me," Catherine said with a sigh.

"Wouldn't that be convenient? But don't take away all my fun."

She didn't respond.

"All right then, let's just move on," Stephen said as he led her across the courtyard to the far side, walking the length of the warehouse.

"This is our supply storage," he said indicating the long building, "Just a warehouse full of old crates, boxes, and barrels. I don't think anyone has died in there, unless you count a few field mice. The next building however is of some interest."

Catherine looked ahead to the familiar two-story building. It stood directly across the courtyard from the residences.

"I can see it from my room. So, what is it?"

"The main floor houses our swimming pool. It's not huge, but it's sufficient for some recreational swimming. I use it occasionally on some of the hotter days when I want to cool off, but that's not exactly the original intention for the pool. Like the majority of amenities on the compound, they built it to facilitate certain contracts. There has in fact been several drownings in that pool over the years. Some have wanted to stare their contractor in the eyes as they drown; others wanted to be tossed in and left alone to die in the deep water. They made the pool rather deep to facilitate the use of cement shoes, so it's a decent swimming pool. They even installed a diving board. Don't worry; it gets thoroughly cleaned on a regular basis."

Amazed by his nonchalant attitude towards the morbidity of this dreadful topic of conversation, Catherine wondered how anyone could possibly be so heartless.

Stephen continued, "The second story is currently vacant, but I've been trying to convince Hawkins to put in a pub or a billiard hall, something useful like that. The roof however is the main attraction for this building."

"How so?"

"The building was intentionally built across from the client apartments in the residences. From the roof, a sniper can see into every front room window on this side. In fact, I just finished using that very spot the other day for my last contract."

"The other day? How often do they do this?"

"Twelve to fifteen a year, at the most for each contractor. They like to evaluate the shit out of everything here, so they try to spread them out. I am required to meet with our illustrious doctor before and after every contract. Should she decide at any time that I'm becoming mentally unstable, she has the authority to put the kibosh on my contract."

"You certainly don't seem very mentally stable to me."

"Really? Why is that? Is it because I kill without remorse? Because I long for the thrill of the kill that I've been unable to find since the first? I may have unorthodox needs, but I assure you that I am of sound mind. I know right from wrong; I know that inebriation is no excuse for murder. Not a day goes by when I don't regret what I did to Lisa. I'm appalled by what I did, and have been imprisoned for it. All the lives I've taken here however, have been at the request of the client. It has been nothing more than assisted euthanasia. No murder; no regret."

"Now you're trying to make it appear altruistic."

"Altruistic? No. I wouldn't go so far as to suggest any honour in it. After all, I do have ulterior motives. I am providing a service, however. A service that you, my dear, have requested. So don't go condemning me for what goes on within these gates."

Catherine fell silent. She realized that he was right. She had been directing her anger towards the man who she, in a roundabout way, hired for her own motives. Not that she was ready to apologize, but maybe she could lighten up on him a little bit.

"What about the water tower?" Catherine deflected, "I suppose you've thrown several clients off the catwalk."

"Actually," Stephen thought a moment, "no, I don't believe anyone has used the water tower to complete a contract. That's our water supply."

Stephen wasn't entirely certain, but it appeared to him as though Catherine was trying to stifle a laugh.

The tour continued beyond the pool and past a small-fortified concrete building that Stephen described as weapons storage. He indicated several points of interest along the way where clients had perished by unique and exotic means. There was a spot where a skydiver struck ground after he discovered that they hadn't securely fastened the chute to his pack during a dive. Another location served as the ideal spot for a big Western movie buff who wanted an old-fashioned quick-draw at ten paces.

"It was really quite impressive." Stephen recalled, "Had the client been packing more than just a paintball gun, he would've won the draw hands down. He hit his contractor square in the chest, before he was felled."

"Sounds exciting." Her tone carried with it a hint of trepidation. "So, what about those who wish to die peacefully in their sleep?"

"Are you serious? Look at this place. Any possible way you can think of to die, they will try to accommodate. Not many want the quiet way out."

"You just said, not many. Surly there have been some."

"Sure, there have been a few, I think. I don't pay much attention to those. They bring in a doctor to prep the patient before one of us administers the drugs and they pass away quietly in their own bed. I've never done it though. Seems like a waste to me."

"Okay, so when your time is up, how do you want to go?"

Stephen's eyes lit up, "Oh, I'll likely never be approved as a client here, but if I had the option- Come, I'll show you.

The tour soon brought them to an open intersection where the buildings ended, offering a panoramic view before them. To their immediate right was a large, racetrack that had a pair of modular trailers sitting in its centre. There appeared to be a couple of workers welding the trailers together.

"What's going on there?" Catherine pointed to the track.

"Meh, I don't know. That's Kevin's thing. Has something to do with his latest contract." Stephen pulled her back on task. "What I wanted to show you is over here."

To the left, a short distance away stood a large, wooded area. Before the Farm, the area had all been flat farmland, so the trees, that the Department of Forestry had transplanted there, looked rather out of place before the golden prairie backdrop.

"That, as far as I'm concerned, is the highlight of the entire facility." Stephen boasted.

"I never pegged you for an outdoorsman."

"I'm not much of a camper, no, you're right about that. But what I most definitely enjoy, is the thrill of the hunt. When the quarry knows you're there but has absolutely no idea where you're hiding. He steps into your line of sight, and *blam*! You have a trophy for your wall."

"Oh gawd, please don't tell me that you collect heads."

Stephen laughed, "Heavens no. I was speaking figuratively of course. I'm not that crazy." He indicated the woods, "Sure-dead Forest, as we like to call it-"

"Classy."

He ignored the interruption, "The forest was designed for the purpose of war-games. It is a popular area for those who want to go out with a fight. Just like the quick-draw, the client uses paint balls while the contractors use live ammo. It's fun though. Some of them have managed to get in a few accurate shots in before they were taken down. That's how I want to go, out with a fight."

Catherine stared blindly into the woods, "My grandfather was killed in World War II. They told my grandmother that he fought and died on the battlefield with honour. Is that what these men wanted? To die with honour?"

Stephen looked back to her with a glint in his eye, much like a proud father whose child just spoke their first words. "I think that's what most people want, for their deaths to have meaning. It would be a good feeling to be able to leave this place with the knowledge that they have made an impact on others' lives."

"It's a shame that my death will mean nothing."

"Come on. That can't possibly be true."

"Oh, I assure you it is. I doubt anyone would even notice I was gone. I was ostracized by my family, lost my child, and was abandoned by my boyfriend. I flipped burgers, I waited tables, and I sold my body for sex. Sure, some of the girls might wonder where I am, but they have likely assumed that I left the business because I wasn't very good at it. So, I'm telling you without a doubt, my death will be nothing more than a tiny blip on the radar."

"Why are you ostracized?"

"They didn't approve of my life choices." Catherine wasn't certain why she was revealing such personal experiences to this appalling man. What made her think she could trust him enough? "They said they expected so much more from me."

"They kicked you out?"

"No, I left."

"Your situation changed after losing your child. Did you ever ask if they would take you back?"

"They offered, but they added conditions."

"Which were?"

"They said I could live under their roof so long as I returned to school. I was to get my GED, and after that, I would have the choice. Either I go to university and live at home, or I get a job and find a place of my own."

"And this was a problem why?"

"I couldn't go back to my old life."

"Because your new life is so much better?"

"You don't understand."

"No, I understand you perfectly. You made some horrible decisions and you suffered for it. The problem is you didn't learn from your mistakes. Your family offered you an opportunity to turn your life back around again, but you were too darn stubborn to accept it. You forged ahead on that same destructive path, in a continuous string of bad decisions until the weight of it became too great for you to burden. Then, what do you do? You come here to enlist our help, bury your gloomy face in your book, and then chastise me for interrupting your little pity party. Well, I'll tell you this, my dear, you have it all wrong. You aren't depressed; you're scared. You're too scared to admit that you made a mistake. Why else would you choose to become a whore when a perfectly lucrative alternative was available to you-"

A sharp slap, which left a sting on his left cheek, cut Stephen's speech short. Catherine stood before him, mouth agape and lost for words.

"How dare you?" Was about as much as she could vocalize.

"Look, it wasn't my intention to offend you, but I won't apologize for what I said. I'm not one to mince words, and it was something you needed to hear."

His cheek stung again from a second slap, although he barely winced.

"If that's how you wish to release your frustrations so be it, but I hope you will, at the very least, consider what I'm telling you. Bad things happen that we have no control over. It's an unpleasant fact, but it happens to everyone. But it's not these unfortunate events that define us but how we deal with the situations and running away solves nothing."

Stephen flinched, but a third slap never arrived. She had considered it. Her upper body tensed in preparation for the next strike, but her eyes revealed her conflict. She obviously didn't appreciate his blunt approach, but it seemed as though she was beginning to realize the truth behind his accusations.

Catherine's shoulders began to relax, and she let out a capitulating sigh, "You know, for a guy who seems to think he has me all figured out, you have an awful lot to learn about tact."

Stephen laughed, delighted by the change of mood. "It's funny you should say that. Years ago, my wife found a T-shirt that she said, for obvious reasons; she had to buy for me. It read, "*Tact is for people not witty enough to be sarcastic.*"

"She was right. Very fitting for you."

Stephen was pleased to see, for the first time since he had met Catherine that she allowed herself to laugh. At that moment he realized how truly lovely she was, as if the smile had transformed her. From that moment on, the conversations took on a very different quality, friendly and sometimes even playful banter.

The tour ended with their midday meal, which they ate together, and discussed literature until Catherine had to leave for her session with Dr. Lough. She knew that at this particular session, they would have much to discuss.

**

Captain Hawkins stood at the window outside the atrium, peering in at the couple who sat together eating their lunch. As his office window looked out upon the courtyard, he had noticed the two of them earlier that morning, when they left together for a walk into the compound. Even as they walked away from him, it was plain to see that Catherine kept herself guarded. She had her arms crossed tightly at her chest and she walked two arm lengths away from her tour guide, Stephen.

Hawkins had considered following them to see what would transpire, but he thought better of it. He couldn't risk that they might discover him spying on them. Therefore, he remained in his office, typing out his daily reports, biding his time until their return.

He was shocked to realize that it was well over an hour before he saw any sign of them again. He watched their approach with renewed confidence. She walked right next to Stephen with her arms relaxed at her sides. Judging by her stern expression, she was unlikely ready to be friendly, but it was most certainly a beginning.

As he watched through the window, while the two of them continued their discussion over lunch, Hawkins wondered if that could have been the beginning of something more. Was he right? Would he possibly be able to save this one, or would it end in heartbreak and the completion of the contract?

As if on cue, Catherine laughed at something Stephen had said and very briefly touched his arm. He'd seen that action before and thought he knew what it meant. For the first time since Catherine had entered the Farm, it appeared as though he may have made the right decision. Only time would tell.

CHAPTER FOURTEEN

Everything appeared to be in order. Ian Montgomery sat up against his headboard, stretched out on his bed with his laptop open in front of him. The screen displayed the profile page for the PALM social network account. The group's logo, a splayed red hand, took up the top left corner of the page. To the right of the logo, the page displayed the name of the group's creator, Grant Niomey, an anagram of his own name. Immediately below, he had meticulously written a few paragraphs about their cause to draw interest from his church backers.

However, something Dr. Lough said during their session still stuck in his craw. *No one followed through, an empty threat.* That was something he would not tolerate. He had set his plan into motion, but there was still much preparation to do if he was going to put his organization back on the map.

Ian clicked on the *Forums* tab, where he had posted his earlier message. *Protest rally at the Killing Farm this Thursday at 8 AM.*
Bring everyone!

In the field below his post, was a link that read *34 comments*. He clicked the link, which revealed a thread of responses, all apparently positive. Some were to the point and said that they would be there; others messaged back and forth to coordinate a carpool. Overall, it seemed as though 16 protesters would attend the following morning's festivities. He had hoped for more, but not bad for such short notice. He thought his plan might legitimately work.

A highlighted icon at the top of the screen indicated there was one unread private message. He dragged his mouse upwards to click on the icon and another thread appeared. This one was a two-way conversation between him and his protest leader, Byron Daniels. He read the high-lighted post.

Everything has come to fruitation.

We are good to go.

Despite the obvious, and rather humorous grammatical error, *fruitation* ha, Ian knew precisely what his loyal friend was attempting to say. Byron acquired everything on the list and was prepared to deliver the goods. Ian kept his response short and concise.

Genesis 8:15-Please, let a little water be brought, and rest yourselves under the tree. -MRS.

He was confident that Byron would fully understand the contents of the message. He doubted it was necessary to speak in code, but better safe than sorry. Byron was correct. Everything was about to come to frui-tion. By morning, he would have the package in his hands, and then the real work would begin. He just prayed that the noisy protesters would distract Hawkins and his outfit long enough for him to pull off the exchange unnoticed.

It would not be long now before the entire world heard Ian's message.

**

Stephen Carlisle sat comfortably in a black leather chair in the administra-tion building's waiting area, patiently biding his time until his turn to see Dr. Lough. The client who currently occupied the doctor's time was the lovely Catherine Dean.

Stephen wondered what they were discussing. He wondered if Catherine had told her about the morning they had spent together and if they were talking about him right at that moment. Perhaps there was a connection, or perhaps she was humoring him until she could use her session as an excuse to leave.

He was astonished at himself. All these useless thoughts did nothing but fog up his brain. He felt foolish, like a giddy teenager, wondering if the pretty girl next to him "likes him" or "likes him-likes him". He knew Dr. Lough would eventually ask him about his feelings towards her, but he was fully prepared to dodge the question. She was unquestionably an attractive woman with a certain sex appeal. Sure, she had been around the block, so to speak, too many times to count. Nevertheless, she was done with that life, and most certainly was not proud of her choices in the matter. He most definitely wanted to sleep with her, he couldn't deny that, but beyond getting laid, his feelings for her were unknown to him. He hated that.

With an audible click, the door to the offices swung open, Dr. Lough appeared and held the door to allow Catherine's exit.

"See you tomorrow, Dr. Lough," Catherine said as she passed. "Thanks."

"Have a good evening," the doctor replied cheerfully.

Stephen caught Catherine's eye as she crossed the waiting area and she smiled at him. Was that a wink? He wasn't certain. She was out the door before he had a chance to figure it out.

"Come on in Stephen," Dr. Lough called.

Stephen stood and followed her through the open door and down the corridor to her office. She offered him a seat and a glass of water, both of which he gladly accepted, and the session began.

"So, tell me Stephen, if I may be so blunt, what did you do to her?"

"I beg your pardon?"

"A very different woman walked into my office this afternoon. She talked openly, she answered my questions freely; and did you know that was the first time she had thanked me?"

"Glad to hear she's coming around. Did she talk about me?" He felt silly for asking.

"Quite a bit, yes."

"What did she say?"

"Well, I of course can't reveal any details of our conversation, but it would seem as though you somehow got through to her. What did you say to her to break that icy exterior?"

"I told her what she needed to hear."

"Which was?"

"The truth."

"The truth about what?" Dr. Lough was clearly agitated.

"I told her that she was a childish, self-centered coward."

Dr. Lough gasped at the statement, but Stephen continued.

"Not in those exact words, of course. I told her that she was given many opportunities to change her course in life, and she turned down every offer of help. The path she took was one of her own choosing and now she needs to be accountable for it. Instead, she is running away like a selfish child."

"Mr. Carlisle," she said aghast, "you could have undone everything I have been working to accomplish. You could have pushed her over the edge right there."

"Judging by what you said when I came in, I would suspect that I accomplished the complete opposite."

"Still, you could have done irreparable damage. Did you not think-"

"Could have, should have," Stephen confidently took control of the conversation. "You're missing the point. You and Captain Hawkins are so wrapped up in doing everything by the book; you have forgotten that your clients are human beings. We don't always see the mistakes we have made on our own and sometimes we just need a kick in the ass to remind us."

"That may be so, but it's not your place to give anyone a kick in the ass." Dr. Lough attempted to regain control, "The reason Travis and I are so *by the book* is because we have to be. We have to document everything for the insurance agencies, in addition to the Court of Queen's Bench. We are accountable for every contract carried out at this facility and we are scrutinized for it; so, you're damn right I'm going to cover my ass!"

"Wow, I thought this was supposed to be an evaluation, not an interrogation. If you're as harsh with your clients, you'll be hard-pressed to save any of them."

Dr. Lough relaxed back in her chair and took a breath. "You are right, and I'm very sorry; but I can't afford to have you undermining what I'm trying to accomplish."

"But it would seem to me, by the sounds of it, I helped you today."

"Don't go counting your chickens yet. She opened herself up to me today, but it's far from a breakthrough. You got her thinking, which is good, but she still doesn't trust you, or anyone else for that matter. She continues to insist that she needs to be here."

"You can't expect me to work miracles in just a couple of hours," he joked, "I need two to three days at least."

"It is definitely something though, so what I suppose I should have said was thank you."

"No worries. It's not like I didn't enjoy myself."

Dr. Lough opened her notebook, "I am glad to hear that. This gives us a good place for us to start today. I would like to hear your thoughts on Catherine."

"You know my thoughts on her; I certainly haven't kept them secret. She made a series of awful decisions, that she had paid dearly for, she's too proud to accept help from her family, and now she wishes to take the coward's way out. Another bad decision."

"That's not what I was asking. You seem to have taken a special interest in Catherine, which you haven't done with any of your other clients, women included. I'm curious as to why you are offering her so much of your attention. Furthermore, why are you are trying so hard to talk her out of it. She leaves, you lose a contract."

"I was under the impression that's what you want. For her to leave on her own accord."

"Undeniably yes, it is, but it goes against your nature. You have never shown compassion towards a client before, and that interests me."

"I'm nice to one pretty girl and now it's the Spanish Inquisition?"

"It's not an inquisition, Stephen, I'm merely curious."

"Have you considered the possibility that I could be trying to bed her?"

"I considered that. If that were the intention, however, there would be no reason for you to talk her out of the contract."

"Perhaps I wanted her to believe that I am a gentleman, sensitive to her situation."

Dr. Lough laughed. "Not the way you handled it."

"Maybe I-"

It was Dr. Lough's turn to cut him off this time. "Come on Mr. Carlisle; don't try to play me the fool. I know you better than that; possibly better than you know yourself."

Stephen's jaw tightened, as his demeanor shifted. He couldn't dodge the question any longer, but he wasn't about to give her the satisfaction of the win. "What exactly do you want me to tell you? Do you want me to say that she is a blatant reminder of Lisa? Should I confess that when I first saw her in the atrium, it brought back a flood of memories that I had tried so hard to forget? I killed my wife and got off on the thrill of it. Now you have confronted me with her doppelganger in a frighteningly similar situation. What did you think would happen? Was I supposed to see her and instantly fall in love, or is it supposed to give me a repeat performance of the original thrill? There isn't a day that goes by that I don't regret what I did to Lisa. I do not want to relive it, so you're damn right I'm going to try to talk her out of it. Now, does satisfy your blatant curiosity?"

"Yes, it does, and I'm sorry. I told Captain Hawkins that the whole thing was a bad idea."

Stephen laughed at the irony. "Are you kidding? It was a brilliant idea on his part. Diabolical, but brilliant. Think about it. It's a no-lose situation for him. Worst-case scenario, it doesn't work, and I complete the contract as planned. The risk to my feelings is inconsequential. Best case, we fall in love, and he saves us both. In the middle, I kill her and may or may not find what I've been looking for. No matter the result, he comes out pristine. Hawkins can be a real asshole, but he knows what he's doing."

"You are an impossible man to peg Mr. Carlisle. One minute you're chastising us for our decision, the next you're condoning it."

"I like to mix it up a bit. That said, just because I find it to be a smart business decision doesn't mean I have to like it."

"Very true." She digressed. "I think we've beaten this topic thoroughly enough. Perhaps it's best to move on to a different subject."

"I'm at your disposal," he relaxed into his chair. "What do you want to discuss now?"

"Let's talk about how you plan to carry out the contract."

"I don't know yet, I have yet to receive instructions, and as far as I know Catherine has not yet decided."

"Well," She folded her hands on the desk in front of her. "That's not entirely true."

"She has decided?"

"Not exactly, no. She has granted Liberum Arbitrium."

**

Something about what Kevin Richards read seemed very suspicious, but he couldn't quite put his finger on why. He sat in front of his computer with the browser opened to a page dedicated to the PALM organization. He was currently skimming through the latest thread, that Grant Niomey, the site's creator started, to schedule a protest for the following morning.

Richards scrolled down to see the previous protest announcements. The last post, dated five months earlier, began with someone named, Byron Daniels. Before that was just short of a month, and before that, damn near on a weekly basis, each one started by Byron Daniels. So why, after a five-month hiatus, have they suddenly started up again? Why is the previously silent creator suddenly calling the charge? Why now? It seemed suspicious that this would occur just hours after Hawkins had brought up the organization for his elaborate hoax.

He read the name again at the top of the page, Grant Niomey. It didn't sound familiar. There was no one on site with the name Grant, first or last. He recalled one of the guards, Lee Stafford, who had mentioned a sister named Naomi, but he couldn't see that lecherous slime-ball being any sort of a religious fanatic. It seemed a bit of a stretch.

He scanned the list of comments for any other name that might ring a bell, but none jumped out at him. Maybe, he thought, he was looking for a mystery that wasn't there. Perhaps the conspiracy buff in him feared the worst. Could this just be a coincidence?

No. He knew better than that. There are no coincidences. Something was going on, the answer was somewhere in that thread and he was going to find it.

ECE-80050

A tire struck another pothole, once again jarring the occupants of the large, reinforced truck. The sound as the shackles clinked together, echoed off the cold, grey steel walls and pierced Andrew Chan's ears. The discomfort was unbearable. The bench, where he sat, was as cold and hard as the walls, and strong bolts anchored the shackles on his ankles and wrists to the floor, which pulled him down into an awkward, slouched position.

Still, the discomfort he felt at that moment paled in comparison to the pain he would have had to endure had he remained in the general population back in prison. He knew what sort of atrocities happened to snitches in prison; in fact, he had dealt a few punishments himself during his several stints on the inside. However, he was more than just your typical snitch. He didn't just throw a few colleagues under the bus. Chan gave up the entire hierarchy, forty-six members, from pawns to king. His death was set in stone, so he made a deal to ensure it happened on his own terms.

The breaks squealed and the truck rolled to a stop. The two guards, who occupied the secure space with him, raised their rifles, to reinforce their feeling of control over their prisoner, in a pathetic show of dominance.

The truck lurched forward once again. Clearly, they hadn't yet arrived at their destination as he had assumed, and the guards relaxed the grip on their rifles. They hadn't driven far however, before they once again rolled to a stop and, as they did before, the two guards flexed their egos.

A sudden clatter of metal upon metal echoed through the mobile prison cell, and bright sunlight temporarily blinded the three of them. As his eyes began to adjust to the change, Chan looked out through the open doors to the compound beyond. The area certainly didn't look like much from where he sat. It appeared more like an old western town than a modern military facility. The roads were dirt, the corner of the building he could see was simple red brick, and beyond that building stood a massive water tower.

While he assessed his new surroundings, one of the guards unlocked the shackle anchor, while the other pulled Chan to his feet. With one in front and the other behind, they escorted him out of the prisoner transport and into the bright compound.

He hadn't realized there would be an audience. The courtyard where they stood was alive with activity. People converged on their location from all different areas of the compound, some in uniform, others not. They talked excitedly among themselves, likely all aware of what was about to transpire.

A man in military dress uniform approached the driver. Chan didn't know enough about the military to identify the rank insignia, but by the way he carried himself, it was clear he was a high-ranking officer.

They escorted Chan across the courtyard, toward the red brick building he had seen upon his arrival. He stood in front of the wall, his shackles removed, and the guards slowly backed away with their rifles trained on him.

The officer spoke. "Andrew Chan, you have been convicted by the Court of Queen's Bench on several counts of manslaughter, and trafficking. In light of the deal, you have made with the Crown Prosecutor, the life sentence has been waved and you have been granted your request for a swift execution. Do you have any final words?"

"No."

"Then, by the power vested in me by the Supreme Court of Canada, I hereby carry out your sentence. Gentlemen?"

Three men carrying rifles stepped out from behind the officer and assembled themselves in a line before Chan. None dressed in uniform, but all three seemed accustomed to taking orders. The crowd now lined the circumference of the courtyard. Men and women in uniform prevented them from getting too close, so even the small group of twenty to twenty-five people appeared larger than it was.

"Ready!"

The three bolt-action rifles snapped shut, dropping a round of ammunition into each of their respective chambers. The air filled with whispers of excitement, some in anticipation, and others in protest. Chan stood firm, unwavering. Death was never his first choice, but he wasn't afraid of it either. Especially when he considered the alternative.

"Aim!"

Chan suddenly found himself staring down the barrels of three assault rifles. He began to swallow uncontrollably, beads of sweat formed on his forehead. The reality of the situation sank in. This was it. Good or bad, this was the end. Everything he was. All he stood for. He had busted his ass to become a prominent member of the organization, and just like that-

"Fire!"

CHAPTER FIFTEEN

Day Four

Though the previous night had brought slightly cooler temperatures to the area, a warm morning breeze that blew across the unkempt fields ensured that it would turn out to be another beautiful day. A perfect day for a little bit of mayhem.

Byron Daniels crouched in the tall grass short distance from the tall fence line, binoculars in hand and a full backpack over his shoulder. He peered through the binoculars at the line of protesters, signs in hand, who quietly approached the front gates. Byron had gathered the group together a half kilometre down the road, where he set them up with signage. He planned to give the occupants of the Farm as little warning as possible before the official protest began, so he had instructed them to hold the chanting until they were in place. After that, Byron ran off by himself, circled around out of sight of the compound to where he now waited for the commotion to begin.

As the line of people reached the gate, they formed a walking circle and started to chant in a rhythmic beat. The guard, after having no luck dispersing the intruders, quickly disappeared back into the guard-house, presumably to inform his superiors of what had transpired. With a satisfied grin, Byron watched as more guards began to converge on the front gate, and right on cue the rally started to escalate. First, a single protester ran to the gate and began to hammer his sign against the heavy wire fence. As the initial guard emerged once again from the guardhouse, a few more stepped up and joined the cause. Soon the uprising was in full swing, and it pulled more and more personnel away from their regular morning duties.

Byron hoped that this would be enough of a distraction to buy him enough time to complete his own task. He checked his watch, 8:11; he was behind and needed to hustle. Crouched low in the grass, he followed the fence line to the north, with one eye on the compound, looking for guards. He hoped all their attention was on the main gates, from where Byron could hear the loud cheers and shouts. He prayed that things didn't go too far where anyone got hurt, then again it would only further serve their cause.

He moved swiftly now through the field and worked his way towards the back of the compound where large, wooded area stood. It had been a frustrating process to get him to that point. Ian wasn't exactly clear in his instructions.

Genesis 8:15-Please, let a little water be brought, and rest yourselves under the tree. -MRS.

MRS, he understood, as they had used the phrase Maintain Radio Silence before, but what had he meant by the passage? It took Byron a while to decipher the meaning behind Ian's cryptic message. He had opened his bible and turned it to Genesis 8:15. *Then God said to Noah, "Come out of the ark".* That wasn't right. He continued to read on until he came upon the correct passage in Genesis 18:4. Ian would never have made an error like that. It was clearly a message.

"8:15" had to be the time and "under the tree", the place. What tree? There weren't too many trees in that part of the prairies, at least not natural ones. He then pulled up satellite photos of the compound on an Internet map program. There it was, clear as day. The only wooded area in miles and located within the gates of the Farm.

That's where his friend would be waiting.

As he neared the trees, he crawled closer to the fence. He hadn't realized until that moment that the nearest tree inside the compound was a good ten metres, at the very least, away from the fence. Obvious security measures, which would leave their hand off more exposed. He hoped that Ian had accounted for that.

"Careful not to get too close my friend," came his friend's disembodied voice. "The fence is electrified on this end of the compound."

Crouched in the tall grass, Byron called back, "I've got your gear, where are you?"

Ian leaned out from behind a tree and waved. He was just a stone's throw away, but they still needed to raise their voices to hear each other.

"We are going to have to time this," Ian hollered. "Take a look in the tree above me, about a quarter of the way up."

Byron lifted his binoculars to his eyes and adjusted focus on a camera that security had bolted directly to the tree. A number of the branches were cut away to give a clear sight line for the camera to complete a full sweep of the area.

"We will have about a ten second window." Ian continued, "Plenty of time if we do this right. I can't see the camera from here so on your go, we rush in, you lob the pack over, and I retrieve it. Quite simple."

"Are you going to at least tell me what this is all about? Like, what the hell are you doing inside the Farm?"

"I will fill you in later my friend. Right now, time is of the essence. Who knows how long the protest will keep their attention. All I ask is that you get that pack clear of the fence."

"Consider it done."

"On your mark."

Byron watched as the camera panned across the field towards his location and waited until the lens had passed.

"Okay, on my mark, in Three... Two... One... Mark."

Byron shot himself out of the grass at the same time as his friend Ian burst from the tree line. He stopped short of the fence, spun around, and turned his back to the compound. He crouched down, grabbed the pack two handed and launched the pack upwards and over the high fence. He turned back just in time to see the pack land at Ian's feet. With no time to waste, they both dove back into concealment before the camera's focus returned.

"Thank you, my friend; I am in your debt." Ian's voice called out.

"What else can I do for you?"

"I don't need anything more at the moment, but I have to get back before they notice I'm gone. I do ask however that you return on Tuesday morning. I'm going to need a ride"

"Why? What's going on? What are you planning?"

Only silence followed.

"Ian?"

There was no response. His friend had left. All he could do from that point on was wait for further contact, and barring that, for whatever was about to happen on Tuesday. There were however so many unanswered questions. Nevertheless, what choice would he have?

He was quite certain that the confrontation at the front gates would be in full swing; therefore, he didn't want to arouse suspicions and show up late to the party. With few options available to him, he made his way back around to the front of the compound. He remained out of sight until he found his way back to his vehicle, which soon took him far away from the conflict.

**

"I don't understand why you did that."

"Did what?"

"You gave me the freedom of choice."

"I thought you would appreciate that."

Stephen had waited for the breakfast rush to die down before he broached the subject. Catherine had invited him to share her table earlier but the conversation up to that point had been sporadic at best. They passed the time with polite small talk until the area cleared out enough to talk freely.

"There has to be some form of exit strategy that would appeal to you," Stephen continued.

"Why? Frankly, I don't care how I go, just as long as you can make it happen. I have no desire to return to my old life. You, on the other hand, are searching for that same thrill. I'm offering you an opportunity to find it."

"It hasn't worked so far, what makes you think you'll be any different?"

"Because you like me."

Taken completely off guard, Stephen nearly choked on his coffee. Catherine smiled.

"Even if that were true, and I'm not saying it is, what would that have to do with anything?"

"Think about it for a second. What was different about Lisa from everyone else that you've killed since?"

"Everyone else was under contract."

"That's part of it, yes. What else?"

"I'm not sure what you are getting at."

Catherine shook her head in disappointment, "You loved her."

Stephen set his fork down and considered the implications of what Catherine had said. It now seemed so obvious. He couldn't believe he hadn't thought of it before. He slumped back in his chair in defeat.

Catherine's expression dropped in concern, "What's the matter? Doesn't seem plausible? I thought you'd be happy about it."

"I don't know how I could have missed it. It is very plausible, but damn," Stephen sighed, "talk about your double-edged sword."

"Why would you say that?"

"Because for me to achieve total ecstasy that first time, I lost everything I loved most in life. First my wife, then my freedom. If what you're saying is correct, my only chance of achieving my goal is to fall in love again, and then sacrifice that love." Stephen suddenly backpedaled, "Not that I meant you. That couldn't be farther from the truth."

"Is that so?" She teased.

"You are horribly presumptuous."

"Am I? How many of your other clients have you stalked before you took them on personal tours? Of those, how many had you sat down to dinner with, and then had breakfast with the next day?"

"None. But-"

"There you have it, you like me."

"And you call me tactless," he said defensively.

"Oh, come on, I'm just teasing you. Why do you have your knickers in a bunch?"

Stephen sighed and reached into his pocket. When he removed his hand, he held a small wallet sized photograph. He set it down on the table and slid it across towards Catherine. She picked up the photo and stared at the woman in the picture with amazement.

"She could almost be my sister."

"That's Lisa."

"I- I don't understand."

"Hawkins chose me for your contract because you reminded him of my wife."

"What exactly are you saying?" She asked as she looked back and forth between Stephen and the photo. "Are you suggesting that Hawkins orchestrated this whole thing?"

"Well, not the whole thing. The decision to come here was your own, and you happened to look like my ex-wife, which would have been a fortunate coincidence for him. He had no control over that. Once he saw the opportunity however, I gather that he wasted no time to exploit it."

"To what end?"

"I suppose he wants us to rescue each other. According to Dr. Lough, she warned him against it. She saw it as a potential volatile situation."

"Yeah, no shit."

"Nothing much we can do about it now. No matter the outcome, Hawkins comes out smelling like roses. We might as well make the best of it."

"I suppose you're right, but it sure would be nice to stick it to him."

Around the room, several radios began to squawk out barely intelligible orders and the military personnel jumped up from their lunch and ran for the exit. The commotion, however, didn't seem to faze the unlikely couple. They sat in uncomfortable silence for a few moments while Catherine decided whether to ask her next question. Reluctantly, she came right out, and asked.

"Do you know what you're going to do with your Liberum Arbitrary?"

"Arbitrium," he teased. "If I told you, it wouldn't be a surprise now, would it?"

"If you can't tell me, who can you tell? Come on," Catherine suddenly became conscious of the irony that she was flirting, still she continued, "how are you going to kill me?"

"Perhaps I don't want to kill you anymore."

"And why would that be?"

"Maybe, because I like you."

**

The electronic ring of the telephone broke the silence while Captain Travis Hawkins sat alone in his office drafting an email. He had just completed his daily report for the previous day and was just about to send it off to General McGovern, when the phone broke his concentration. He checked the digital display that read *GUARDHOUSE*. He wondered why Sergeant Morgan would be calling that morning, as there were no clients or deliveries expected.

He picked up the receiver and placed it to his ear. "Good morning, Walter. What can I do for you today?"

The voice on the other end sounded urgent, "Captain Hawkins, we have an incident."

"What is it Sargent?" Hawkins always reverted to standard protocol when he dealt with official matters.

"PALM has decided to make another appearance today, but this time they are making a lot of noise."

"PALM? Now?" he considered the implications. "Thank you Sargent, I will be right out."

He didn't wait for a response. He hung up the phone, grabbed his uniform jacket and hat then headed for the door. Within minutes, he was outside the building, and could hear the shouts the moment he opened the door. As Hawkins made his way toward the front gate of the compound, his steps took on a great sense of urgency.

The sounds became louder as he neared the gate, and he began to realize that the timing could not possibly have been better. He wasn't sure what had set them off, but he was fully prepared to let them make themselves known. This would back up his lie quite nicely. All that remained was for Ian Montgomery to catch wind of it.

A crowd had already gathered by the time he reached the gate, and more were on their way. Official and unofficial personnel alike shouted through the fence at the protestors, exchanging insults and profanities. He slowed his pace as he scanned the crowd for Ian, but unfortunately saw no sign of him.

He approached the throng and tried to gain control of the situation.

"Stand down!" He shouted out to no one in particular.

Those who occupied his side of the fence immediately fell back from the gate. Even the non-military personnel quickly heeded his call. Those on the opposite side, however, continued their chaotic aggression with not so much anger as determination. Something fueled this sudden incursion, something more than simple unity for the cause. He would investigate this further, but first he had to get these assholes away from his gate.

The protesters largely ignored his shouts for order, and continued to call out Bible verses while they hammered against the gate with their signs. It was a long time since Hawkins had seen the group so aggressive. He got the attention of a nearby security guard. "Sergeant, please."

The guard removed his side arm from its holster and handed it to Hawkins, who aimed the Beretta into the air. The sound of a single shot attracted the attention of everyone in the area. Some of the protesters covered their ears and ducked for cover, while others shouted obscenities directly at Hawkins. He handed the pistol back to the guard and held up his hands, open palmed to the antagonists, in an offer of peace. Though they didn't go completely silent, Hawkins no longer needed to strain his voice to shout over them. "Now that we have that under control, I should like to know what is happening here."

Hawkins met blank stares from the protesters. None seemed to want to take responsibility for their presence.

The Sergeant, who had proffered the pistol stepped forward, "Sir I-"

Hawkins quickly silenced the officer with the raise of a hand. "Thank you, Sergeant; I will require your full report shortly. In the meantime, I wish to know who is behind this rabble."

Again, he met only silence.

"Seeing as no one appears prepared to take responsibility for this action, I shall address you all at once. I recognize most of your faces from past rallies so it shouldn't come as a shock to you that I find this highly unusual. First off, since you haven't been around for a while, I had assumed you had given up on us."

"We will never give up on defilers of God's will." A man shouted from the back.

"Fair enough." Hawkins continued without falter, "but what surprises me the most is the degree of anger that you are displaying here today. In the past, you've always held peaceful protest. Why the sudden fit of rage?"

The man who had previously spoke stepped forward. The larger man seemed out of place, as he lacked the arrogant demeanor possessed by his colleagues. "It has been decided that it is time for our voices to be heard. It is time for you to listen."

"And was it you sir, who made this decision?" Hawkins asked.

"Well, no."

"Then why doesn't the one responsible step forward? Why does he leave it up to you to speak for him?"

"He ain't here."

"He ain't?" Hawkins balked, "Very well then Mr.-"

"Barker."

"Mr. Barker. I guess that it is you and I then. I'm listening. What are your voices saying that must be heard?"

"Well, I, uh-"

"Come on Mr. Barker. You came all the way out here to pay us a visit; surely, you have some form of message for me. There is no media, no public awareness of this rally, so enlighten me. What must be heard?"

Randy's face held an expression similar to that of a deer in the headlights. This man knew nothing. Hawkins looked around to find that the crowd around him had grown, and further realized that Stephen Carlisle and Catherine Dean were among the new faces. They stood together, off to the side talking between themselves. Another cursory glance revealed to his disappointment, no sign of Ian Montgomery. He turned back to the confrontation at the gate.

"Very well," Hawkins turned his attention back to Randy Barker, "I think you and I are done here. Continue to make noise if you wish, but I can't be bothered to deal with impromptu rallies with little to no purpose. Good day Mr. Barker."

As he turned to walk away, the protesters burst out into a cacophony of angry voices. Randy Barker raised his voice over the noise for Hawkins' benefit, "I promise you will regret ever opening this place."

"Your idle threats are lost on me Mr. Barker, as I have done nothing to warrant regret. But I assure you that any illegal action that you or your friends take against this facility will be met with the full force of the law."

Hawkins ignored the remaining shouts behind him and made his way through the crowd as they dispersed. As the path before him cleared, he noticed, standing at the entrance of the apartments, was the man he had hoped to impress. He had in fact witnessed the event, even if only in part.

Hawkins felt that the encounter had gone well and now trusted that it would work in his favour with Mr. Montgomery. He would however have to wait to find out, as Ian had disappeared into the building.

**

Heavily laden backpack in hand, Ian Montgomery wasted little time making his way back to the main area of the compound. So far, he hadn't run into any resistance, but he couldn't be too careful. He stuck close to the buildings, prepared to find cover if the need arose, and moved swiftly yet carefully through the streets. He wasn't so much worried about someone noticing him wandering around the farm, as the clients were free to explore the compound. The contents of the backpack on the other hand would be extremely difficult to explain.

Since Ian had yet to encounter another person since he retrieved the package, it seemed as though he was right. The commotion at the gates had successfully drawn attention away from his task. He silently raised his head and thanked God for keeping him safe from those who would oppose his cause.

Once the narrow street opened into the courtyard, he had a clear view of the living quarters as well as the front gate. Not a soul stood between him and the front door to the guest residence. It appeared as though the full complement of the Farm's inhabitants gathered before the main gate to observe the excitement. To be safe, once out in the open, he returned to his performance of frailty and stumbled towards the front door of the building.

The diversion was certainly a success, but he was curious about the lack of commotion at the gate. There was no chanting or shouting and Ian was too far away to be able to hear what anyone was saying. He stopped at the residence entrance and watched his handiwork. Hawkins was front and centre talking to one of the protesters. Who was that? Randy Barker perhaps.

Whatever Hawkins said next obviously irritated the protesters, as they burst into a commotion of insults and profanities. He still couldn't discern what was happening, but it didn't matter, he had what he needed from the situation. He no longer required the distraction; the flock had done their job and could go home. Hawkins turned away from the gate, along with the compliment, ignoring the shouts behind them.

Ian briefly made eye contact with the captain, and with a nod, he turned back to the entrance. With his salvation slung heavily over his shoulder, he would allow the rally to run its course. He entered the building and made his way up to the privacy of his own room where he could examine the contents of the pack uninterrupted. It had all come together, and God would soon have his justice.

**

The view from Kevin Richards' bedroom window had often been advantageous, this day more than most. Located at the front of the building with a Southern view, it gave him an ideal line of sight to the front gate. On most days, this gave him firsthand knowledge of who was coming and going, to and from the compound. On this occasion however, it gave him box seats to the morning's festivities.

He had used a homemade parabolic microphone that he had put together from pieces of an old television set and a transistor radio. He had little difficulty eavesdropping on the conversation between Captain Hawkins and a flock of angry protesters. He had to hand it to Hawkins on this one. He made a good show of it. Every point he made appeared deliberate to anger his opponent. It worked too. Although, who was he performing for?

He leaned out his open window, and there he stood on the steps below him. Ian Montgomery watched Hawkins from the entrance to the building. Curiously, he carried a large, apparently heavy backpack over his shoulder. At first, Richards wondered where his target was going, until the client turned on his heels and disappeared into the building. The question then became, where did he come from, and what was in the pack?

Richard left his perch at the window, drew the curtains, and crossed the room to his desk. He pulled out a pen and note pad, and wrote two words. *Ian Montgomery*. Directly below, he wrote two more, Grant Niomey and began to cross out letters. Very quickly, he had his answer.

Kevin tore the sheet from the pad with all the fervor of a three-star general and strode triumphantly from his apartment.

CHAPTER SIXTEEN

Ian Montgomery was relieved that, because of the disruption, Dr. Lough had postponed his morning session with her until later that afternoon. It gave him an opportunity to sort through the unauthorized care package he had received earlier. One by one, he pulled each item from the pack and laid them out on the bed.

He had grouped a multi-head screwdriver, pliers, wire cutters, duct tape, and a soldering iron together at the end of the bed. In a small pouch on the side of the pack, he located a small coil of solder, which he placed next to the iron. At the bottom of the pack's main compartment were two carefully wrapped packages and a small spool of 22gauge wire. He placed the wire next to the tools then carefully lifted the first package from where it rested and set it down on the bed. He unwrapped the brown paper to reveal a ratty shoebox. He lifted the lid to examine its contents and took inventory as he laid each piece out. Circuit boards, electronic switches, cell phone batteries, and a small bag of assorted resistors were among the selection of electronic devices contained in the box. He checked each item meticulously for quality before he placed them down upon the comforter. The last items he pulled from the box were two long slender rods, each wired with a pair of leads.

He then turned to the final package in the backpack and lifted the bulk from its seat. The generic brown paper that covered this specific package had a waxy texture to it. He carefully opened the wrappings and smiled at what would have appeared to an untrained eye to be two large bricks of modelling clay. Satisfied with the contents, he re-wrapped the clay and returned it to the backpack.

Ian stood before the collection he'd laid out across his bed. Everything on his list was there, but he knew he would need some help if he expected to assemble the device correctly. He sat down at the desk and opened his laptop. On the Internet browser, he selected the link to his anonymous e-mail account. After he typed in his password, the inbox opened on the screen that showed one new message from an unknown sender. When he clicked on the message, it revealed an e-mail with no subject line, no text in the body, and an attached PDF file. A second click and his laptop displayed a detailed wiring schematic of an electronic device.

Ian had no idea who the unknown sender was, but considering the calibre of friends Randy Barker associated with, he knew not to ask too many questions. Whoever it was, the nameless colleague came through with flying colours.

He examined the schematic for a good starting point. He pinpointed a small circuit board he recognized from the items on the bed. As good a place to start as any. He retrieved the soldering iron, the solder and a selection of parts, and then Ian Montgomery sat down to work.

**

The atrium was quieter than usual as they approached the lunch rush, since most of the staff were busy filing reports and cleaning up after the rowdy protest march earlier that morning. Stephen Carlisle didn't mind the seclusion, however. He sat alone, a steaming cup of coffee in hand and a book opened on the table in front of him. Feet up on the opposite chair, he was fully engaged in the story of Aloysius X.L. Pendergast. Stephen found the FBI agent to be an admirable character. He was brilliant, rather egocentric, very eccentric, and clearly belligerent. It was easy to see why anyone would find his character appealing.

"Is that my book?" A familiar voice startled him from behind. Catherine moved around the table, pulled the chair out from under his feet and took a seat.

Stephen straightened in his chair, "I'm sorry?"

"You're reading my book. I was looking for it, and I couldn't find it. Give it back."

"Well," Stephen teased, "I figured that since you seemed to be enjoying my company so much, you wouldn't need your Special Agent anymore."

"Who are you to decide who I wish to spend my time with?" She snatched the book back from him. "And look what you've done. You dog-eared the page. Hasn't anyone ever taught you how to take care of a book? I'm surprised you are well read enough to have taken on a series like this."

"Ouch. Take it easy. I'm sorry I took your book."

Catherine closed her eyes and let out a breath of air. Her shoulders relaxed and her expression softened. "I guess I should stop taking out my frustrations on you."

"Hey, don't worry about it. I'm a big boy. I can take it. Besides, you aren't entirely far off."

"What do you mean?"

"I have a bit of a confession," Stephen shrugged his shoulders, "I haven't actually ever read it."

"You are welcome to have it after I'm done. I won't exactly need it anymore."

He leaned forward, "No, what I meant was, I've never read a single Pendergast novel."

"Really?" Catherine was legitimately shocked, "But you seemed to know all about him."

"While you hid your face behind your book, I took the opportunity to read the back panel. From there, I took a guess at his personality."

Catherine flipped the book over and skimmed the synopsis. "That was a good guess."

"I may take you up on the offer though."

She looked up from the book, "What's that?"

"I would like to borrow it when you are done."

"Borrow it?" She scoffed. "It's not like you will be able to return it to me."

"True enough." His expression suddenly changed, "Hey, aren't you supposed to be in with Dr. Lough?"

"I was, but she cancelled the morning session. I'm supposed to meet her at one o'clock instead."

"She must have been busy with all that happened this morning. I'm at two, so I'll pass you on your way out."

A server came by to drop off Stephen's coffee and offered Catherine a cup of her own, which she accepted. They each nursed their respective hot beverage, and continued to learn about each other's interests and shattered dreams. Soon the conversation developed into a serious discussion about their moral beliefs. It appeared they were both, more or less, on the same side of the fence when it came to the decriminalization of drugs; however, their views on legalized prostitution became clearly divided.

"I don't understand how you could possibly be against it?"

"What's not to understand?"

"For God's sake, you used to be one."

"Yes. And look what it did to me. You have no idea what it was like."

Catherine vividly remembered every detail of her last day at the Garden, sitting up against the headboard of the comfortable queen-sized bed. She had the burgundy sheet pulled up to cover her naked body. She watched the man she only knew as Brad, zip up his trousers then shove his scrawny arms into his white, pit-stained dress shirt. He watched her all the while he got dressed, with a big ridiculous grin on his pock marked face. It took all she could muster to return a passible smile, while she desperately waited for him to leave.

"That was fun. I'll see you again next month." Brad tried, and failed, to appear suave.

Fun was a relative term, dependent on the eye of the beholder. From Brad's point of view, it was certainly fun. He had the pleasure of a beautiful naked woman crawling all over him, touching him all over his body. Kissing him places where other women wouldn't dare.

For Catherine, on the other hand, fun wasn't a word that ever came to mind. There were plenty of other descriptive words she found to be more suitable. She was disgusted by the taste of his sweat and appalled by the smell. She felt dirty when he licked her, as his tongue was dry and rough. She gagged when she took him in her mouth and clenched her teeth behind a forced smile when he entered her. Fortunately, for her, the act itself took no more than a few moments before he slumped over on the bed next to her, out of breath. The worst of it was over, all she needed to do was look pretty and smile until he left, so she could shower.

"*I'll see you again next month*, he said. That would be the fourth consecutive month." She shuddered as she recounted the incident to Stephen. "Why couldn't one of the buff hockey players or handsome executives have come back month after month? Instead, I got stuck with the pathetic mama's boys who would never get laid if they didn't pay for it."

"Maybe, but for that brief time they were with you, you made them feel like so much more than that." Stephen attempted to reassure her.

"But at what cost? Any dignity they gained, they stole from me, and that doesn't ever come back. Every time one of them left, they took a piece of me with them. I would stand there alone, in front of the mirror and wonder how anyone, even Brad, could find me pretty. All I ever saw in the mirror was an ugly whore.

"I would step into the shower and turn on the water, as hot as I could handle. There wasn't enough soap in the entire building to get me clean. How much more could I possibly endure? How many more clients could I satisfy before they began to realize how disgusting I was? How many five-dollar tips did it take before I realized that I had made a huge, fucking mistake?"

"I'm sorry that your life turned out this way for you," Stephen interjected, "but the new policy has done fantastic things for the profession. The escorts are off the street, they're clean, they're safe, they have healthcare. The child prostitution rate in Canada is at its lowest in recorded history. What more could anyone expect?"

"But the sheer number of prostitutes in the country is at an all-time high. How many of these new recruits would have ever chosen the profession, if it had remained on the streets?"

"So what?" Her arguments had Stephen shocked, "it's their bodies. If they're comfortable with it why not? Now that it is a widely accepted field, it is no different than paying an electrician to wire your basement."

"But an electrician doesn't get violated on an hourly basis," Catherine said with venom.

"I don't know. Have you seen their paychecks?"

Catherine's expression remained stern, so Stephen digressed, "it's only a violation for the unwilling, or without consent. I feel bad for those who do it out of necessity, but you can't deny that decriminalization has improved the conditions."

The chime of Stephen's phone cut off Catherine's retort.

"How can you have a cell phone anyway if you're a prisoner here?" She asked as he opened his instant messaging.

"My calls are restricted to Hawkins' and Dr. Lough's phones, and it has limited, and heavily monitored Internet access."

Stephen's face displayed obvious surprise as he read the message from Dr. Lough. "Well, I'll be damned."

"What is it?"

"Dr. Lough has rescheduled my next psych evaluation."

"So?"

"It's been moved up to one o'clock."

**

Kevin Richards left the scorching heat of the mid-day sun and entered the dining hall. He had spent the morning crawling around under the trailer, running the wires for the backdraft simulation and he was ready for a burger and a beer. Unfortunately, burgers weren't on the menu that day, and because it was a dry facility, he would have to settle for a grilled chicken sandwich and a coke. At least he would be able to get fries with that.

He scanned the dining hall for a place to sit and noticed an unlikely couple sitting together at one of the tables. It was baffling enough that his colleague, Stephen Carlisle sat across from his own client, but more than that, they appeared to enjoy each other's company. Not a common occurrence at the Farm, so Richards felt obligated to investigate.

"Good morning, lovebirds," he said as he took the seat next to Stephen. "And how are we doing this morning?"

Catherine's posture straightened as she pulled back, away from the table. He could see her jaw clench as he addressed her. "You must be Catherine. I am so glad to meet you. Stephen has told me absolutely nothing about you."

Catherine's jaw clenched tighter, but it was Stephen, who answered, "What do you want Kevin? Can't you see we are trying to have a conversation here?"

"Oh yeah? What are you talking about? It must be very interesting to get the two of you at the same table."

"That would be none of your business," Catherine blurted out with ire.

"What the hell are you doing, man? And where the hell have you been crawling around? You're a mess."

"Oh, I've been wiring up the modular trailer for my next contract. Had to get under it."

"Wiring it up for what?"

"The guy wants to die in a fire, so Hawkins asked me to rig a backdraft. I'm going to add something extra though, to make it a bit more exciting."

"Damn." Stephen suddenly forgot all about Catherine, "That'll be freakin' cool. Hey, could you put in a camera so we can watch the action?"

"I tried; Hawkins won't allow it. Some privacy thing."

"Shitty."

"You men and your damned explosions." Catherine interrupted.

"Am I wrong? I don't know about you, but I've never seen a backdraft like that. At least outside of the movies anyway. I'm looking forward to it."

"You men aren't happy unless you're destroying something."

"It's not just men though, is it?" Kevin answered. "I think it's a part of humanity. It's the same thing with car accidents. How often do people slow down to see if anyone is hurt, or worse?"

Catherine scoffed, "Who's to say that they aren't looking to make certain that everyone involved is okay?"

"To what end?" Kevin added cynically. "If someone is seriously hurt, are these good Samaritans going to jump out and help? Not likely. They would be into much of a hurry to care. They are just looking for a little bit of carnage to make their future anecdotes more exciting."

"That's incredibly cynical, don't you think?" Catherine continued the debate.

"Is it? I would call it realistic. When the suits at the office are chitchatting around the water cooler, no one is going to care about the minor fender bender, but if there are emergency response teams involved; well, now you have a story."

Stephen leaned forward resting his arms on the table. "I don't know, he's got a good point with the whole anecdote thing, but for me it's the adrenaline rush. I mean, personally I couldn't care less about the aftermath of a car accident because I didn't see it happen. A certain progression occurs during an event, it's like a dance. With the car accident it starts with the impact, then the bumper crumples while the rear wheels lift off the ground. The airbags inflate, heads strike the bags, the vehicles' momentum takes them into the path of more potential impact and then all is still. It's the same thing with an explosion. It starts out as just a tiny spark, which turns into a flash, which quickly grows as the energy pushes outwards destroying everything in its path until it has completely engulfed it all in flames. It only lasts a few seconds, but what a rush."

"You've put an awful lot of thought into this," Catherine chided.

"Okay Catherine," Kevin turned to her, "you seem quick to criticize the others, where do you suppose the fascination comes from?"

"Action movies."

"How do you figure?"

"It's quite simple really. Hollywood glorifies violence to the point of drawing the audience into the action. What would be better than your very own live action sequence?"

"Come on," Stephen argued, "people always blame the movies for all the bad in the world. If it's not the movies, it's video games, or Dungeons & Dragons, or Catcher in the Rye. There has always been violence through-out history, long before any of those ever existed."

"Yes, there was, but for the purpose of warfare or rebellion, not for entertainment."

"Not true, look at the crowds that would gather at public executions."

"People gathered to bear witness to a system of justice, not to gawk at the bloodshed."

Stephen began to tense, "First of all, no. The average citizen couldn't care less about the system of justice, and even if they did, how do you know what was going through their minds? History was written by those who were there, in the moment. Sure, it sounds noble, but if you were one of them, how would you write history? Would you say you were there to watch the bastard's heads roll, or you were there to bear witness to justice? Which makes you sound more heroic?"

Kevin stepped in smugly, "Did you not just agree with me when I said that bloodshed makes a far better story at the water cooler?"

"Sure, and the bloodshed made the history books, but the storytellers always come out clean. They always have the appearance of objectivity."

"It's not like you were there," Catherine scolded. "Can you not ever give somebody the benefit of the doubt? Are you so closed minded that you can't believe any opinion that differs from your own?"

It was then Stephen's turn to scoff. "Ah, yes. Are you still referring to the peasants, or are you now talking about our discussion about decriminalization?"

Kevin laughed, "I think it's safe to say that everyone in this room is of the same mind when it comes to their opinions of euthanasia."

"Don't be so quick to assume Bud," Stephen responded. "There may be some here who just might surprise you."

"And who would that be?"

"I believe he is referring to me," Catherine said defensively.

"And why is that?" Kevin directed his question at Stephen. "Is she experiencing a moral dilemma regarding our little utopia here?"

"I'm not sure, we haven't got that far into the conversation yet, but she sure has some interesting ideas about prostitution."

"I'm sitting right here you know."

Kevin looked up as a familiar face entered the dining hall from the apartments. He locked eyes with Ian Montgomery for a moment and smiled. Ian quickly looked away and sat down at a table on the other side of the dining area. He turned his attention back to the conversation at hand. "So, you are okay with the Farm, but oppose prostitution?"

Catherine let out a sigh before she responded, "All I said was, prostitution ruined my life and I wish that it had never been legalized."

"But you're blaming an entire profession for a choice that you made."

"See? Those were my words exactly," Stephen declared.

Catherine looked across the table at the faces that stared back at her. She wasn't accustomed to this many people taking an interest in what she had to say. "I have had this argument with Stephen, and I don't feel like rehashing it. But, yes, I used to be a prostitute, and just look where it got me. It never should have happened."

"And I told her that her downward spiral began long before the brothel opened. She can't blame an entire profession for her downfall."

"I wouldn't have joined the profession if it hadn't been legalized."

"You made the choice. No one else made it for you."

Kevin interjected, "I think we need another opinion on this matter." He raised his voice over the din of the dining hall. "Hey Montgomery, come over here for a second. We need your opinion on a certain matter."

"Leave him alone," Catherine warned through clenched teeth. "He clearly doesn't want to be bothered."

"He's fine. He's a part of this too. I want to hear what he has to say about it." He shouted again, "come on Montgomery. We're having a friendly discussion over here. Come and give us your take."

**

Ian shut his eyes tight and tried to ignore the call, but unfortunately, for him, the ignorant contractor persisted. If he were to get any peace, he would have to confront him directly. Ian grasped the armrests of the chair and took a deep breath. He pushed himself to his feet and silently limped over to their table. "What do you want?"

"Good morning, Mr. Montgomery," Kevin mocked with a smile that dripped with condescension. "Please, have a seat. Have you met Stephen and Catherine?"

Ian reluctantly lowered himself into the seat next to Catherine. "I've seen them around."

"Well Ian, may I call you Ian?" Kevin continued without waiting for the response. "We're just having a little moral discussion here, and we want your opinion."

"Kevin," Catherine pleaded, "please."

He raised his hand to stop her interruption. "We would very much like to hear your thoughts on the subject of decriminalization?"

"I'm not certain how comfortable I am talking about this with you."

"It's okay Ian. We are not here to judge you."

"Is that so? Just like Stephen isn't here to judge Catherine?"

"You heard that, eh?" Stephen winced.

"How could I not? You weren't exactly quiet about it."

Kevin smiled. "Well then, that saves me some time filling you in. So, what's your take Ian?"

Ian took a moment to consider. The truth was, he had never been afraid to speak his mind in groups; in fact, he rather enjoyed it. His concern was, he didn't want to blow his cover, and his lie needed to be convincing enough to hide his true intentions and still sound plausible.

"All right then," he appeared hesitant, "as far as the drugs are concerned, I couldn't care less. If these kids want to kill themselves off with mind-altering chemicals, so be it. Survival of the fittest I say. As for prostitution, I'm forced to agree with Catherine. If the government was hell-bent on saving these girls, they should find them alternate solutions, not enable them."

"You will never see an end to prostitution," Stephen snapped, "it's as inevitable as death and taxes. As long as it's still around, wouldn't you rather be certain that it's safe for everyone involved?"

"Of course, I want them to be safe, but safe doing something else. By offering shelter and healthcare to them, the government has effectively taken away the deterrent."

"Everyone has the right to health and well-being, no matter what career path they take. You can't deny anyone their God given right to happiness."

For a moment, Ian lost sight of his ruse as he stood up and slammed his fists on the table. "Don't you dare presume to lecture me on God's given right. You would allow those filthy whores success and happiness, while I'm forced to suffer through the loss of both my health and my wife?" Ian suddenly remembered himself, faked a coughing fit and sat back down in a slump. Ian closed his eyes tight. He wished everyone around him would disappear. The other three looked around at all the surprised stares.

"I, uh. I should go wash up for lunch." Kevin started to stand, avoiding eye contact with Ian. "I'll see you guys around."

Ian struggled out of his chair. Catherine moved to help but he brushed her off. "No, you stay. I wasn't that hungry anyway."

The three of them watched silently as Ian stumbled out of the dining hall, head down, deliberately avoiding everyone in the room. Catherine turned back and looked into Stephen's remorseful eyes. When she looked to Kevin however, she didn't see remorse or guilt. His face was smug, and he may have even been smiling. Could he be that cruel and sadistic to get joy out of emotionally torturing a dying man?

Kevin suddenly realized the others were watching him. He looked to Catherine whose face conveyed an expression of sheer disgust. He cleared his throat as he slid his chair back under the table. "Well, if you two will excuse me, I had better go and wash up."

Stephen and Catherine sat in silence while Kevin strolled out of the dining hall, whistling *Swingin' on a Star*.

CHAPTER SEVENTEEN

Ian Montgomery waited until he was behind the locked door of his private apartment before he relaxed. He was furious that he had allowed them to goad him in such a way. All his preparations could have been for nothing if his outburst had revealed his true intentions. He would proceed as planned, he had to, but he would have to be far more cautious. His own temper could have blown it for him.

He found himself staring at his inventory laid out on the bed. This had turned out to be a far more daunting task than he had originally thought. The schematics he understood well enough, but those small-scale welds proved difficult for his less than steady hands. As he examined what he had done so far, he decided that, though it didn't necessarily look pretty, the functionality appeared passable. He couldn't be certain of course until he turned the device on, but he had some degree of confidence.

He checked his watch to confirm that he had a couple of hours before he had to meet with Dr. Lough. Plenty of time for a bit of tinkering. Ian logged onto his laptop and pulled up the schematic. He then pulled the soldering iron from its sleeve and plugged it in to the outlet above the writing desk. He pulled a page from his complimentary morning newspaper and laid it out to protect the wood surface of the desktop. Finally, he selected the desired components and set to work on his crude, but hopefully effective device.

**

Dr. Lough's hand stopped on the knob on her office door, while she took a moment to listen to the two voices conversing inside. She knew it wasn't terribly professional to eavesdrop on her clients, but she wanted to hear how well the two of them got along. Unfortunately, the tones of the voices were a lot more hostile than she was prepared to allow.

The voices stopped the moment she opened the door and casually walked in. "Good afternoon. I apologize for the schedule change, but in the light of this morning's events-" She deliberately changed the subject to feign ignorance. "Is everything okay?"

"Yes, fine." Catherine chimed in.

"Dandy." Stephen added.

Valerie frowned. "You two will have to be far more convincing than that if you expect me to take you for your word. We will talk more about it in a moment. First, can I offer you some water or coffee?"

Stephen silently shook his head, while Catherine spoke out, "No thanks. The coffee here is terrible."

"You're preaching to the choir. I've been asking for better coffee for years, but the military folk seem to like this sludge."

All three laughed uncomfortably.

Dr. Lough took a seat and opened one of the folders she carried in with her. They sat quietly for a few moments while Dr. Lough quickly scribbled a few illegible notes on the page. When she finally looked up, she took a deep breath and a moment to settle, before she continued with the session.

"Okay then, the three of us have a few things to discuss. First, would either of you like to tell me about the conflict that I walked into the middle of?"

"No." Catherine spoke up.

"What's there to tell?" Stephen blurted out over top of her.

Very well then, perhaps we will come back around to it later. In the meantime, as per our conversation yesterday, Catherine, you have granted Stephen *Liberum Arbitrium*, the freedom of choice."

Catherine nodded bashfully.

"I'm sorry Catherine, I know that I am putting you on the spot here, but I need you to acknowledge this. Did you grant Stephen Liberum Arbitrium?"

"Yes, I did," she answered with contempt.

"And do you understand fully, that by agreeing to this you have relinquished all decisions regarding the completion of a validated contract to Stephen?"

"Yes."

"And Stephen, do you fully understand this responsibility granted to you?"

"Yeah, I know what it is, but I don't understand why she would-"

Valerie quickly cut him off. "We will get to that in a moment Stephen. First you have to tell me if you understand."

Stephen slouched down in his chair and huffed out a deep sigh, "I understand."

"Good. Now that the formalities are over with, we can discuss this further. Stephen, do you have a question for Catherine?"

"Nothing I haven't already asked."

"He thinks I'm a coward," Catherine chimed in.

"I never said that."

"You didn't have to. I can read between the lines."

"All I said was; I think you have given up prematurely."

"So, I'm a coward."

"No!"

"Stop this," Valerie shouted above their bickering. She wanted to get a conversation going between the two of them, but not like that. She had to regain control of the session. "This is counterproductive. We need to get through this, and I will not allow you to waste our time at each other's throats. Catherine, please allow Stephen to say his piece, and when he is finished, I will give you plenty of opportunity to respond. Now Stephen, what makes you so certain that she gave up prematurely?"

"You disagree?"

"It's not my place to agree or disagree with either of you. I'm not here to take sides, I can only listen and offer advice as I see fit."

Catherine would have spoken out in defiance, but Valerie's stern expression immediately silenced her. "Go ahead Stephen," the doctor urged.

"Okay," Stephen leaned forward in his chair and rested his arms on the table in front of him. "Do you know about chaos theory? The Butterfly Effect?"

While Valerie nodded in agreement, Catherine's perplexed expression suggested that she didn't understand. He explained for her benefit. "I have always been fascinated with Chaos theory. It asks; *if a butterfly flaps it's wings in Brazil, will it cause a tornado in Texas?* Meaning a small local action, causing a greater global reaction. The theory also suggests that every action has an infinite number of possible reactions. Every moment of your life, you make some form of a decision. Do you turn left or right? Do you walk or drive? Do you hit the snooze button one more time? Each decision you make sends you on a certain path. Some call it destiny; others call it the luck of the draw. Some even believe that every possible outcome occurs in other parallel realities. It doesn't matter what you call it, you will never know where that other path would have taken you; so how can you possibly know if the decision you made at any one single moment, was the wrong one? On top of that, you make thousands of those decisions every day. If you did make a wrong decision, which *one* was wrong? Perhaps it wasn't the decision you thought. Catherine isn't happy because she doesn't like how her life turned out, because she made a series of bad decisions."

He directed his next question to Catherine. "Can you be absolutely certain, that your life would be better had you chose differently? What if you hadn't got pregnant and dropped out of school? What if you hadn't become a prostitute? What if you hadn't stepped foot onto the Farm's shuttle bus? What if, what if, what if?"

We have all made thousands of wrong decisions in our lifetime, whether we are aware of them or not, and you're willing to destroy yourself over three or four. At this point, the smartest decision you can possibly make is to turn your life around. You are still young, twenty-four years old. How many potential decisions do you think you could have ahead of you? One million? Ten million? A billion? They can't possibly all be bad."

Stephen was about to push it further, but he thought better of it and decided to leave it alone. He had made his point. He sat back in his chair and folded his arms across his chest to demonstrate his cessation.

While Catherine sat stunned, Valerie responded, "Well then, I have never heard you object so passionately towards a client. I had no idea that you felt so strongly."

"She's throwing her life away," Stephen added

"Catherine, do you wish to respond?"

"I'm not even sure how to respond to that. I mean, so what? I'm not talking about how my life could have been, I'm unhappy with how my life is now."

"Then change it."

"Do you think I haven't tried? I was out on my own, working to try to make a living so I could rebuild what I once had. I thought I could make good money working at the Garden, but I sucked at it. Did you know that in the three years that I worked there, I only had four returning customers, none of which was much to brag about? How do you think *that* made me feel? I wasn't worth fucking a second time." Catherine laughed at her next thought," I couldn't even succeed at rock bottom."

Stephen attempted to sound sympathetic. "So then why didn't you take up your parents' offer and go back to school? You could've got your equivalency, to open your options."

"I couldn't do that."

"Why the hell not?"

Catherine lost her temper, "because that would have been admitting defeat."

Stephen gawked at her for a moment, dumbfounded by what he had just heard. "Are you kidding me? Did those words seriously just come out of your mouth? You are perfectly willing to end your life because you can't cope with the hand you've been dealt, but asking your family for help is admitting defeat?"

Catherine stumbled, "that's different."

"How was it different?"

"If I go home, I will have to live with the shame of failure for the rest of my life. How can I look anyone in the eyes after this?"

"Can I cut in here?" Valerie spoke up. "This is a great debate, but it's starting to get heated again. Stephen, you've brought up some excellent points, but you need some work on the concept of compassion. Catherine will continue to get defensive if she feels like she is under attack."

"I'm not attacking her. I'm trying to-"

Valerie stopped him with a raise of her hand. "It's all about perception. She can't guess your intent. On the other hand, Catherine, I hope you are listening to what he has said because he made some impressive observations."

Catherine averted her eyes to keep herself from crying.

"It's alright Catherine. I can see that this is making you uncomfortable. If it's okay with you, I would like to excuse Mr. Carlisle and talk to you a bit more, one-to-one. Yes?"

"I didn't mean to hurt you, Catherine," Stephen apologized. "I was only trying to help you understand."

"Okay," Dr. Lough said as she began to gather up her files, "I think we have done enough damage for one afternoon. That said, I also believe we made some progress here. I learned some interesting details about both of you today."

"Like what?"

"That's for another time, Stephen. In the meantime, I would like you both to think about what we discussed here today. Good stuff."

"What's to think about?" Stephen turned an accusing eye on Catherine. "She shouldn't be here."

Valerie looked at him puzzled. "And why would you say that, Stephen?"

Stephen looked her square in the eye and replied confidently, "because she doesn't want to die."

CHAPTER EIGHTEEN

"We will talk more about it in the morning. Mr. Montgomery and Mr. Richards should be arriving any moment. Good night, Travis."

Dr. Lough hung up the phone and closed the file on Catherine Dean. She opened the bottom file drawer next to her and examined the contents. The drawer contained ninety-six file folders. Only three folders were green, the remaining were all red. Not a great record of accomplishment. She looked at the white folder in her hand and wondered in which colour folder she would transfer Catherine's files. She wasn't able do much for the terminally ill patients, but in Catherine, she saw potential to add a fourth green file to the mix.

She slid Catherine's folder into the front of the drawer, closed it and turned her attention to the second white file on her desk, Ian Montgomery. She opened it up and began to read over her notes. Valerie heard the coughing in the hallway before she heard the knock at her door.

"Come in."

The door opened, and Ian Montgomery slowly made his way into the office. He appeared to have deteriorated even more than she had observed the previous day. Dr. Lough wondered if his condition had worsened, or if his time spent at the Farm has affected him mentally. Either way, in her professional opinion, he looked like shit.

She stood to assist him. "Good afternoon, Ian. May I give you a hand?"

"I can manage thanks." He practically fell into the chair.

"How are you doing today?"

"As good as one would expect. I'm still dying."

"I hope your time here has been comfortable."

"Look," he coughed, "I appreciate what you are doing here, and yes, your staff has treated me very well, but I don't have the energy to pretend.

I don't want to be here, biding my time in my apartment, and I certainly don't want to sit here and talk to you about my feelings. I'm tired. I'm done. I just want to get this week over with so I can move on to a better place."

"I understand and I'm sorry." She leaned forward in her chair. "I do have some news for you that may help relieve some of your stress."

"Yeah? What's that?"

"Because of your terminal condition, which is clearly causing you great discomfort, Captain Hawkins submitted an application to headquarters to move up your end date. They have approved the request. We were able to knock twenty-four hours off your contract and we will be able to proceed on Monday instead of Tuesday."

Ian's eyes widened and his jaw went slack. Otherwise, he remained silent.

"Are you okay, Ian? I thought this would be good news."

No- yes, sorry," he fumbled his words. Yes, that's fantastic news, I'm just a bit surprised, that's all. What happened to Hawkins big speech about procedure?"

"Procedure is crucial, as it protects all who are involved from legal action. That said, we are an organization whose goal is to protect the well-being of our clients. We are rigid, but compassionate. In certain situations, if there is another option, we are not so cold to ignore it."

"I don't know what to say."

"That's okay. Your silence speaks volumes."

Ian leaned back in his chair, lost in thought and Valerie continued, "I wanted a few minutes to chat with you about this before Mr. Richards arrived. I have asked him to join us for the last half of our session. Are you okay with that?"

Ian's attention snapped back, "Richards, why?"

"Because of the interruption this morning, I was forced to rearrange my entire schedule. We also need to discuss the contract itself, and I felt that instead of cancelling or condensing any sessions, it would be more productive to involve both of you in the conversation."

"Shit," Ian said under his breath.

"Is there a problem?"

"No. It's fine. You're full of surprises today."

"I promise, I will try and keep the surprises to a minimum from here on. While we are waiting, I would like to discuss the details of the contract.

You have stated that you wish to die the same way as your wife did, in a fire. Why is that?"

Tears began to well up in the corners of his eyes. "I should have been there. In Fort Mac, I mean. If it weren't for this damned cancer, I would have been. Perhaps I could have saved her, or at the very least, died with her. She was everything to me." He wiped the tears with the back of his hand. "You know, she wanted to stay with me? She wanted to stay home and take care of me, but I told her to go. If I hadn't got sick, I could still be with her right now."

"Hello."

"Hi, sweetie." Ian recalled the last time he heard her voice.

"Ian, I was just thinking about you. How are you feeling?"

"I'm doing okay." Ian stretched out on the sofa covered in a thin flannel blanket. He sat comfortably in the glow of the muted television. "I'm very tired."

"I'm sorry. I should be there with you. I should be taking care of you."

"No, you shouldn't. You should be there for your sister. I can take care of myself for a few days."

"Have you eaten?"

"I warmed myself up some of the stew." he lied. His stomach was too upset to eat. "How are Sachi and the baby?"

"They are both doing wonderfully. They named her Anna-Marie. She's so beautiful. Check your email, I sent you pictures."

"I will." He closed his eyes to picture her face. "I miss you, Kat."

"Aww, I miss you too. I'm going to throw a small baby shower for Sachi and a few of her friends tomorrow night, and I think I'll be going home on Monday, so just three more sleeps."

"I can't wait." He closed his eyes and listened to her breath on the other end of the line, "I love you Kat."

"I love you too. I will call you tomorrow."

"Okay. Give my love to Sachi, Ben, and Anna-Marie."

"I will. Have a good night."

"You too, sweetie."

Dr. Lough listened to his account with sympathy, before she offered her own insight. "I understand how lost you must feel and it's so easy to blame yourself. We don't know what would have happened if you had gone with her. We will never know which path was the right one." She realized, to her amusement, that she just quoted Stephen Carlisle. "Blaming yourself won't fix anything; all it will do is push you further into a state of depression."

He glared at her through watery eyes. "I think worrying about a few hurt feelings is moot at this point. Don't you think?"

"I'm afraid you are confusing depression with sadness. Sadness is an emotion, something you feel in reaction to an event. Depression is a state of mind. It doesn't need an event to trigger it. Depression is always there, and it feeds off your emotions. It, not only controls your actions, but it can also affect your decision-making process."

"Can depression also cause cancer? If that's the case, I will be as over-joyed as I need to get rid of this thing. But unless they can find a link in the next forty-eight hours, I don't think depression is a big concern for me."

"I assure you, Mr. Montgomery that-"

Another knock at the door interrupted.

"I think we should continue this conversation privately afterwards, if that's okay with you."

Ian's shoulders sunk as he quietly nodded.

She called out, "come in."

The door swung open, and Kevin Richards walked confidently into the room. A curious smile formed on his lips, once he saw there was a third person in the room. "Hello, Montgomery, what a delightful surprise. Hiya, Doc. I see we have company. What's on the agenda for today?"

"We were just discussing the change to the timeline. Please Kevin, take a seat."

As Kevin pulled a second chair up to the desk, Ian slid his chair closer to the wall, to put as much distance as possible between himself and that maniac. He embellished the move with a few more coughs.

Dr. Lough stood and moved over to the side table where she poured a glass of water from a pitcher. She placed the glass before Ian and then offered the same to Kevin.

"I'm good, thanks."

She returned to her seat and crossed her legs. "As I had started to tell Ian, because of the incident this morning, I had decided-"

"Hey, yeah," Richards interrupted. "What was that all about anyway?"

Valerie recalled what Travis had told her, "The PALM organization decided to stage another protest rally. I'm not certain what sparked this one. We suspect other motives."

"What makes you think there was an ulterior motive? Could it not have been a simple demonstration?" Ian jumped in defensively.

"At first it didn't seem out of the ordinary, but Captain Hawkins thinks their spontaneous violent outbursts concentrated on the front gates may suggest an underlying motive. On top of that, the lack of media attention makes him think that the protest rally was a ruse, perhaps a distraction for something much bigger."

Ian, once again, swore under his breath. He hadn't considered the media. "Is there an investigation?"

"Captain Hawkins has a team scouting the perimeter for anything out of the ordinary and he has beefed up security at the gate, but other than that, I haven't heard anything unusual."

"You aren't imposing curfew, are you?" Kevin jumped in,

"Heavens no." Dr. Lough clicked her pen, as if to signify a switch of topic. "However, we seem to have gone rather off track. Captain Hawkins has the investigation under control, and we have other matters to discuss. The events at the gate are not your concern."

Kevin shrugged, while Ian sunk back in his seat with a frown.

Valerie continued. "Okay. As you are now both aware, we have authorization to move up our timeline by twenty-four hours. Now that you have had a few minutes to process, Ian, do you have any concerns?"

Ian had to choose his words carefully. Perhaps he could still get out of this mess. "On the contrary, I couldn't be happier. But that gives us less than 2 days. Will all the preparations be completed in time?"

Kevin laughed. "No worries here. I could be ready this evening if you wanted."

"What a relief." His heart sank.

"Kevin," the doctor interjected, "why don't you fill him in on what you have been working on."

"What, and spoil the surprise?" He smirked.

"I think we have surprised him enough for today."

"All right." He adjusted in his seat to get more comfortable. "There's not a hell of a lot to tell. Maintenance has finished building the satellite apartment. They are just painting the walls and it will be ready for furniture. They have done a damned good job of it too. It's nicer than my own apartment. I may have to ask Hawkins for a transfer, though I may feel differently once we are done with it. "Kevin cleared his throat once he realized he was the only one laughing. "Anyway, we used all flammable materials, so once I add the accelerant, you won't be able to fart without starting a fire."

Neither so much as cracked a smile.

"Tough room." He wrapped it up. "I've installed an igniter so we can set it off from a distance. We just need to wait until you're asleep."

"Do you have any questions, Ian?"

"Not really, I'm just so glad he gets so much amusement out of this."

"You gotta have a sense of humour around here, buddy. This place is too damned serious."

"I don't *gotta* do anything. And I am most certainly not your buddy."

Dr. Lough made certain to keep her tone calm. "Come now, Ian. Remember, Kevin is here for your benefit. His sense of humour may be," she considered the word, "unorthodox, but I assure you, he means well."

"Oh yes," Kevin stated with mock sincerity, "I mean very well indeed."

"And as for you Mr. Richards, I'll ask that you keep your sarcasm to a minimum and show some consideration for our client."

Richards leaned in, to whisper to Ian, "You know you're in trouble when she uses your surname. I guess I had better play nice." He finished with a wink.

Ian directed his questions to Dr. Lough. "So, what are you telling me? Am I supposed to just lay there and wait for the fire? Can I at least take something to knock me out?"

"We cannot render you unconscious. You need to be able to escape in the unlikely event you change your mind."

"But-"

"But, if you will allow me to finish, I can give you something to help you relax. If you have truly come to terms with your death, you should have no troubles falling asleep."

Ian nodded.

Kevin gladly jumped in. "Don't worry bud; the way we have set this up, you won't have to wait long."

Ian ignored him and continued to address the doctor. "Thank you for everything you are doing for me. You are a good doctor, you've been very kind to me, so don't worry. Your conscience is clear." He turned her psychology back on her, "Don't think of it as losing another client, think of it as having gained a client's respect and admiration."

Ian struggled to his feet and Valerie stood to reassure him. "Please Mr. Montgomery, I-"

He raised his hand to stop her. "No, Dr. Lough. I am tired. This session has taken a lot out of me, and I would like to get a cup of tea and go to bed."

She nodded. "Okay Ian. Get some rest and I will talk to you in the morning. If you like, I could meet you at your apartment, if you'd find that more comfortable."

"No," he said hastily, and then brought it back. "I like to be able to get out a bit, while I still can, you know?"

She nodded, as Ian turned to leave. "Good night, Ian." He exited the room and closed the door behind him.

Once alone, Kevin, who had silently watched the exchange with a mischievous grin, turned to Valerie. "Was it something I said?"

**

"Shit!" Ian Montgomery cursed as he slammed his bedroom door behind him. "Shit, shit, shit!"

They moved the timeline up twenty-four hours. "Shit!" In order to keep up his ruse, he had begged and pleaded for them to move up the timeline, but he never expected that they might actually do it. After all, they had procedures to follow. "Shit!"

It was too late to dwell on it. He had dug his hole, and he would have to double his efforts if he was going to get himself out of it. Especially if he had to continue to waste so much time rehashing painful memories with that pain-in-the-ass shrink. Once he had calmed down and steadied his resolve, he then noticed something terribly wrong.

"Shit!"

The housekeeping staff had been through his room. They made the bed with tight hospital corners; the small kitchenette was spotless and organized. Fresh new towels hung in the bathroom and a band of paper, wrapped around the toilet seat read *Sanitized for your Comfort*. Even the carpet had the telltale lines made by a vacuum cleaner.

"Shit!"

Ian wasn't concerned about the information on his laptop, as he protected it with a strong password, but the backpack on the other hand, how could he have been so careless? He ran to the back of the bed and lifted the skirt. He lay on his stomach and peered into the darkness towards the head of the bed. To his relief the bag remained where he had left it. Still, had it been disturbed? He couldn't tell.

He reached under and grabbed hold of the strap to pull the heavy backpack out into the open. At first glance, everything seemed to be there, but he had to be certain. He took inventory of each item, laying them out on the bed. He accounted for everything including the two solid bricks wrapped in brown wax paper.

He laughed at his own paranoia. No, he wasn't paranoid he was too smart for that. In a game of cat and mouse where strategy is paramount, one must exercise a high degree of caution. That's not paranoia, that's smart business.

He picked up a circuit board and a small timing relay. This was far more complex than he hoped, even with the schematics. He fired up his laptop and stared at the diagram. He tried to concentrate, but his mind continued to drift back to his conversation with Dr. Lough. He was so preoccupied with his plan; he had forgotten how painful his memories were.

Ian leaned back on the rear two legs of the chair and rubbed his eyes. He had to concentrate; there was too much work to do. One day less. Shit. He got up and went to the counter where he dropped a pod into the coffee maker. He placed a mug under the spout and started the machine. The smell of fresh coffee filled the room. He closed his eyes and took a deep breath.

It was going to be a long night, and he was going to need a lot of coffee.

ECE-80062

Shannon Coulter sat alone at her table in the atrium, watching Amanda, the lovely young server, move efficiently from table to table. She served food and topped up coffees. She was very good at her job. Coffee cups were rarely empty, and the food was always hot. She was well liked and appreciated by all her customers, so there was no reason why she wouldn't have been able to serve Shannon her morning apple juice.

However, Amanda didn't bring her the juice that sat on the table in front of her. The glass of amber liquid placed before her was delivered by someone else, someone she was familiar with, Stephen Carlisle.

Shannon wasn't stupid; she knew exactly what was in the glass of apple juice. She had signed the papers the previous evening with Captain Hawkins and had her final meeting with Dr. Lough. They were very kind and understanding people and Shannon appreciated all they had done to help her make the right choice. She was certain she had.

She stared blindly at the juice. It reminded her of urine, of the countless samples the doctors had taken from her over the past several years. It was a rare disease and she had refused the risky surgery, so they had to keep an eye on things.

She had Pheochromocytoma, a rare tumor that formed in her adrenal gland. This caused her to produce too much norepinephrine and epinephrine, which in turn wreaked havoc on her blood pressure, heart rate and metabolism. As the surgery was high risk, she opted for chemotherapy. The cytotoxins that surged through her body destroyed her immune system and caused her to lose all her hair. Worst of all, it failed to help.

Though surgery was still an option, it was also uncertain. It could help, or make matters worse, and she had lost the will to fight. Shannon decided that quality of life was more important than quantity and requested a referral to the Farm.

She reached for the glass. It felt cold in her hand. She remembered her wife, Cass, who held her hand through every appointment and every procedure. She wondered what Cass was doing at that moment.

She remained with Shannon through all the vomiting and the hair loss. She held her when she was too scared to go to sleep yet too tired to stay awake. Nevertheless, Cass wasn't there when Shannon left for the Farm. Cass couldn't face her decision. She begged her not to go. She didn't understand.

"Please don't do this. I love you. I don't want to lose you."

She could hear Cass's voice echo in her head. Shannon wanted so badly to see her again. To hold her in her arms, comfort her, to assure her that everything would be okay.

Of course, everything would be okay because she had made the right decision. The best decision for her, and if Cass couldn't understand that, then-

Shannon looked at the glass of juice in her hand. It was still full. If she were so certain she had made the right decision, it would be easy to lift the glass to her lips and pour the cold liquid down her throat.

She imagined Cass, lying on their bed alone, face buried in her pillow as she cried, wondering if it was over yet. Did she have someone there to hold her hand, to comfort her through the difficult time? Whom could she have called? Who would have understood her pain? Did anyone understand Cass like Shannon did?

She placed the glass on the table and stared at the tainted apple juice. The surgery was such a huge risk. It could end up killing her anyway. Shannon looked up from the glass and saw Amanda watching her intently. After a moment, a smile formed on her face. What did Amanda know that she didn't?

She looked down at the glass. It lay on its side, the contents spilled over the table and onto the floor. She could hear the splatter as more juice dripped from the table into the puddle that had formed on the floor below. She needed a cloth. She needed a mop.

More importantly, she needed a phone.

CHAPTER NINETEEN

Day Five

"Well, it doesn't sound like that turned out quite the way I had planned."

Captain Hawkins and Dr. Lough sat across the desk from each other in his office where they discussed the events of the previous day. "I made a huge mistake. It sounds like they were ready to kill each other yesterday. I was stupid to think they would fall for each other."

Valerie gave Travis a wry smile, "On the contrary, I wouldn't start writing your resignation quite yet. If I were to make an educated guess, I would say that he's in love with her."

"How can you say that, if he tore into her every time she opened her mouth?"

"He did, but if you think about it for just a moment, you'll realize that every comment that he jumped on was self-destructive. She had a hundred excuses for why she needed our help, why her life isn't worth saving, and he argued the contrary. He defended Ms. Dean from herself."

He considered what she sold him, not quite certain if he bought it. "What are you saying? Are you suggesting that he wants to talk her out of it?"

"I believe that to be the case, although he has tried very hard to hide it. If you had seen his body language, I think it may have hurt him to listen to her self-deprecating remarks. It made him uncomfortable. That's likely why he responded so harshly. He didn't like the idea that someone else took away his control of his own emotions."

"Well, I'll be damned, I hadn't considered that. Do you suppose it's mutual?"

"I'm not entirely certain yet, as she continues to keep somewhat guarded. But I think so. She is certainly curious about him, but whether she has fallen for him or not remains to be seen. She doesn't like to talk much about her feelings; however, I have no issues convincing her to talk about her past. Unfortunately, she glosses over the good and focuses heavily on the bad. She has what some like to call the Eeyore complex."

"Eeyore?" Hawkins stifled a laugh, "You mean the donkey?"

"Precisely. Like Eeyore, Catherine perceives everything to be a million times worse than it actually is, and she desperately wants others to know exactly how horrible her life truly is in her mind. I think Mr. Carlisle may have hit the nail on the head yesterday. It's very possible that she knows in her heart she doesn't want to die, but she needs everyone to acknowledge that her life really is that bad."

"So, we got her then." Travis said excitedly.

"Now hold on there a second cowboy. You're going to have to leave that champagne in the fridge a couple more days. We can't just deny her contract and send her on her way. If I release her and she goes and kills herself anyway, we can still be liable for negligence. I need to convince her to come around."

"And if you don't?"

"I call in a third party, government appointed psychiatrist who will evaluate her. Based on their decision either we continue with the contract, or we turn her over to their care."

"Why the runaround? We've never had to do this before."

"Well, if I talk them down, it isn't an issue," Valerie explained, "If I have justifiable cause to preserve the contract, I have the authority to make that decision. This time I don't have cause. If she doesn't come around, I am not authorized to make the call."

"This is the part of the job I hate." Travis sighed, "Clients like Montgomery are no-brainer, but this depression stuff? I don't even fully understand why they allow it here. It's not as if they're terminal or anything. There is nothing physically wrong with them."

Valerie scolded him for his remark, "Travis, you should know better than that. Depression is a very real illness. Besides, the legislation states *persons suffering from a debilitating illness*. Nowhere does it say *terminal*. Whether you agree with it or not, crippling depression fits the bill."

"I know that." He quickly backpedaled, "But it's so damn hard to evaluate."

"That's why you have me here, honey. The thing you need to remember about depression is you can't just chalk it up to a sign of weakness, because that couldn't be farther from the truth. In fact, in most cases the patient has shown an incredible amount of strength for so long, the pressure builds up to the point of cracking their psyche like an egg. Once this happens there are a flood of emotions the patient can no longer cope with, and they end up needing some form of assistance."

"I understand that. My youngest niece suffers from depression. She is on medication and deals very well with it. She would never end up in a place like this."

Valerie straightened up in her chair, "If that's the case, I would let her know how proud you are of her. You can't however always tell what is going on inside their heads. Medication is great because it helps to balance their hormones and it allows them to think a little more clearly. The problem being, drugs can't eliminate the underlying catalyst. You just mask the problem instead of fixing it. For some, it's enough to keep them going. Others may not be so lucky and continue their downward spiral into oblivion."

"And Catherine?"

"Well, the next two days will be critical. Can we reach her in time? It's possible, but she has some sturdy blinders on. As it turns out, you may have been right after all. I now believe that Stephen may still be our best hope. He is not afraid to tell it like it is, which we may find incredibly tactless, but it forces her to listen."

Hawkins tried to hide his smug expression. He was right, and it all seemed promising. He prayed that the two of them could pull this off without resorting to a third party shrink. Perhaps if they turned this contract around, it would help to bring them closer together. Lost in thought, he hadn't realized that he had been staring into Valerie's beautiful green eyes.

"What?" She asked, feeling self-conscious.

Hawkins decided to give it a shot, "Have dinner with me tonight."

"We eat together every night."

"Not here, let's go into the city. We'll have a nice dinner, just the two of us."

"You mean like a date?" She asked, pleasantly surprised. Then she added, "But it's more than an hour's drive."

"So what, it'll be nice to get away. What do you say?"

Valerie tried to hide some of her eagerness. "Why not, let's do it. Catherine is my last appointment. We should be done at five. Pick me up at my apartment at five-thirty. I'll even let you drive."

Hawkins beamed. As far as he was concerned, the meeting couldn't possibly have gone better. "I'm looking forward to it."

**

It hadn't even been an hour since Byron Daniels had checked his messages, but he was restless. He needed answers. Though he wasn't optimistic, he still anxiously waited for the page to load. He didn't have long to wait, however, and there it was, at the top of the page. A little red dot that indicated a new message. He clicked the icon.

Matthew 8:05- Therefore do not be anxious about tomorrow, for tomorrow will be anxious for itself. The Lord is our shepherd. -MRS

There was no need to look this one up. Byron already knew it would be misquoted, and already knew what it meant. Tomorrow morning at 8:05, Ian was going to need a quick getaway.

**

He watched anxiously as the numbers on the tiny digital display counted down. It had been a meticulous process soldering and re-soldering, to piece together unfamiliar components, until he had before him, a crude but potentially effective device. He would soon find out if his efforts would come to a positive conclusion. The results came in three, two, one,

Click.

Just as Ian had hoped, the small micro-switch closed and completed the circuit. If he had this device hooked to a detonator, the results would surely have been much louder. Though he was pleased with the outcome, he wanted to be certain he could re-create it. He reset the micro-switch then dialed up the digital display with a small termination screwdriver until it read twenty seconds. He picked up the terminal wires and touched the two stripped ends together, to produce a tiny spark. The display once again began to count down the seconds.

As he watched, everything he had overheard through the bug in Hawkins' office ran through his mind. That afternoon Richards was to have completed setting up the last-minute details for the fire. An igniter in the floor will light the gasoline-soaked carpet. The fire will grow bigger and hotter as it feeds off the furniture. It shouldn't take long for the fire to burn up enough oxygen to prime itself for the perfect backdraft.

That of course was not how it would go down.

In the middle of the night, when everyone was asleep, Ian would sneak into the apartment and rewire the igniter, so it will also engage his own wireless device. He would then plant explosives on the gas meter for the administration building, tied to the micro-switch. The following morning, when Richards pushes his button, the fire will start, and his timer will begin a five-minute countdown. He won't be in the apartment though. He would be out of there long before Richards pushed the button. He would be well hidden somewhere, where he could watch the show, then make a quick escape. The timer will run out and-

Click.

Once again, the small micro-switch closed. His test had been successful. He eyed the backpack on the bed, which still contained the C-4 and detonators. It truly would be an event to remember. One detail remained. His escape.

This was the reason for the second block of C-4. There would be a second explosion while everyone concentrated on the destruction of the administration building. This one would be at the fence line by the wooded area where he made the trade-off with Byron. After the fence came down, his friend would be there waiting to drive him to safety. He would be well on his way home before they even realized he was gone. The plan was perfect.

All those years he had spent on the fight against decriminalization would finally come to a head. The destruction of the administration building may not necessarily take down the entire operation, but it would certainly be a critical blow. It might cause the politicians to think twice before they rebuild. Surely, they wouldn't be stupid enough to cross PALM again after this display of strength. No matter the outcome, everyone will know he had struck the first blow, and if they were to decide to force his hand again, he would have plenty of time to begin plans for another assault.

Ian's confidence was increasing. Nothing would stop him from defeating his nemesis. Just to be certain there would be no surprises, he once again picked up the tiny screwdriver and dialed up the digital display to read twenty seconds.

**

Good morning, Ms. Bentley,

Based on the series of reports you have aired over the past several years, it is clear to me that you have an interest in the goings-on at the various facilities, founded by the diversification strategy. In this specific case, I am referring to the facility you know very well as the Farm.

I would hazard a bet, however, that your knowledge of the Farm is limited to what Captain Hawkins and his associates have allowed you to know. I therefore wish to offer you a unique opportunity. I offer you firsthand knowledge of an upcoming contract.

Come to the Farm for precisely eight am, Monday morning and bear witness to the conclusion of an actual contract. A contract where a client will be burned alive in a fiery inferno, while he sleeps. A contract that will be approved and carried out by the Farm's administrator, Captain Travis Hawkins. I call upon you to show the world what really goes on beyond the high fences.

You need not worry about the guard at the gate. Inform him that you have been invited by the client, as a witness on his behalf. He then cannot deny you entry.

I trust, in the meantime, you will keep this correspondence in confidence, as we don't want anyone to have the opportunity to prepare for your arrival.

As I will be understandably preoccupied at the time of your arrival, I regret that I won't be able to meet you in person. I will therefore thank you in advance for your attendance and for what I am certain will be a very informative report.

Respectfully,
Ian Montgomery

CHAPTER TWENTY

It was still quiet in the dimly lit atrium when Catherine first emerged from her apartment that morning. All she could hear was the faint clatter of pots and pans from the kitchen as the staff prepared for the Saturday morning breakfast rush. Catherine however welcomed the silence. Unable to sleep, she decided to escape her room to sit among the fake foliage and read. Fortunately, for her, the kitchen staff had already made a pot of coffee, which went a long way to help her relax. Nonetheless, she couldn't quite concentrate on her book. The conversation the previous afternoon haunted her thoughts. Stephen's arrogant presumption sickened her. Just who did he think he was, analyzing her like that? He was a bloody contractor, not a shrink. What gave him the right to call her out in such a way?

Her mind continued to run in circles, going over the conversation repeatedly in her head. *Can you be absolutely certain that your life would be better had you chose differently?* What a stupid question. Of course, her life would be better. If she hadn't got pregnant, she wouldn't have had to become a prostitute and she most certainly wouldn't be at the Farm. *Then why don't you take up your parents' offer and go back to school?* How could she possibly face her family every morning after everything she had done? They had raised her to be an intelligent, independent woman, and just look what she had become.

He was right about one thing, she had made so many stupid decisions the last several years, the best tracker on the planet could never find his way back down the correct path. It was far too late to turn back, and she was far too scared to continue forward.

Because she doesn't want to die.

Well, that couldn't conceivably be farther from the truth. Why would she be there if she didn't want to die? Why would she put herself through the daily reminders of how badly she screwed up? Of course, she wanted to die, that was the dumbest thing she had ever heard. What could she possibly have to live for?

Because I like you.

Well, there was that. Did he truly mean what he said or was he just looking to get a reaction from her? Perhaps he just wanted to get into her bed before he completed the contract, or to put one more notch on his belt. On the other hand, maybe he's the kind of predator who loved to play mind games with his victims.

On the other hand, maybe he liked her.

That was highly unlikely. What was to like? She was a mess of a woman. Not necessarily unattractive, but used and abused with a ton of emotional baggage. What could he possibly see in her?

"You will never find out how it ends if you sit and stare at the same page all morning."

Catherine snapped out of her self-pity to find Stephen standing next to her table with a pot of steaming coffee and an empty mug in hand. As he spoke, he topped up her coffee, filled his own and set the pot down in the centre of the table. He then took a seat across from her.

"Are you okay?"

"That's pretty stupid question, don't you think?"

"Not at all. You only have two more days until you get the closure you' desire. By rights, your mind should be at peace. After all, you have nothing left to fear. Instead, you look as though your mind is in conflict."

"That's because you've been messing with my head."

"Ah, then I have given you reason to doubt."

"Would you stop that?" Catherine snapped.

"Stop what?"

Catherine looked into his unreadable grey eyes, unable to tell if he was sincere or playing games. She hated that he could manipulate her like that, but it was so hard to resist his charismatic tenacity.

"Why do you always have to make this so damn difficult? Can't you see that I want this pain to end? It's your job to free me from the heartache, not cause me more."

Stephen sat forward in his chair and rested his arms on the table. He leaned in close to be certain he had Catherine's full attention. "*That* is exactly what I am talking about. If you were truly at the end of your rope, there would be no more room for pain. You would be completely numb to everything I had to say. Instead, you fight with me. You argue your position and try to justify why you are here. If you believed in your heart that you belong here, there would be no reason to justify your presence, you wouldn't give two shits about what I had to say."

Catherine's eyes began to tear up while the pitch of her voice rose slightly. "I argue with you because you keep telling me and everyone else within earshot that I don't belong here."

"Why the hell do you care what I think? Or anyone else for that matter? I'm just the guy you hired to kill you. Dr. Lough is your psychologist; she's the one whose impressions you need to be worried about. What I say doesn't make a lick of difference."

Now tears streamed down her cheeks. "But she listens to you. She said herself that you made some good points."

"The best literary villains often make a good point, which doesn't mean you have to agree with them. Just because someone sounds like he knows what he's talking about, doesn't mean he's right. The arch nemesis is always smart; otherwise, he wouldn't be much of an adversary. Take your beloved Pendergast and his brother Diogenes. Aloysius knows his brother is brilliant, but he would never trust him."

Catherine managed to smile at the analogy. "I see you've been brushing up on your reading. Yes, you are most definitely more suited to Diogenes' personality."

"Ha, ha," Stephen laughed joyfully. "It seems we can see eye to eye after all."

Catherine found herself smiling as she stared into the face of a handsome man who sat across the table from her, looking proud of himself. They shared a moment, as his eyes locked with hers, but soon she grew uncomfortable and averted her gaze. Desperate to break the tension, Catherine quickly changed the subject.

"So do you know yet how you're going to do it?"

"Do what?"

"Don't play coy. You know what I'm talking about."

Stephen leaned back in his chair and crossed his arms upon his chest. "I'm not sure. I haven't decided yet."

"With all the possibilities this facility has to offer, you must have some idea how you'd want to take me out." She threw his own words back at him.

"Touché," Stephen laughed, "although I never said that I don't have ideas, I merely stated that I haven't decided. Liberum Arbitrium doesn't happen every day. I would hate to squander it."

"So then, what are you thinking?"

Stephen folded his hands on the table and leaned in towards her. It was beginning to get noticeably louder in the atrium. As, they talked, others began to make their way down for breakfast. Other residents now occupied several tables around them, and Stephen's eyes darted around the room, very aware of their close proximity.

"Look, can we talk about anything besides your contract right now?"

"Yeah, sure." Catherine found herself rather grateful for the change of subject. "Like what?" Catherine reached up to swipe the stray hairs out of her face, and her sleeve slid part way up her arm. She caught Stephen staring at her scars. "Not that."

"You cut?"

She looked away from him, "I used to."

"Some of those look pretty fresh."

Catherine squeezed her eyes tight, and tears formed in the corners. "Please… don't. I can't-"

"Okay, I won't push." Stephen let out a deep sigh and rubbed his chin in thought. "Tell me something good."

She looked at him quizzically as she wiped the tears from her face. "What good?"

"Well, there has to be something good in your life, it can't all be shit."

Catherine turned her head and attempt to hide her blushed cheeks, "I don't know, I-"

"Come on, there must be something you love, something you're proud of."

Catherine looked back at Stephen, surprised to discover what appeared to be genuine interest in what she had to say. She began to speak but stopped herself, afraid to share that one last vestige of individuality.

"Please," he pushed, "enlighten me. What do you have to lose?"

"It's silly." She turned away again.

"I promise I won't laugh. Come on. You can tell me. The suspense is killing me."

Catherine scanned the tables around them. The restaurant was nearly at capacity. The dull drone of a dozen or so conversations filled the air, which gave Catherine confidence that if she spoke quiet enough, her response would remain private.

"My voice."

"Your voice?" Stephen's response was louder than Catherine had hoped.

She tried to take the conversation back down to little more than a whisper. "I'm a singer. Not professionally, I mean I've never had any formal training, but I'm proud of my voice."

"What do you sing?"

"Back in school I was the lead soprano in our choir. I had several of the solos. We did very well in our competitions, and even had the opportunity to tour Central Europe and sing in the old cathedrals. After that, I did a little bit of musical theatre. I played the part of Marian in The Music Man. I loved that. The last decade though, the best I've been able to manage is the occasional night of karaoke."

Stephen smiled as he listened to Catherine's anecdote. The way he looked ate her in that moment made her feel like he actually cared. Then he surprised her again. "Sing for me."

"What? No."

"Please, I want to hear this magical voice of yours."

"I can't sing here. Are you crazy?"

"Wait, I have an idea." Stephen stood and began to head for the exit. He stopped just short of the door, turned around and yelled across the room. "Well, are you coming?"

Stephen disappeared through the open door. Catherine looked around to find all the attention was on her. Catherine suddenly felt uncomfortably self-conscious, so she gathered up her novel and followed her contractor out of the building.

**

Kevin Richards held the flaming lighter up to the window and slowly traced around the frame. There wasn't so much as a flicker. The maintenance workers did a fantastic job sealing the windows and vents. Even the rubber seal around the exterior door prevented any outside air from seeping in. The only airflow into the room came from the small space under the bedroom door. That was no concern to him, however. He needed that little bit of oxygen to keep the fire from completely burning itself out.

He flipped the lighter closed and scanned the outer room. It was a very nice-looking apartment for one that was destined to go up in flame. The workers put a lot of effort into the place to make it look comfortable and inviting. There was a fresh coat of paint on the walls, the floor carpeted and the rooms were furnished.

Richards opened the door to the bedroom and walked in. It was more impressive than the outer room. It had a comfortable queen-sized bed with a burgundy duvet centered on the left wall, with a polished wood end table on each side. One table held a brass-reading lamp, and on the other sat an ice bucket with a bottle of champagne and a single glass. A thirty-two-inch television sat on the matching dresser across from the bed and the windows were dressed with curtains to accent the bedding. The prominent piece in the room, however, hung above the bed. Though quite a bit smaller, it was the exact same print of Logan's Pass that hung in the administration office. A lot of thought went in to ensure Montgomery's final night was as comfortable as possible.

Richards went over to the window to confirm the potential escape route. The hinges were well oiled, and it opened with ease. There should be no obstacles for an easy exit. If Montgomery were to reconsider, there would be nothing to stop him. Of course, Kevin was confident that the issue was moot.

He shut the escape route, exited the bedroom, and closed the door behind him. He knelt in front of the exterior door and pulled up the edge of the carpet. He rolled it up just a few feet before he exposed a pair of small wires that poked up through the small hole he had drilled in the floor. He reached into his pocket and pulled out a small igniter with two small screw terminals on its bottom end. He screwed the two wires down under the terminals, then fed the excess wire back into the hole, which was the perfect size to allow the device to sit flush with the floor. He then rolled the carpet back into place and tucked the edges under the baseboards.

He ran his finger along the bottom of the baseboard, until he found the small plastic tube that he cut flush with the wall. He found that the carpet covered a bit too much of the tube for his liking, so he pulled a penknife from his pocket and trimmed the carpet down around the hole. Once he found it satisfactory, he crawled to the other side of the room where he did the same for the second tube. He wanted to be certain to get a good spread of accelerant.

He bent down to blow the excess carpet fibres away from the tube, when there was a knock at the door behind him. He stood and cautiously opened the door. The older man who stood before him was professionally dressed in a white shirt and black tie. The badges on his arms held the logo of Regina Fire and the epaulettes on his shoulders displayed the five gold bars of a Chief. The Fire Chief greeted him with a smile beneath a bushy grey moustache, the same colour of his thinning hair.

"Good morning. You must be Mr. Richards."

"Yes sir." He resisted the urge to salute.

"I am Chief Inspector Glenn Spaulding of the Regina Fire Department. Captain Hawkins told me I would find you here."

Kevin extended his hand. "Good to meet you, sir. I didn't realize you were coming."

The Chief accepted the handshake, "Captain Hawkins applied for a fire permit, so I am here to see what kind of department presence you'll require."

"I think you'll find that, the way we have this set up, you won't require much presence at all. I was just finishing up here if you want to see what we have done."

"I would appreciate that. Thank you." Spaulding climbed the three steps into the trailer.

Richards backed up into the apartment, to allow him to enter. "All the exterior walls, as well as the dividing wall, have a two-hour fire rating. This will keep the initial fire contained in this room until the backdraft is initiated."

"How do you plan on starting the fire without putting yourself in danger?"

"I won't be anywhere near it. I have installed a fuel pump under the trailer that, when remotely engaged, will pump ten litres of gasoline into the room through the two tubes, there and there."

Spaulding knelt closer to where he pointed. "Clever. How will you prevent the fire from traveling down the tube to the pump and reservoir?"

"It was quite simple. The tubing I selected has a low melting point, and I have installed a back flow preventer at each entrance point to keep the fire from jumping. The supply lines will fall away long before it has time to spread."

The inspector nodded. "Continue."

"Once the carpet is saturated, I will signal the igniter which is installed in the floor, and nature will take it from there. The fire will feed off all the furniture and deplete the oxygen, priming the room for the backdraft."

"Spaulding's face revealed nothing. "Show me the other side."

Kevin opened the door to the bedroom and let the Chief to enter before him. Once inside, Spaulding examined the room. "That window opens?"

"Absolutely, it serves two purposes. First, it acts as an escape route, should it be required. Second, it ensures a sufficient supply of air to feed the inferno."

"You've done your homework."

"I have a good understanding of fire, sir. I used to be a firefighter at CFB Halifax."

"A firefighter?" Spaulding scowled. "And now you start fires? It seems to me that you are fighting for the wrong side."

"Believe me sir, when I tell you that I have a great deal of respect for the flame, perhaps even a greater one. When I worked for the department, I studied fire to learn how to fight it. Now, I study fire to learn how to control it. I understand fire, how it moves, how it grows, and I have learned how to bend fire to my will." Richards smiled. "Trust me. I will have more control over this fire than your fighters with their hoses."

Spaulding cleared his throat as he wiped the sweat from his brow. Averting his gaze, he changed the subject. "I would like to see the pump and igniter.

"Certainly."

Richards led the inspector out the door and around back of the trailer. Spaulding carefully examined the equipment, while the entire time he kept one suspicious eye on the contractor. Satisfied with the installation, he crawled out from under the trailer and distanced himself from Richards.

"Okay, then. Everything appears to be in order. I see no reason why Captain Hawkins can't proceed as planned. Uh-" He fumbled for the words, "Good work."

"Is there something wrong, sir?" Richards enquired.

"You know your stuff, Mr. Richards, perhaps a little too well." He took a step backwards, "I honestly think you would benefit from a few more conversations with Dr. Lough on the subject." He nodded. "Captain Hawkins will have my report by the end of the day."

Chief Inspector Spaulding turned and walked back in the direction of the administration building. His pace was hurried, but not panicked. Richards leaned against the side of the trailer; arms crossed and watched him disappear around the corner of the storage building. The inspection had gone according to plan, which meant the preparations were nearing completion.

Richards reached into his pocket, pulled out his pocketknife and crawled back under the trailer.

**

Captain Hawkins shook the hand of the inspector, before he climbed into his white sedan and drove out of the compound. The inspection itself went off without a hitch. Spaulding approved the precautions taken, and in addition, would have a water-truck present at the event to aid in the cleanup. Spaulding himself would also be on hand to observe.

The chief's one concern involved the contractor, Kevin Richards. Though warranted, it didn't come as a surprise to Hawkins, as Richards' "unhealthy passion for fire", as Spaulding put it, was the very reason he selected him for the contract. Besides that, he was confident in Valerie's ability to stay on top of things and sound the alarm at the first sign of trouble.

Still, the conversation began to weigh heavily on his mind. Prior to his station at the farm, he never would have associated with the likes of Richards or Carlisle, or any of the contractors, for that matter. Ever since, he had embraced their worst qualities, and used them to his advantage.

Travis wondered what kind of monster he had become, to sacrifice his morals to avoid a medical discharge. He wondered if Valerie suffered through the same moral dilemma each time a contractor or client revealed to her their innermost secrets. Was she too, a monster?

The two of them were to spend the evening alone together. He wondered what kind of monsters they would let out of the closet.

CHAPTER TWENTY-ONE

Catherine stepped out of the residence building, into the crisp morning air, to find Stephen moving quickly away from where she stood. He paused and turned back for a moment, just long enough to motion for her to follow, then continued towards his undisclosed destination.

Stephen was more than halfway across the courtyard before she resigned herself to follow. She picked up the pace slightly, in attempt to close the gap, but remained somewhat weary of his intentions, and made little effort to catch up entirely. By this point, it became abundantly clear that his intended target was the storage warehouse. She recalled him saying that the building held little of interest, so she wondered what could possibly be contained in there that would generate such excitement in him. Catherine shivered at the thought of walking into a dark, unoccupied building with a potential sociopath. While she welcomed death, torture wasn't something she wished to experience.

With each cautious step, she slowly moved closer to the building. By the time she got there, the door was wide open and there was no sign of Stephen. Catherine took a deep, calming breath before she stepped through the doorway and into a scene of utter chaos. Dozens of wooden crates and cardboard boxes of varied sizes were stacked up along the walls and in the centre of the storage area. In one corner were stacks of stuffed military issue duffel bags. Though she couldn't see Stephen through all the clutter, she could hear a shuffling sound coming from the far end.

She cautiously made her way through the piles of boxes until she stumbled upon Stephen, in a furious struggle to remove a canvas drop cloth that covered a large unseen object.

"It's caught under the wheel in the back; can you give me a hand?" Stephen called out, once he was aware of her presence.

Careful not to trip over the spilled contents of several boxes, she approached and grabbed hold of the heavy blanket. Stephen gave the heavy object a shove while Catherine tugged on the thick material. Together, the two of them managed to free the drop cloth from its encumbrances, and it fell to the floor. There before her was an old upright piano, quite like those she remembered from school. The cover had managed to keep the bulk of the dust off the instrument, but the age of the piano was apparent by the flaked varnish and the oily stains left behind by sweaty hands. Years of disuse took its toll on the instrument.

Stephen lifted the hinged cover to expose a full set of grungy keys. He ran his fingers across the board with a slight frown, as a cacophony of notes rung out and the room filled with sound. Then starting with the low C., his fingers dexterously moved up the scale ringing out each note in turn until he reached the high A.

"It's pretty close." Stephen analyzed the tone, "A few of the notes are off slightly and the low F is missing altogether, likely a broken string. Aside from that, it's relatively passable. It'll do in a pinch."

Catherine's head flinched back slightly, "What will do in a pinch?"

He sat on the bench and began to plunk out a series of notes with his right hand. She immediately identified the tune as the introduction to the song *Goodnight My Someone* from *The Music Man*. As he repeated the segment, he looked back to her expectantly.

"What?" Catherine asked defiantly.

"Sing."

"No."

"Come on, there is no one else around. I want to hear that angelic voice you're so proud of. I'm coming around again, sing for me."

Once again, he repeated the intro, and once again, she ignored the cue. "I don't want to sing for you."

Attempting to entice her further, Stephen brought his left hand to the keys and began to fill in the chords. He played beautifully, without the need sheet music. His fingers effortlessly danced across the keys, clearly demonstrating his years of training. Catherine found herself lost in the music and the song swelled inside her. When the lead in came around again, she couldn't help but add her voice to the mix.

Catherine's body visibly straightened as she took a breath deep from her diaphragm. Resting her tongue gently on the back of her lower teeth, she opened her mouth to allow the beautiful sound to fill the room. Divine overtones hung in the air while she gently sang the words in time with Stephen's accompaniment. He turned and watched the sheer joy on her face as she sought out each note with perfect tone. When she finally came to that ultimate note, she expertly reached that high E with angelic precision.

As the song ended, Stephen turned to face Catherine. He smiled with the pride he hadn't felt in a long time, truly impressed with the performance he had just witnessed. Before he had an opportunity to share his compliments however, Catherine knocked him backwards with the full weight of her body. She threw herself into his embrace and forcefully locked her lips with his own. Her hands grasped the back of his head to pull their faces tighter together while their tongues performed their own intimate dance. Stephen's hands slid down her back and grabbed hold of her tight ass and their bodies pressed even closer.

When they finally broke apart to catch their breath, they stared into each other's eyes for a moment before Stephen broke the silence. "That was lovely."

"What, the kiss or the song?"

"Take your pick."

She moved in to kiss him again, this time with less raw passion, but a tremendous amount of feeling.

"You never told me you played piano." She said after she pulled away a second time.

"It never came up. My mother forced me to take lessons from the time I was six until I turned thirteen. After that, I never really had a use for it, aside from playing at my cousin's wedding. Occasionally, if I found myself alone in a room with the piano, I would get all nostalgic and play something, but how often does that happen?"

The truth was, up until he was arrested for murder, it happened every opportunity he could find. In fact, he sought out unoccupied pianos wherever he went. He loved the feeling of the smooth keys beneath fingers and the sounds he was able to create with them. It would take him to a place of joy and comfort that he couldn't find anywhere else. After Lisa's death, he had lost interest in music and found a new passion. It was certainly nice to be back.

"Will you play something for me?"

Stephen looked into her eyes, and for the first time since he met her, he saw signs of actual happiness there. It was at that moment he realized he had reached her. Turning back to the piano, he began with an elaborate arpeggio before he settled into the song. His fingers effortlessly glided across the keys ringing out each note and each chord with a passion he hadn't experienced since he first arrived at the Farm. He had chosen a personal favorite, Piano Man by Billy Joel. He sang along, and though he knew that his singing voice paled in comparison to his playing, it was a hell of a lot of fun.

Enamored by the music, Catherine moved in behind him and wrapped her arms around his neck, resting her cheek on the top of his head. She had never found herself so drawn to a man's talent. In the past, she had always been attracted to shallow qualities, such as appearance and charisma, characteristics that Stephen also had in abundance. Now this new quality had suddenly came to the surface. Musical prowess.

The song ended as Stephen pounded out an embellished encore and then, as the last of the tones began to dissipate, he relaxed into Catherine's embrace. There they remained, in each other's arms, until she broke the silence.

"You never cease to amaze me."

"Hey, we've just met," Stephen teased, "I have plenty of surprises up my sleeve."

Catherine swung her leg over his, straddling his lap. She placed a hand on either side of his head and pulled him in for another passionate kiss.

"Feel free to surprise me again any time." She said seductively.

"We don't have a lot of time left for surprises." He responded candidly. "Apparently I still have to kill you on Tuesday."

Catherine immediately dropped her hands and pulled back from him, a look of extreme revulsion on her face. "Why would you say that? Why now? How could you be so heartless?" Her eyes began to well up.

"I'm sorry, but I'm speaking the truth. A small dose of reality if you will."

"Don't you have any feelings for me?"

Stephen stood and sat Catherine down upon the piano keys in a loud explosion of discordant tones. Backing away from her, he spoke clearly and concise. "I can't afford to have feelings for you. I've lost one woman I loved by my own hands. I won't do it again."

Catherine stared at him, dumbfounded, watching to see if he would turn back to face her again. When he didn't, she finally found the words that were eluding her. "Are you saying that you're falling in love with me?"

When he did finally turn around, tears began to form in the corners of his eyes. When he finally spoke, there was a slight tremble to his voice, as if he feared the consequences. "What is going to happen on Tuesday?"

"I don't know. You-"

Stephen interrupted her with a burst of anger, "Well you better damn well figure it out because you have two choices of how you want to leave the Farm, by foot or in a body bag. If at this point you still don't know, you have a serious decision to make."

"What I was going to say before you interrupted me," she said, angrily poking her finger in his chest, "is, I don't know. You haven't told me how you're going to do it yet."

The room fell silent. Catherine's stubborn determination completely baffled Stephen. He was so certain that he had gotten through to her; he would've put money on it. Not even his phony tears did anything to change her mind.

"Then why should it matter to you whether or not I'm falling in love with you?"

With that, he turned without another word, and walked out, leaving Catherine by herself in the quiet storage space. As she watched the door close behind him, she let out a defeated sigh. She turned back to the piano and began to plunk out the first few notes of *Goodnight My Someone* before she slammed the lid down in frustration. She decided she gave Stephen enough of a head start and she exited the building into the mid-morning sun.

**

"You are very welcome and enjoy your afternoon. I'll meet up with you this evening."

While Dr. Valerie Lough closed her office door behind Ian Montgomery, she couldn't help but feel saddened by his departure. He had seemed like such a kind and gentle man who had faced adversities at every turn. Soon his suffering would end. None of it seemed right to her. Was there anyone he still needed to contact? Was there anything left unfinished?

Valerie thought back to all the conversations they had over the last six days, some hostile, but most were friendly and rewarding. She had learned as much from him as she hoped he learned from her. In his heart, he never wanted to die, but accepted the inevitable. He fought through his illness, he fought again through the death of his wife, but after a while, he began to tire and the will to fight ran out. She respected his determination. He would have been an amazing man to know under better circumstances.

Still, there was something odd about him too. Some underlying secret he had left unsaid. Of course, it was common for any client to omit certain details, but this seemed different. She couldn't quite put her finger on what it was about him that bothered her. Not that it mattered any more, in less than twenty-four hours it would all be finished. The approval had gone through, and she was just about finished typing out her final report for Travis.

Travis. She was giddy just saying his name. For two years, she wondered if there was a mutual attraction, going over, repeatedly in her mind what she would say, and what they would do. She began to think it would never happen, and finally she would have the chance to explore the possibility.

"Have dinner with me tonight. Just the two of us."

She leaned back in her chair and sighed with a deep breath. She hadn't realized how lonely she had been until she started thinking about their date. The busy days and her nights alone in bed had taken their toll on her. It became clear, how much she wanted it to work, how much she needed it.

Moreover, she was hungry. With everything going on that morning, she had only been able to stop long enough for a coffee and a bran muffin. With a few final additions to her report, she attached it to an email and sent it off to Travis. Finally, she logged off her computer and headed back down to the atrium for some lunch.

CHAPTER TWENTY-TWO

Captain Hawkins sat behind his desk, massaging his temples, while he waited for Stephen Carlisle to elaborate on his unexpected response to Hawkins' most recent request.

"I need you to make a decision on how you are going to fulfill Ms. Dean's contract." was all he had said. The request was simple enough. The end date drew near, and Hawkins still needed to submit the method for approval, which he normally had long before this point in the contract.

"No."

Was that it? There had to be more. Perhaps it was his typical sarcasm, which usually led into a ridiculous ultimatum. *No, not unless I get an extra serving of pudding after dinner tonight.*

"No."

The reply made no sense on its own, and Mr. Carlisle didn't appear to want to expand on it. Hawkins decided to offer a bit of encouragement. "What do you mean, No?"

"I don't know. I think the word *no* is quite self-explanatory. Don't you?"

"Let's pretend for a moment, that it isn't so obvious. Indulge me." Hawkins pressed, frustrated by Stephen's indifference.

"It's quite simple really. I won't be fulfilling Catherine's contract."

Hawkins began to see an element of hope. "Is there something you know that I don't? Is Ms. Dean backing out?"

"Oh no, she is far too stubborn for that. She would rather die than ask anyone for help. So no, she is not backing out."

"Then what is the issue?"

"There is no issue. I believe with absolute certainty that she is wrong, and I will not be responsible for her death."

"I appreciate your concern Mr. Carlisle, but it's not up to you to decide whether or not her request is valid. Dr. Lough is fully capable of making that decision. Now, as for the contract, if you don't want it, you have to tell me now so I can make other arrangements."

"Well, that's the thing." Stephen leaned the chair back and balanced upon two legs. "The two of you are always looking for clients you can save. You keep telling me that they are *too few and far between*; well here's your chance. It is obvious that Catherine is the perfect candidate to get her release papers, and if you can't see that, I'm done."

"Done what?"

"This, everything. If you continue with Catherine Dean's contract, I quit."

The response surprised Hawkins, and he nearly burst out in laughter, "That isn't exactly a fantastic incentive. There are few things that would please us more, than having you resign as a contractor. You certainly serve a purpose here and you always come through for us tremendously, but we would love to see you give up the life of contract killing."

"Then I suppose it'll work out great for everyone here but Catherine." Stephen said sarcastically.

"Don't worry; we won't sacrifice Catherine for the sole purpose of getting you out of the business. We have a bit of time remaining to try to change her mind. That said, should it not turn out as we hope, I am obligated to remind you of something. You have a little better than a year remaining on your sentence before you can apply for early parole. Should you decide to leave this facility, you will have to serve the remainder of your sentence in the federal prison system. I guarantee you won't have any of the freedoms there that you have here."

"Is that what you had planned all along? Stephen accused Hawkins. "You assign me this contract to put me in a precarious situation where I'll likely either succeed or quit."

"You make it sound underhanded. I saw it as a low-risk gamble. My hope was that you two would hit it off and talk each other out of remaining here. If it worked, we've saved two people. If not, the contract continues as planned with nothing lost."

"Low risk to whom, you? Perhaps you had nothing to lose. What about us? Did you consider all the possible outcomes? Suppose I fell in love with her, but she still wanted to die. Do you not think that could have negative consequences?"

"Is that what this is all about?" Hawkins asked, as he leaned forward and rested his arms on the desk. "Have you fallen in love with Ms. Dean?"

Stephen suddenly realized that in his angry rant, he ended up saying far more than he had intended. He wasn't comfortable talking about his personal feelings. It was bad enough having to talk to Dr. Lough, he sure as hell wasn't about to share his thoughts with Hawkins.

"You're missing the point here." Stephen dodged the question, "It doesn't make a lick of difference what transpires, all you care about is how clean your reputation remains once this is all over. Your intentions were self-serving."

Hawkins wasn't interested in continuing with this argument, the same argument he had with Valerie a few days earlier. It was clear that Mr. Carlisle wasn't willing to expand on his slip up and it didn't matter. He had heard enough to know that everything had come together as he had hoped. Stephen Carlisle all but admitted to his feelings toward Ms. Dean, who in turn, according to Valerie was waffling.

"You're right Mr. Carlisle. I may not have considered every possible angle. If I have caused you unnecessary grief. I apologize."

"Don't patronize me Captain, I know you better than that. I am quite aware that it's far too late to change the situation, but you do have some control over the outcome. Surely, I can't be the only one able to see that this contract is bullshit. Send her home!"

If only it were that simple. Hawkins leaned back in his chair and took a deep, calming breath. "Okay Mr. Carlisle, you win. I can't help but agree with you. Due to Ms. Dean's hesitancy, it has become clear to me that the contract is no longer valid. My recommendation to Dr. Lough and the board will be to void Ms. Dean's contract. If they back me up, we will release her under the care of an appointed psychiatrist.

"Thank you, Captain. That's all I needed to hear. If you stick to your promise, you will continue to have my full cooperation."

Captain Hawkins wasn't terribly concerned about such a promise. He was relatively confident that would be the outcome anyway. Even if Valerie couldn't change Catherine's mind, she would end up in the care of a third party who would take Hawkins off the hook. At that point, whatever happened to Catherine, Hawkins keeps his promise and Carlisle leaves the business. Another win-win.

Still, there was the chance of the contract approval, if not by Dr. Lough, then possibly by the other shrink. If this happened, Hawkins would need a backup contractor. Since Carlisle wouldn't do it and Richards already had another contract, he would have to use Ryan Melville. The evaluation period for Melville was complete, so there was no reason they couldn't utilize his services. The Liberum Arbitrium contract would require amendment, of course, which would take time, but at least there was an alternative.

Though his bases were covered, Captain Hawkins hoped he wouldn't require Melville's services. If all went according to plan, Ms. Dean would go home with a pulse, and Mr. Carlisle would apply for early parole to be with her. Best-case scenario, everyone gets exactly what they want.

**

"I think I hurt him."

Catherine fought back tears while she faced Dr. Lough across the paper-cluttered desk. She had an hour to sit and think about her argument with Stephen before she had to make her way to the administration building for her session, and her own actions mortified her.

"I didn't mean to, but he cornered me, and I panicked."

"Why don't you tell me how it happened?" Dr. Lough said in a gentle tone.

Catherine recounted the recent events as they had transpired, beginning with the conversation in the atrium that led into their excursion to the warehouse, then finished with the lovely duet. She wasn't quite ready yet to discuss the kiss.

"It really was a beautiful moment, and I appreciated what he was trying to do, but when he asked me what was going to happen on Tuesday, I told him I didn't know because he hadn't yet decided how he was going to kill me. I think he hoped that, if he brought me back to a happy memory, I would fall in love with him and change my mind about the contract."

"So, was he wrong?"

"It was a sweet gesture." Catherine dodged.

"But was he wrong?"

"Of course, he was wrong, I mean, well yes." She began to flounder, "I don't know, I mean… what other choice do I have?"

That was the very moment that Dr. Valerie Lough became certain that she would be able to save her patient. What she had just heard was a definite cry for help. Catherine had just taken her first step towards admitting there could be other options. She only needed help to recognize them.

"How about we take a few minutes to explore the possibility of other choices."

"I just told you, I don't see another choice."

"That's okay," Dr. Lough remained calm, "humour me for a moment. What is it that you want more than anything?"

Feeling defeated, Catherine could feel her eyes begin to water again, "I just want the pain to go away."

"Okay, that's good. Can you think of anything that might help to take away some of that pain?"

"Death." Catherine said without hesitation.

Valerie clenched her hands tight together in her lap and concentrated on keeping her poise. "Okay, I think that we have death covered for the moment, so for now why don't we take that one off the table. What else can you think of that could potentially help take away the pain?"

"I don't know. I can't think of anything."

"Okay," Valerie wasn't going to back down so easily, "how about I throw a couple ideas your way and tell me what you think. What about companionship?"

"You mean like a dog?"

"Sure." It was definitely an uphill battle. "A pet could certainly go a long way towards filling a void. They are loyal and need your care, but that's not quite what I was getting at."

"Then you mean a lover."

"That's a pretty big jump from pet to lover. Why don't we start somewhere in the middle? How about a friend?"

Catherine laughed, shaking her head at the thought of it. "I've had lots of friends, none of which did me much good. All we ever did was go out, party, and get drunk.

"That's not the kind of friends I'm talking about. Those friends are fine, as they serve a purpose. Everyone needs to unwind occasionally. What I'm referring to is someone who you can call up in the middle of the night and say *hey, I'm bottoming out here. I need to talk,* and she'll be there to listen."

"I couldn't burden them like that."

"For the kind of friend, I am talking about; it would never be a burden."

Catherine was about to argue the point when she remembered Sarah Fulton. Sarah was her best friend throughout junior high and high school. The two of them were practically inseparable. They sang together in choir, sat next to each other in class, and ate lunch together every day. When they weren't together, they were usually talking on the phone, gossiping about boys or the latest episode of Survivor. Sarah was someone Catherine could talk to about anything.

"I had a friend like that once." She said quietly. "She was my best friend in school."

"There you go, see? What happened to her? Do you still keep in touch?"

"No, I have no idea where she is right now. I screwed that one up too."

"How so?"

Catherine began to explain what had come between them, and as she spoke, she started to realize how much she missed her friend. It all began one lunch hour when Catherine, Sarah and a third girl named Jennifer sat, and watched a group of boys playing hacky sack. Both Catherine and Sarah found the oldest boy of the group, Patrick, to be incredibly attractive and each girl vied for his attention. It just so happened that he already had his eye on Catherine.

Despite a minor affliction with jealousy, Sarah's disappointment was short lived, and she remained supportive of Catherine's relationship with Patrick. She gave them their space as needed, yet was always there to lend an ear or discuss who would be the next contestant voted off the island.

As time went by however, Sarah expressed concerns about a side of Patrick that she found to be less than desirable. He took her out all the time. She would cut classes and sometimes missed several days of school at a time, he got her hooked on drugs and alcohol, and he took her back to his apartment to do, god knows what. Catherine was no longer the person that Sarah knew her to be, and one evening during a particularly boring tribal council, she decided to confront her on the subject.

"Gawd damn it. If they don't vote Jonathan off this time, I'll lose my shit."

Sarah and Catherine had sat on opposite ends of the couch, both with their legs curled up under them and their arms rested on the respective armrests. While Catherine stared blankly at the screen, Sarah watched Catherine, searching for any sign of the friend she once knew.

"Hey Cat?"

"Yeah?" She remained glued to the television.

"What the hell are you doing?"

Catherine turned and looked at her with such confusion; her eyebrows disappeared into her hairline. "I'm watching Survivor. What the hell are *you* doing?"

Sarah turned to face her friend. "That's not what I meant. I meant, what are you doing with your life? You spend all of your time with Patrick, you cut class all the time, and you're doing drugs."

"I'm having fun."

"You're ruining your life."

Catherine's face turned red as she turned angrily to Sarah. "You don't know what you're talking about. You're just jealous. You hate the fact that he chose me over you. You're jealous because I spend more time with him than I do with you. Frankly, I don't give a shit. I love him, and I'm not going to break up with him just because you can't handle it."

"Love him? You barely know him. You are infatuated with him because he gets you high and gets you off. You don't love him, and he certainly doesn't love you. He's a no good, drug addicted slime-ball, and he will keep you around as long as you serve his purpose. You are so much better than he is. You can do so much better than him."

"Who the fuck do you think you are?" Catherine shouted. "What gives you the right to tell me who I can and can't date? You're supposed to be my friend."

Tears began to fall from Sarah's eyes. "I am your friend. I love you, and I don't want you to get hurt."

"Well, you sure have a shitty way of showing it."

"Cat, please, you have to listen to me." The tears flowed freely.

"I don't have to listen to shit. You aren't my mother."

"Well, that's a relief; you don't listen to her either. At least at the end of the night, I can leave."

"Then maybe you should just do that." She turned her back on Sarah.

"That's not what I meant. I only-"

"Get out. Leave me the hell alone."

That was the last time they spoke to one another.

That evening, a distraught Catherine snuck out of her bedroom window and into the arms of Patrick who had parked around the corner awaiting her arrival. He took her back to his basement apartment where he spent the remainder of the night comforting her the only way he knew how. That was when a certain event occurred that started the ball rolling towards Catherine's downfall.

"The funny thing is, at the time I thought my pregnancy was a blessing. I thought that we would be a family and grow old together in marital bliss." Catherine scoffed at her own comment. "What a pathetic naive little girl I was."

"Don't go chastising yourself too strongly. People make questionable decisions all the time in the name of love. Sometimes it works out, but a lot of the time it ends up coming back to bite them. It's a common occurrence. As for terminating your friendship with Sarah, I think you can both share the responsibility for that. You need to understand that Sarah was only trying to watch out for a friend she thought was in trouble. On the other hand, she could have shown a bit more compassion, perhaps by talking it out with you rather than attacking Patrick's character."

Valerie stood and moved around her desk to sit in the chair right next to Catherine. She hoped that a less professional, more intimate position might help to solidify her next point. "Everyone makes bad decisions Catherine, but it shows strength to learn from them."

CHAPTER TWENTY-THREE

For the first time since Hawkins first occupied his office more than two years previously, his desk was in a state of disarray. Several files were open, with their contents spilled out over one another, and he frantically worked to sign and organize everything so he could get out early for his date with Valerie. He couldn't recall ever being so anxious, and he had one hell of a mess to show for it. At least by his standards.

Unfortunately, however, he didn't have the time to dwell on the subject as he expected a knock on the door at any second. He had just buzzed Ian Montgomery into the office by way of the intercom system, for his final briefing before the completion of the contract.

He quickly typed a few more words into his e-document when a light knock sounded at the door.

"Come." Hawkins called out stoically, so as not to reveal any form of impatience in his voice.

The door swung open and in shuffled Ian Montgomery, who grinned from ear to ear. That was the happiest Hawkins had seen him since his arrival. In fact, it was likely the happiest he had ever seen a client since inception.

"Well, you appear to be in good spirits today, Mr. Montgomery. Please have a seat."

Ian cheerfully accepted the offer, "Why shouldn't I be? Today's the day I finally have the end in sight. You're damn right I'm in good spirits."

His joy was infectious. "I'm glad to see some optimism around here for a change. Though, I must admit, I am sorry there wasn't more anyone could do for you."

"Don't worry, Captain," Ian grinned, "we all get what's coming to us in the end."

Hawkins gathered up the papers on his desk into a pile. "Okay, so this is how it's going to go down. I'm sure you've seen our little setup on the racetrack."

"I have. It doesn't look like much from the outside."

"Just wait until you see what we have built for you. I don't think you'll be disappointed."

"Can't wait. So, when do I check in and," he winked, "when is check-out?"

Hawkins acknowledged the joke with a smile. "We just have a few things to settle here first. I have some papers for you to sign, and then we can meet Dr. Lough over at the new apartment."

He struck a key on his keyboard, and the muffled sound of the ink-jet printer emanated from the drawer. While he waited for the document to finish printing, he continued. "This evening, when you are ready, you will go to bed in your new apartment. Dr. Lough will offer you a mild sedative, if you wish, to help you relax."

"That won't be necessary."

"Well, the offer is there, should you change your mind. Either way, you will be fully cognizant in the unlikely event you decide you don't wish to proceed with the contract. If you decide to abort at any time, there is a telephone in the room with a direct line to me, as well as a large window which has been constructed for an easy escape."

Ian chuckled, "I don't think I am in any condition to be climbing through windows, but I can assure you, Captain Hawkins, I will not require your assistance." He exhaled a large sigh. "Still, it's nice to see that you and the good doctor truly have compassion for your clients."

"Thank you, Mr. Montgomery. We do our best."

The printer went quiet, and Hawkins pulled the large document from the drawer.

"Now, most of this," Hawkins began as he placed the stack of papers before his client, "is just typical legal red tape, obligations, liability, stuff like that. You are more than welcome to read it, but it's more for the lawyers and upper command than for you."

Ian quickly flipped through the legal jargon. "I'll pass thanks."

Hawkins reached over and turned to the next section. "This part, however, is for you. It states that both parties, yourself, and the Farm, have completed their obligations outlined in the contract and that you wish to continue with said contract in accordance with section C383 of the Canadian Human Rights Act."

"In other words," Ian played, "I've worn out my welcome and, one way or another, I am leaving the Farm."

"That's one way of putting it, I suppose."

"In that case, give me a pen."

The two of them went over the document together, where Hawkins indicated a dozen or more places for him to either initial or sign. When they finally came to the end, Hawkins signed, dated and witnessed it himself.

"Well, Mr. Montgomery, this is my least favorite part of the job. I get no pleasure from signing the order to euthanize. The only saving grace is that I respect the wishes of our clients and end their needless suffering."

Ian smiled, as if struck by an epiphany. "You're a good man, Captain. Your conscience is clear."

Hawkins cleared his throat and digressed. "Come. It's time I showed you to your new quarters. Dr. Lough will be waiting for us."

Hawkins assisted Ian to his feet and escorted him out of the building, where his golf cart waited for them.

**

Catherine's sat alone in the business centre and stared at the display of the computer, trying to build up the courage click on the *send* button. In order to satisfy her curiosity, she had decided to take a slight detour from her usual route back to her apartment from Dr. Lough's office.

She had logged on to the social network and opened her profile page. It had been quite some time since she last logged on, so there were thirty-three pending notifications waiting for her. She quickly scanned through the list and found little of interest, mostly invitations to events she would never attend and online games she would never play.

On the side of the screen, she found an icon labelled *find friends*. She clicked on it. In the text field, she entered the name Sarah Fulton. A long list of personal profile pages with names that contained the two words quickly filled the screen. Out of the entire list of variously arranged names, only eight were exact matches and two hyphenated with another surname. She ignored the links that were obviously wrong and selected each potential page, looking for anything that might be familiar to her. Some pages had photographs of children or landscapes, which didn't tell her much about the person, so she continued, hoping for a break.

She had gone through all the exact matches, so Catherine selected a hyphenated name. As the page opened up, the first thing she noticed was all of this individual's information was restricted to her friends only. She could only view the profile pic and a couple of unhelpful statistics. Not that it mattered of course, because she recognized the face staring back at her immediately. Her old friend, now Sarah Fulton-Peters, stood in the photograph with a very handsome man and a little girl not much more than a year old.

Delighted she had found her friend; Catherine couldn't help but want to reach out to her. At the top of the page, she selected the icon that read *send message*. She began to type.

Hi Sarah, it's me. SURPRISE!! :-)

I see by your profile pic that you have found yourself quite a lovely family. I'm so happy for you. You certainly deserve it.

I just wanted to write and tell you that you were right. I didn't want to hear it at the time, but you were right, and I am so sorry for all those horrible things I said to you.

So, I may be a bit out of the loop these days on Survivor, but I would really like to have my friend back. I realize that I don't necessarily deserve it, but would you consider giving me another chance? I could really use a friend to talk to right now.

I hope to hear from you soon.
Catherine.

She had already read the message several times over, but decided to give it one last perusal before she sent it off. That was of course if she could build up enough courage to send it. So much time had passed; what if Sarah ignored her message, blocked her, or worse sent a harsh reply? The last thing she needed right then was another rejection. What if-

Catherine began to laugh to herself. There she goes again with the what-ifs, just as Stephen had said. He was right. As much as she hated to admit it, he was right. Catherine was paralyzed by what-ifs. She finally understood what he had been trying to tell her. She can't change the past, and she can't avoid the future, so what's the point in going crazy, dwelling on the maybes.

She had no control over how Sarah would respond, but she had complete control over what she said, and she wanted to be certain she was clear on how she felt about her old friend. She made a minor change to the letter.

Luv Cat.

She was about to send the message when she remembered one last thing, she wanted to add to the end.

P.S. I've met someone, and I would like to talk to you about him. I would be very interested to hear your opinion.

Message sent. Okay.

**

The golf cart came to a stop before the front door of the modified trailers. Hawkins leaped from the driver's seat, and then circled around to the other side to assist Mr. Montgomery. By the time they reached the door, the familiar whine of another golf cart came up from behind them. Hawkins turned to see Valerie's lovely face smiling back at him from behind the wheel. She parked the cart next to the other, slid out of the seat and approached the two men.

"Good afternoon, Ian. Hello, Travis. I'm sorry I'm late."

"Not at all." Hawkins replied, "We just got here ourselves."

"Excellent. Why don't we go inside? We can talk more in there."

With a nod, the three of them walked up the three metal steps and through the front door of the trailer.

"Holy shit!" Ian looked wide-eyed around the common room. "Awful fancy for something you plan to set on fire, isn't it?"

Hawkins answered, "We wanted to be certain that your final night with us would be as comfortable as possible."

"Well, you've outdone yourself. This is incredible."

"Wait until you see the bedroom." Valerie added.

Ian smiled at the doctor. "It's been a long time since such a pretty woman has invited me into a bedroom."

Dr. Lough tried to hide her smile, while Hawkins snickered.

"I'm sorry, Doctor. I didn't mean to embarrass you."

Hawkins quickly came to her rescue. "That's okay, Mr. Montgomery. No harm done." He opened the bedroom door and stepped aside to allow Ian to enter before him. "Please."

Ian stepped past Hawkins and stopped, just inside the room. The decor in the room was beautiful, but the painting above the bed immediately drew his eye. He recognized it right away.

"That's-" A tear began to well up in his eye.

Valerie stepped in behind him. "We thought you might want something familiar with you tonight."

"I don't know what to say."

"You don't have to say anything, Ian. Let's have a seat, and we can talk."

Ian sat down on the edge of the bed and Valerie sat next to him. Hawkins remained standing, leaned up against the doorframe.

"Can you tell me what you are feeling right now?" Valerie asked.

Ian sniffed. "I thought it would be easier than this."

"If you aren't ready, there are other options for palliative and end of life care. You can change your mind at any time. You don't have to do this now."

"No, I am ready. It's just," he looked up at the painting, "I wasn't expecting to ever see that again."

"Do you want me to take it down?" Hawkins inquired.

"No! Please- I mean, it's beautiful. It was very thoughtful." Ian scrutinized Hawkins for a moment and a smile began to form.

"What?" Hawkins straightened his stance. "What is it?"

"I'm sorry, it's nothing. You've surprised me, that's all. You're not at all what I expected."

"How so?"

Ian turned his head and stared at the painting while he spoke. "Everyone jokes about *The Killing Farm*, making up slogans like, *we aim to please* and *our service is to die for*. Most people think that you are just a bunch of hired assassins or hitmen, out to rid the world of the weak and dying population." He turned back to Hawkins. "Of course, I never took any of that seriously, but I expected you to be colder and more distanced. I can see now, that you really care about your clients, and play an active role in the time we spend here. I don't think you are the devil others have made you out to be."

"Thank you, Mr. Montgomery. That is kind of you to say. The truth is, not a day goes by when I don't have to wrestle with my own conscience, so I certainly appreciate your feedback."

"Now, Ian," Valerie changed the subject, "as the resident medical authority, it is my duty to ask you one final time. Are you absolutely certain that it is your desire to surrender your life to the Government of Canada under section C383 of the Canadian Human Rights Act, for us to carry out the act of assisted euthanasia as per our contract with you?"

"Yes, I am."

Hawkins stepped in, "Well then, Mr. Montgomery. It is my duty to inform you that you have satisfied all the requirements of your contract, which will be carried out tomorrow at 0800 hours. Do you have any further questions?"

"None that I can think of."

Valerie turned to face Ian with a pleading expression. "Please remember that this is not written in stone. You can still change your mind at any time up until the end. You do not have to go through with it."

"Speaking of which," Hawkins added, "should you have a change of heart, we have made it easy for you."

Hawkins approached the window and pulled the curtains aside. He grabbed hold of the locking mechanism and gave a sharp tug. With an audible click, instead of the pane sliding to the side, the entire window and the section of wall below it swung open like a door. Through the opening, Ian could clearly see the racetrack and the wooded area beyond.

"Wow." Ian laughed. "You guys thought of everything. I was curious how you expected me to climb through that window in my condition."

"We take our contracts very seriously, Mr. Montgomery. Along with the escape route, there is also the telephone on the end table. We will be off site this evening on personal business, but the telephone is directly linked to my cell phone, so you will have no issue reaching me if necessary."

Ian noticed that Dr. Lough began to blush, which led him to believe there was more to the *"we"* in Hawkins explanation than he let on. "As I said, that will be unlikely, but I appreciate your concern."

Hawkins shut the secret door. "One last thing. I have spoken to the kitchen. You have a few hours until dinner, and they will prepare any meal you desire."

Any meal Ian desired. That was going to take some thought. Food was one thing he never really had to put much thought into, before he lost his wife. He would eat just about anything that Kat had put in front of him. She was a tremendous cook.

Beef stew. It was the last meal that she had ever made for him before... Ian began to tear up.

"Are you okay, Ian?"

"Sorry, yes, I'm fine. I just remembered something, that's all. Can they make beef stew?"

"I don't see why not."

"With potatoes, onions, carrots, and dumplings?"

"It'll be hot and ready for you at dinner time."

"It's my favorite."

"I understand."

Ian reached up to wipe the tears from his own eyes. "It's been an eventful day, and I'm exhausted. If you don't need anything else from me, I think I will take a little nap before dinner."

"Of course." Hawkins reached out and shook hands with Ian. "Goodbye, Mr. Montgomery. I wish you all the best in your journey."

"Thank you."

Valerie took both his hands in hers. "Take care, Ian. Remember that we are here if you change your mind."

"I know."

"Pleasant Journey."

The room fell silent, there was nothing more to say. Hawkins stepped aside to allow Dr. Lough to pass through the doorway before him. Hawkins turned back to Ian with a nod before he shut the door behind him.

Jay Newman

ECE-80070

It was a cool, calm morning. The sun rose slowly over the horizon, and the light, cool breeze chilled the perspiration on his forehead. It was the perfect conditions for a morning jog, but Meldrik White's lungs burned from the exertion. Still, he pushed on. It had been many years since his body had allowed him to perform his daily run. SARS had put a stop to that.

When he first got sick, he wrote it off as a typical flu. Fever, chills and an annoying cough. Since the virus never progressed enough to put him in the hospital, as other cases had, he wasn't concerned. As the symptoms faded, he went straight back to living a normal life. Still, the cough persisted. At first, it was a minor annoyance, lingering effects of the SARS virus, but as the weeks passed, the cough continued to grow worse. Soon, minor exertions, such as a simple flight of stairs, winded him. It became more difficult to catch his breath.

Although delayed, the hospital visit Meldrik thought he avoided was inevitable. A severe respiratory infection developed into pneumonia, and he soon found himself in a medically induced coma on a ventilator. There he lay, for twenty-three days, until the doctors were able to get the infection under control. They brought him out of the coma, but the damage was already done.

He endured weeks of physiotherapy to regain his strength. It was a long journey, because the exercises tired him very rapidly. He lost so much time, lying in bed, watching cartoons on the television, until he was strong enough to endure another round of physio. As time passed, he grew stronger, but saw very little improvement in his respiratory system. His doctors warned him that it was likely to get worse, before it got better.

That it did. After his eventual release from the care center, he tried to live the best, albeit strenuous, life possible. Everything that had been so easy for him before became more and more difficult all the time. It was taking its toll, not only on his body, but on his mental health as well. Soon he stopped trying. He lost his willpower and gained a lot of weight. Eventually, his lungs failed him all together. He opted for a transplant, but after a while, his stubborn body began to reject the new lungs. He still had options, but he was so very tired. There was no fight left in him. It was time to go, and he would go on his own terms. The end was now in sight, but he couldn't pass up one last opportunity to enjoy a good run.

Some peripheral movement to his left caught his attention. A short distance away, a wild dog paced him, watching him. Too small for a wolf, possibly a coyote. A beautiful animal, but out of place for the area. Meldrik wondered where he had come from. He wasn't particularly concerned, however. He knew that coyotes were generally timid around humans, but it still seemed strange to have the creature pacing him like that. Fortunately, the path entered a wooded area, and he lost the animal in the trees.

There was considerably less light once he penetrated the woods. Not spooky, per-se, but he definitely had to be more aware of his surroundings. His chest ached while his lungs fought to pull in enough air, but he couldn't give up. He had to push on. He stopped to catch his breath before a large pile of rubble that blocked the path and resisted the urge to vomit. The rocks definitely weren't there by accident. Each boulder was well rounded and stacked very deliberately in the shape of a pyramid. Someone had driven a signpost into the ground before it. A large red arrow pointing to the right, with sloppy white lettering painted upon it that read, *DEETUR*. As whimsical as it all seemed, there was no going forward. He decided to follow the juvenile directions.

The adjacent path continued through the woods. The path opened up into a small clearing and Meldrik White stopped to take in the ridiculous surroundings. They had outdone themselves and he couldn't help but laugh. Ignoring the giant mechanical crane, partially hidden in the trees to his right, he concentrated on the delightful scene before him. A large bowl of birdseed sat on the ground. Stuck in the seed was a small sign that read, *FREE FUD!* Below his feet was a giant red X. A loud clang drew his attention upward, just in time to see the largest anvil he had ever seen bearing down upon him. One last thought crossed his mind.

"That's all, folks."

CHAPTER TWENTY-FOUR

Stephen lay upon his bed, propped up on his pillow, half watching the Fawlty Towers marathon, trying to take his mind off his day. It didn't work. He would just start to get into the show, before his mind would wander back to his argument with Catherine. He couldn't understand where he went wrong. Everything had gone perfectly. The book, the music, the kiss. By all rights, she should have been lying naked next to him right at that moment. How could he have been so stupid? Tact had certainly never been his strong suit, but what made him think he should call her out like that, just when things were about to get good?

The irony of the situation wasn't lost on him either. He knew that he berated himself for a poor decision that was now out of his control. Just let it go and move on. Great advice, but the problem was he couldn't let it go. He was far too concerned that his ill-chosen words may have pushed Catherine away from making the right decision. Was she so tenacious that she would die just to spite him? Could she be that stupid?

A polite knock on the apartment door interrupted his train of thought. He turned up the volume on the television and tried to ignore the knock, in the hope that the caller would go away. To his chagrin, a second, more persistent knock soon followed.

Resigned to get of bed, he called out, "hang on a sec. I'm coming."

Stephen made his way to the front door, swearing under his breath. The last thing he wanted was to be bothered at that moment. He had no desire to put on a happy face and feign interest in anything anybody else had to say. All he wanted to do was sulk in peace.

A third knock came to the door.

"Hold on!" He yelled.

He unlatched the deadbolt, grasped the handle, and flung the door open, ready to shout at the source of the interruption. His voice however caught in his throat once he realized the person who stood before him was in fact, Catherine Dean. She stood in the doorway, looking lovely as ever, staring up at him with a pleasant smile on her face.

Stephen found himself at a loss for words, which didn't happen all that often. Catherine was the last person he had expected to see at that moment. In fact, after their argument earlier, he wouldn't have been surprised if he never saw her again. Nevertheless, there she was, twirling her hair around her finger smiling up at him, also apparently unsure of what to say.

He felt suddenly awkward while they stood at the doorway in silence, so he decided to be the gentleman. "Catherine, I didn't expect to see you tonight. Would you like to come in?"

She silently accepted his gesture with a nod. She stepped through the doorway and into the living room, before he closed the door and turned back to face her.

"Would you like something to drink?"

"Yes please." She finally spoke.

"I'm not allowed alcohol in my apartment, so all I can offer you is water or ginger ale."

"Water will be fine, thank you."

While Stephen filled two glasses with water, Catherine sat down on the sofa and folded her hands in her lap while she waited. When he appeared with the beverages, he handed her one before he took a seat on the sofa next to her. They had both drank a substantial amount of water from their glasses before Stephen was forced to break the silence once again.

"So, what brings you by? I didn't think I'd see you again tonight."

As she turned to face him, he could see the tears began to form in her beautiful almond shaped eyes. "I wasn't certain if I should, but I needed to see you. I wanted to apologize for this morning."

"No, please." Steven stopped her, "You have no reason to apologize. I never should've called you out like that."

"But you are right about everything you said. This is all on me. I brought it on myself."

Stephen began to laugh. "Sounds like a typical Canadians standoff. I'm sorry, no, I'm sorry. After you, no I insist."

She almost smiled.

He brushed some hair from her cheek, tucked it back behind her ear, and as he stared longingly into her eyes, he continued, "Look, you said some things, I said some things. Could we just forget about what happened in the warehouse and move on?"

Lost in his gaze, Catherine could only manage a meek nod. The awkwardness as they sat and stared at each other like that, soon became uncomfortable. She tried to smile at him, but it felt forced and awkward. Finally, she gave up and went with her instinct.

This time the kiss was everything it should have been. It was full of passion and emotion, coupled with raw sexual tension. Their tongues vigourously explored each other's mouths, while his hands slid down her back and grabbed hold of her shirt. The kiss broke only long enough for Stephen to slide Catherine's shirt up and over her head before they returned to the passionate embrace.

Their lips remained locked tightly together even as Catherine felt her bra strap loosen from behind her back. She let go of Stephen to allow the lacy undergarment to fall to the floor, then reached out to lift the shirt off his body. She wrapped her arms around him once again and pulled his bare chest tight against her soft breasts. Her grip remained tight, as she lay back on the sofa and pulled him, very willingly on top of her.

Stephen unlocked his lips from hers and kissed her neck. It took little time before he found a sweet spot just above her collarbone that caused her to arch her back in pleasure. She pushed her neck into his kiss and moaned as his teeth gently scraped across her skin. He continued to move downwards in a long trail of sensual kisses and stopped at her breast. Stephen took her nipple in his mouth and teased it with his tongue, lips, and teeth. He could feel it harden in his mouth as he gently sucked upon it, and he brought his free hand up to massage the other. Catherine grabbed hold of a handful of his hair to keep him longer in that position, while her entire body shuddered with excitement.

Not one to linger in the same spot for too long, Stephen continued his path of kisses down her body pausing once again at her navel. While his tongue probed the small cavity, his hands worked their way around to the button for her jeans. Catherine arched her hips to allow him to easily slide her pants down and reveal a sexy black lace thong.

As he slid her panties off her body, Stephen was pleasantly surprised to find a freshly groomed patch of hair that suggested Catherine had put some forethought into the evening. He planted a series of kisses around the area, before plunging his tongue into her warm petals. A wave of ecstasy shot up her spine and she arched her back pushing harder into his dexterous tongue. The harder she pushed, the deeper he penetrated her, and as he took her over the edge, she cried out loudly in pleasure.

With a firm grip on his hair, Catherine pulled him back up towards her and once again locked her lips firmly with his, with a desire she hadn't felt in so many years. This time as they kissed, her hands moved down to his belt and removed the last remaining clothes that separated them. He was fully hard, and within moments, she had helped to guide him inside her. Each thrust sent shock waves of pleasure up her spine that made her entire body tingle with goosebumps. She bit her lower lip in attempt to prevent herself from crying out, not certain of how thin the walls between apartments were. Soon however, as she came to the brink of orgasm, she could no longer keep the cry from escaping her lips. Stephen quickly followed with a deep grunt of satisfaction before he collapsed down upon her, their sweaty bodies pressed tight, breathing heavily in time together.

As she lay still beneath his bulk, Catherine realized she got great pleasure and joy out of making love to Stephen. Instead of being repulsed, she owned it. She couldn't help but feel, for the first time in a long while, that she had finally got out of her head and could enjoy the moment.

**

The night air was cool and calm as the sun began to set over the prairie. The large floodlight standards around the perimeter of the compound shone down on the buildings and cast long shadows across the ground to give Ian Montgomery plenty of cover for his personal mission.

He had just opened the secret door of his apartment enough to squeeze his body through the gap, and crouched in the darkness behind the modular trailer, where he waited for the fat and lazy excuse for a security guard to drive past on his golf cart. He was a joke and everybody on site knew it. In fact, Ian likely could have stood in plain sight without drawing his attention. Nonetheless, he couldn't afford to take any risks now.

He watched the small red taillights disappear around the corner of the warehouse, and quickly sprang into action. Backpack slung over his shoulder, he ducked around back of the trailer to a location he had previously identified. Earlier that evening, before dark, he went for a stroll around the area, for *one final breath of fresh air*, when he discovered a removable panel that would allow him access underneath the trailer.

He examined the panel to find that only two screws held it in place. Reaching into his backpack, he pulled out a screwdriver and a small pen light. He easily removed the screws and slid the panel to the side. Once he shined the light under the trailer, he immediately identified the gas tank and fuel pump, but was unable to locate the igniter from that position.

He lay down on his belly, put the light between his teeth and used his arms and feet to pull himself under the trailer, dragging his bag behind him. He struggled along most of the depth of the trailer before he saw the connection point of the igniter protruding below the floor. He felt around the contents of his backpack for the familiar shape of his hand-made mechanical device, along with a pair of wire cutters.

The small pen light gave him just enough illumination to complete his task, though the awkwardness of lying on his back with the light in his teeth slowed the process down considerably. He reached up with the cutters and clipped one of the two wires from the igniter. He then stripped the ends to reveal the stranded copper. He had foreseen the possibility of a cramped space, so he had built his remote switch with small alligator clips, soldered to the ends of the wires. He clipped the ends to the exposed copper, connecting his device into the ignition circuit. A toggle switch on the side activated the red LED display, which indicated a five-minute timer. Armed and ready to go, he slid the small electronic box into a cavity above the support joists, returned the tools to his backpack, and worked his way back out from under the trailer where he replaced the wood panel.

He glanced at his watch, 11:18pm. Another twelve minutes, give or take, until the overweight guard circled around again. Ian peered around the corner of the trailer. There was no one in sight between him and the nearest building. He sprinted across the racetrack towards the building on the other side. He began to feel his age, as his lungs burned in his chest. He was out of shape, but he couldn't let it slow him down for the risk of capture. He slowed his pace as he approached the building, but had to put his arms out to cushion himself from running head-long into the brick wall.

Another glance around the corner, and he shot out across the gravel street towards the water tower and the wooded area beyond. His sides ached, but he was too much in the open to stop for a breath; he had to get under the cover of the trees. By the time he did, he collapsed to the ground for a needed and well-deserved breath. Time was of the essence, but all his planning would be for nothing if he suddenly died of a heart attack.

As he lay there breathing heavily, he heard the whine of the golf cart go by, presumably towards the trailer. He had been laying there too long already, time to get moving. He clambered to his feet and navigated through the woods in search of the perimeter fence.

He hid inside the tree line, eying the gap between the trees and the fence and pulled the first of two explosive devices from his pack. Like before, he would have to time his move just right, to avoid the sight lines of the sweeping camera. This time he didn't have a spotter on the other side to tell him when to go.

Device in hand, Ian lay down on his back and began to slide out from under the cover of the branches, until he could see the underside of the camera. He remained back a bit to keep out of the line of sight and watched as the camera swiveled in his direction. Just as it turned back away from him, he rolled out from under the tree towards the fence line and deposited the device just short of the electrified fortification. A quick cover of leaves would hopefully help to conceal his package, and he rolled back under cover before the camera made it back around again.

Two down, one to go.

His final stop would be the administration building. Although the most direct route would have been a straight shot down the middle of the compound, the risk of detection was too high. He wasn't certain of how many cameras watched the compound. He decided it would be safer to work his way around the perimeter, keeping behind the buildings where he was able.

It was a considerably longer trek, but concealment was a far greater issue than time. He moved quickly from shadow to shadow until he once again heard the telltale whine of the golf cart. Plastered flat against the rear of the building and unable to see the roadway from his cover, he had to judge his next move by sound alone. The cart's high-pitched engine became louder as it approached from the east until the sound moved around to the other side of the building. He waited for the noise to subside again before he continued his journey, but instead the sound cut out altogether. The guard had turned off the engine.

Ian's heart began to race. Had he missed a security camera? Had he inadvertently tripped some form of motion sensor? He hadn't considered additional security measures during the night. He dared not move, if the guard found him with the contents of the backpack it would be game over for him. This being a government run facility, they could conceivably charge him with some form of terrorism.

Ian couldn't remember if he had taken a breath lately, so he quickly stole one while he listened. A set of keys jingled faintly, and then a door opened and slammed shut. He thought back to the tour of the facility wondering which building this was. There were no rear doors or windows, solid brick construction; it had to be the weapons storage. Could this possibly be a part of the guards regularly scheduled rounds?

Once again, he heard the door open and close and the same jingle of keys. A few moments later, the golf cart engine came to life and continued down the road; the high-pitched whine trailing off into the distance. Ian exhaled a huge sigh of relief. Routine would dictate another thirty minutes before he came back around again, but that was too close. It was time to pick up the pace, so he wasn't out there any longer than he had to be.

He skulked past the darkened building that housed the swimming pool, circled around the residences, and ran across the walkway to the rear of the administration building. From there, he followed the wall around until he located the incoming utility service. The gas meter was inside the building, but he was able to identify the gas line feeder as it penetrated the building. He removed a small ball of his special putty from his pack and rolled it between his hands to form a long rope, which he then used to surround the black iron pipe at the base of the wall. From his pack, he also pulled out his homemade device; the timer, wired into a detonator stuffed inside the last of the C-4 bricks. He mounted the explosives to the pipe and smoothed the clay into the existing ring.

He paused what he was doing to think about the two people who normally occupied this office space. They had surprised him. They weren't the cold-hearted villains he expected them to be. Contrary to his assumptions, they honestly appeared to care about the wellbeing of their clients. Dr. Lough was a lovely and compassionate woman. She made it her priority to get to know Ian. She listened, never judging, always professional. As for Hawkins, he put an incredible amount of effort into making the apartment perfect for him. It was a shame that their reputation would have to go down with the building, but it was their own fault for conspiring against God's will.

A familiar and unmistakable sound suddenly caught his attention. Ian looked up from his task to see a pair of bright headlights heading straight for him. It was far too soon to be a part of the normal rounds. His mission had obviously attracted some attention. As Ian backed up along the wall, he watched the vehicle approach. He quickly weighed his options. They would surely spot him if he ran for it. If he stayed where he was, they would catch him red-handed. Either way, he was dead in the water unless he could talk his way out of it. He had to think fast before his luck ran out.

To Ian's relief, the golf cart came to a stop in front of the building instead of coming around to the side. He watched in anticipation as the fat guard heaved his bulk out of the cart and painstakingly made his way around toward where Ian stood. Ian jumped into action and grabbed the chunk of C-4, along with the detonator, with the hope that the rotund guard wouldn't notice the ring he left plastered around the gas line.

In a flash, Ian ducked around back of the building and began to circle the walls to the other side, hoping Tubbo hadn't called for backup. He could no longer see the guard and there was no telling where he was at that moment, so Ian stood silently at the corner, where he could watch front and back.

The shine of a flashlight signaled him to continue around front, as the guard came lumbering around the back talking into his radio. "Yeah control, there's no one out here. And nothing seems to be out of place." He added sarcastically, "Whatever it is you think you saw; it doesn't seem to be a threat to national security."

Ian was unable to make out the muffled response on the other end of the radio, but it didn't matter to him. He had evaded capture. He returned to the shadows where the gas line entered the building and waited for the useless guard to drive off. Ian returned the explosive to its perch, once again molded the putty into the existing ring and then wrapped the entire thing in duct tape to keep it in place.

All that remained was to wait. His watch read 12:06am, there was still another eight hours until show time. He needed some sleep, but he couldn't risk returning to the trailer. It looked as though he would have to spend his final night at the Farm under the stars, and it was going to be a beautiful night.

**

They lay quietly upon the bed; their naked bodies entwined together glistening with sweat. Her head rested comfortably upon his chest while his free hand caressed her smooth skin. It had been everything Travis had hoped it would be. Valerie's body was so soft and warm; it felt incredible pressed up against his own.

The evening couldn't possibly have gone better. The long drive into the city was delightful. Valerie's presence was the perfect distraction to keep his mind off the multitude of painful jolts to his spine on the horrible, uneven gravel road. It was nice to be able to chat freely about anything and everything, while they avoided work-related topics. It was the first time he had the opportunity to get to know Valerie as a person, rather than a colleague. They shared anecdotes and discussed their personal interests and hobbies. Even though he had worked with her for over two years, he had just learned that as a teenager, Valerie was a champion youth bowler. They both shared amusing stories about themselves and had laughs at the other's expense. Overall, it was a very enjoyable drive.

Dinner was at a small, but busy Italian restaurant in Regina. The atmosphere was quaint, though it was obvious that the location was a bit too small in comparison to the popularity of the restaurant. With the tables so close together, the chairs were nearly touching. The servers had just enough room to move between them with their heavily laden trays. Their server soon arrived, with a basket of fresh hot rolls, to take their order.

While Valerie ordered the seafood linguine, Travis decided on a plate of potato-filled gnocchi in a meat sauce. While they waited for their food, they continued with their conversation, delving deeper into their pasts to reveal some of their most precious and intimate stories. Valerie truly was an incredible woman. She had no qualms about talking about her own experiences, both good and bad. She insisted that there was no shame in bad memories as long as you have grown because of them. She said, "You can't stop unfortunate things from happening, but there is always something to be learned from them."

The meal was exquisite. They each started with a fresh Caesar salad, and a nice bottle of Chardonnay was the perfect accompaniment to the delicious pasta. The conversation remained light while they ate, both extremely cognizant of proper table manners. Despite the fact, they had shared countless meals in the past; the "date" atmosphere seemed to draw out the best in both.

After dinner, they drank coffee and shared a plate of Tiramisu, while they discussed personal goals and desires. Neither of them planned to remain at the Farm for much longer, as they both agreed that the nature of their assignment began to take its toll on them. It was just about time to move on and perhaps even settle down. Somehow, however, they both managed to continue to avoid the topic of their own relationship.

The drive back to the compound was a little bit quieter but highly enjoyable. The topics of conversation were now less about themselves and more about the countless stars in the clear night sky, and the moon that was just a little short of full. The road was quiet, the night had been perfect, and Valerie reached out to hold his free hand for the remainder of the drive.

When they arrived back at the residences, Valerie had invited Travis to her apartment for a drink, which he gladly accepted. Though ultimately, he never received that drink, as he barely had enough time to close the door behind him before she met him with a voracious kiss.

There they lay in each-other's arms, in a position he had yearned to be in for as long as he had known her. He wasn't certain where that evening would lead, but at that moment, it didn't much matter, because at that moment everything was perfect.

CHAPTER TWENTY-FIVE

Day Six

Wrapped in little more than a bedsheet, the nineteen-inch screen on Stephen Carlisle's laptop cast a green glow upon Catherine's face as she quietly logged on to her social networking page. Though Stephen had no issue at all sleeping through the night, Catherine was far too restless, and she was itching to find out if her old friend had replied to her message.

As the page opened, a notification immediately appeared at the top of the screen. *You have a new message from Sarah Fulton-Peters.* With slight trepidation over what might be contained within, she clicked on the link that opened up the message.

> *Hi Cat, I'm so happy to hear from you. It's been far too long. I didn't think I ever would again. Yes, you are right, I have a wonderful family and I would love for you to meet my husband Ty and my daughter Elaina.*
>
> *As for your apology, I don't accept it. I want to apologize to you. I ran into your mom a few months ago and she told me what had happened. I am so sorry. I can't even imagine how awful it must have been. I can't honestly say that I'm disappointed things didn't work out between you and Patrick, but I should have been more supportive. I should have been there for you. I'm here for you now if you'll let me be.*

*On a happier note, tell me about this new guy. Is he
hot? What does he do? Come on girl. Don't keep me
in suspense.*

Please call me so we can catch up.

*TTFN
Love Sarah.*

Catherine read the message repeatedly, looking for any sign of insincerity, but there was none. Sarah, her dearest friend in the world wasn't gone after all. She was there the whole time, waiting for her to reach out once again. Catherine couldn't help but smile.

She looked at the phone number that Sarah had included at the very end of the message. It had a 780-area code, Northern Alberta. Sarah had family in Edmonton, had she gone back there?

"So, what do you plan on telling her about me?"

Startled from her daydream, she turned around to find that Stephen stood behind her reading over her shoulder, still completely naked.

"I'm sorry, what?" Catherine asked, taken off guard by the question.

"What are you going to tell her when she asks about me?" He began to mimic a female voice. "So, tell me about your new boyfriend. Is he rich, is he dreamy?"

He changed the pitch of his voice slightly to suggest a different speaker, "Actually he's a professional contract killer at a government run facility that supports euthanasia. And he plays the piano."

He returned to the original voice, "Oh, he sounds like a keeper, a real catch."

"Maybe I should open with the piano thing before I ease into the contract killing," she teased.

"I think you'd better use a more politically correct term though. How about, a Mortality Encouragement Technician?"

Catherine laughed at his sarcasm, then swiveled the chair around to face him. "You know, I wouldn't have to lie if you could just quit and come with me. The disadvantage of dating a convict, I suppose."

Stephen pulled her close to him. "That is definitely an option that I have considered, but it may not be that simple. I still have a year left to finish of my sentence before I can even apply for early parole."

"Early parole? How is that possible? You murdered your wife."

Stephen looked away for a moment. Was it remorse? "It was all part of the plea bargain that landed me here. They reduced my sentence to involuntary manslaughter. There is a chance that I could apply for early parole, but only if I stop contracting. Still, there is an appeal process. It would take time."

"But less time." She pleaded.

Stephen searched her eyes for sincerity while he asked what he believed to be the most pertinent question of the week. "I need to be clear on something here. Are you bargaining with me, saying that you will go home as long as I go too, or are you saying that you are ready to live your life and you want me to be a part of it?"

Catherine never once broke eye contact while she responded, "I guess what I'm saying is, I want you to be a part of my life. The truth is you were right. I don't want to die; I know that now. "

Stephen kissed her passionately and stopped just briefly to comment, "Thank you. That's all I needed to hear." before he escorted her back to the bed.

**

The reporter, Laura Bentley cautiously pulled her Smart car up to the gates of the Farm and came to a stop next to the guard shack. She rolled down her window as the guard approached.

"May I see your ID please?" He asked sternly.

"Of course." She fished through the assorted contents of her purse for her media access card and handed it over.

Sergeant Morgan examined the card. "I am sorry Ms. Bentley. You should know by now our policies regarding media presence on the grounds. I cannot allow you to enter."

She confidently looked him in the eyes, "I am here at the request of Mr. Montgomery, to serve as a witness on his behalf."

The Sergeant's eyes narrowed and the corners of his mouth turned downwards. "Wait here."

Sergeant Morgan kept her ID in hand and returned to the guard shack. She watched as he picked up the phone to make a call. Though still quite close to her, with his back turned and speaking quietly, she was unable to hear what he said to person on the other end.

He hung up, returned to the vehicle, and handed her back the card. "You can park next to that first building. Lieutenant Murray will meet you there to escort you to the site. You will remain in his company as long as you stay within these gates. Is that clear?"

"What if I need to go to the bathroom?" She smiled.

The guard stared at her with unwavering eyes.

She quickly backed down, "I understand."

Sergeant Morgan turned on his heels and, once again, entered the shack. He picked up a handheld scanner and ran it over his own ID badge. The gate began to rumble open, and she politely waved to him as she drove the small car into the compound.

**

Everything was finally in order and lay out neatly upon the desk before him. The first was a signed document from Captain Glenn Spaulding of the Regina fire Department, declaring that he approved inspection in accordance with the Canadian code standard. The second was a letter from Kevin Richards, stating that he had completed his end of the installation according to their discussions. The third and final document was a fax printout from General Roger McGovern, with an official seal, which gave Hawkins the green light to proceed.

It was all going exactly as he planned, and Hawkins could not have been happier. The best part of his morning was the beautiful woman in the office across the hall, who had woke up next to him just an hour earlier, still curled up together with her head resting comfortably on his chest. It had been far too long, and it was well worth the wait.

There came a knock at the door, and a beautiful face poked through as it opened. "Hey you." Valerie's eyes glistened as he had never seen, and a mischievous grin formed on her moistened lips. "I was hoping you might want some company."

As she stepped in the room, Travis noticed her hair pulled up off her neck, and her white blouse unbuttoned more than usual, revealing the lacy top of her pale pink bra. He stared with desire at her flawless skin. He marveled at how the curve of her neck ran down into the cleavage.

"Who am I to turn down an offer like that?"

Valerie strode into the office closed the door behind her, and then walked around to his side of the desk. When she straddled his legs and sat down on his lap, her skirt rode up to flash her matching pink panties. She wrapped her arms around his neck and kissed him with passion. His warm hands were under her blouse, on her back, pulling her body tight against his own.

Sadly, Travis had to ignore the bulge that started to form in his pants and pull his lips from hers. "I wish we could right now, but it's awfully close to go time and the witnesses could be here any minute."

Valerie exaggerated a pouty frown, "Spoiled sport." She placed her palms flat on his chest and leaned into him. She whispered in his ear. "We should have done this a long time ago."

"I can't argue with that."

"She sighed and sat up straight, but remained on his lap, facing him. "Have you spoken to Captain Spaulding this morning?"

"Yes. He should be on his way now with a truck. He figures they can keep the fire under control with just one. I don't foresee any difficulties."

Valerie stared blankly at the wall behind Hawkins' shoulder. "I wonder if he slept well."

"Captain Spaulding?"

She snapped out of her daydream. "No silly. I'm talking about Mr. Montgomery. He refused my offer of meds, so I'm just wondering if he slept."

"I'm not sure, but-," the telephone cut off his thought. He struggled to answer it with Valerie on his lap. "Yes?"

Valerie's expression took on a note of concern as she watched Hawkins' reaction to the news coming at him through the telephone.

"Fine, let her in. But have Murray keep an eye on her. Thanks." He reached to return the handset to its cradle.

"Trouble at the gate?"

"Yeah. We've had an unexpected visit from the reporter, Laura Bentley. She said she was invited by Mr. Montgomery to act as his witness."

"Why would he invite her?"

Hawkins frowned. "I don't know, but I don't like it."

"Do you have to go meet her?"

"No, Lieutenant Murray can deal with her for now. Shit, I don't want to have to deal with her at all."

Valerie's tongue darted out to moisten her lips. "So? What do we do now?"

Travis rested his hands on her bare thighs and gently rubbed her skin with his thumbs. "Well, as soon as Sargent Morgan calls again, I'll have to go meet the fire department and take them down to the track."

"That's not what I meant."

"Oh." His hands slid up higher, under her skirt. "Well, I am perfectly willing to explore all our options."

Valerie grabbed hold of his tie. "You said you are waiting for Walter's call?"

"Yup."

Her hands slid all the way down his tie and found his belt buckle. "So, we could be waiting another few minutes, possibly more."

"Very possible."

She unbuttoned his trousers and pulled open his fly. "I have always been taught to make efficient use of my time."

"You've learned well." He grabbed hold of her and pulled her on top of his hardened shaft. Lips locked; their mouths molded together in a passionate kiss. While Valerie's hands worked to free Travis from his pants, he reached out and knocked the phone off the receiver. If the Fire Captain were to show up over the next few minutes, he would have to wait.

⁕⁕

Ian Montgomery stretched, in a futile attempt to work out the crick in his neck after a restless sleep in the woods. With only his empty backpack as a pillow, the conditions were less than ideal for a good night's rest. Ian wasn't terribly concerned though. He was confident that he would sleep like a baby, in his own bed the following evening.

Unfortunately, for him, his own bed will be in unfamiliar surroundings. Fully aware he would no longer be able to return to his own life after the attack, he had arranged to rent a new apartment in Montreal under his alias, Grant Niomey. He had arranged to move his valuable possessions and necessities, content that he would have to abandon the remainder of his things. An acceptable loss, assuming all goes according to plan.

In the meantime, one last matter remained. He wanted to witness the fall of Hawkins and the Farm, before he made his triumphant escape through the hole, he was soon to make in the fence line. He needed a vantage point, one where he could see both the trailer and the administration building. He wanted to watch the personnel frantically scurry around as they try to figure out what went wrong. There was one clear option.

The water tower.

A catwalk circled the entire perimeter of the tower, and the ladder that led up to it climbed the backside of the structure. If he remained quiet and still, he should have no issues staying out of sight while he watched the festivities. However, he needed to move. The sun began to rise over the horizon, and he would soon lose his cover of darkness. Others would soon start to mill about, and he had come too far to falter right before its conclusion.

He slowly crept to the edge of the woods and scanned the immediate grounds. There was no one in sight for the moment, but the clock was ticking. He cursed himself for not getting up sooner, but he didn't want to be stuck up on the tower for longer than necessary. This reminded him that he hadn't taken a piss since he woke up. How awkward it would be, if he was hiding on the tower, and was struck by the sudden urge to pee. He moved back deeper in the trees and relieved himself into a bush.

He returned to the tree line to the sound of two voices in the distance. Shit. Two maintenance workers had just passed the water tower and were heading toward the trailer. He watched as the two men approached the unit and attempted to peer into Ian's apartment. Lucky for him, he had drawn the curtains, so they would be unaware of his absence. No one else appeared to be in the area, aside from the two workers. He waited until their inspection took them behind the trailer, then he darted from the trees and sprinted to the iron-rung ladder that reached up to the top of the tower. The muscles in his legs burned, as he ascended the ladder with haste. He didn't stop until he got to the top and collapsed against the backside of the tower.

He concentrated, trying to hear over the sound of his own heavy breathing, for anything that might suggest that anyone noticed his presence. There were no shouts, no alarms. He was safe, for the time being. He sat in silence and listened to the ambient sounds wafting up to him from the facility below. Over time, the number of voices began to increase, but he dared not sneak a look out of fear of someone spotting him. No, he would have to wait until the fire became a distraction.

The next sound he heard, aside from additional voices, was the growl of a large diesel engine that increased in volume as it drew nearer. A firetruck, perhaps? It would make perfect sense. They expected a large fire; they would need a way to extinguish it. He laughed to himself. They had no idea what was in store for them. One truck wouldn't be enough.

He looked at his watch, 7:52am. It was nearly time. Soon they would learn what it means to defy God's will. Soon, they would know what it means to cross PALM.

ECE-80088

Lieutenant Commander Thomas Clayburne stood before a full-length mirror within his private quarters. He looked damn good for a ninety-three-year-old veteran with COPD. The sharp, dark green dress uniform, pip and crown on the epaulettes, three stripes on the cuff, not to mention the array of commendations displayed proudly over his breast.

Through he had finally come to the end of his ninety-three-year journey; he had few regrets. He was sorry he never had an opportunity to travel to Scotland, where both his parents were born. He was sad that he never met someone, with whom he wanted to share his life. Nevertheless, he was married to the army, and they had always treated him with respect and dignity. Mostly, however, he wished to hell, he had never started smoking.

He had smoked most of his life; it's what they did when he was young. Over the years, he had never had the desire or will to quit, that is, up until a few years earlier, when it was already too late. The chronic bronchitis had taken hold, and there was nothing he could do to stop it. He could only wait for the inevitable.

Regrets aside, he had very few complaints. He held a successful career in the Canadian Infantry that began in Normandy with the Second Division. He worked his way up through the ranks in France, Korea and even Vietnam where, by amazing coincidence, he commanded a certain James D. Hawkins.

The week Tom had spent on the Farm was a truly memorable one. He spent a great deal of his time with Captain Hawkins who reveled in the stories of his military career and the time Tom had spent with his father. He found Travis Hawkins to be a kind and honourable officer, a trait he came by naturally.

Tom was proud of the man who stared back at him in the mirror. He had lived a long and admirable life that he was ready to leave behind with his head held high.

He made one final dress inspection. His shirt was clean and pressed; his tie was straight with a tidy Windsor knot. His jacket, neatly buttoned, held his service medals that shone brightly. He had even taken the time to spit-shine his boots in the traditional fashion. Atop his head, he proudly displayed his officer's cap, with the crest of the PPCLI.

Lieutenant Commander Tom Clayburne saluted the decorated veteran in the mirror and proudly exited his quarters. He made his way down the outer corridor and through the atrium towards the door out to the compound. He grasped the brass handle and pulled the door open.

"Attention!" shouted Captain Hawkins upon his appearance.

The sight before him brought tears to his eyes. Hawkins must have called in some favours. The number of military personnel that stood at attention before him eclipsed the normal compliment of the Farm. A score of service men and women lined either side of the pathway, while a third row of seven stood off to the right cradling traditional rifles. Hawkins stood to his left with Dr. Lough and a member of the Canadian Highlanders at the ready with a set of bagpipes.

"Royal Salute!"

The Lieutenant Commander straightened his posture to receive that great honour.

"Present Arms!"

The seven riflemen brought their arms to the ready.

"Ready, fire!"

Seven shots carried across the compound.

"Fire!"

A second round filled the air.

"Fire"

Twenty-one shots in total, in honour of the humble Veteran Officer, before they lowered their arms.

As the sound of the rifles died down, the Highlander lifted his pipes and began to play *Scotland the Brave*. Hawkins stepped forward and extended his hand, which he gratefully accepted.

"Thank you for your service, Sir."

"Thank you for this honour."

Hawkins released the handshake, snapped to attention, and followed up with a salute. Dr. Lough stepped forward and extended her own hand. Tom ignored the handshake and moved in for a hug.

"Thank you." He whispered in her ear.

"Pleasant Journey." She whispered back, and then kissed him gently on the cheek.

Clayburne straightened and stood before the men and women who honoured him. With immense pride, he snapped to attention and saluted them. It was time to move on. Steady as he could, he walked between the two rows that directed him along the pathway towards the open courtyard. He had never in his life felt so appreciated and revered, and as he passed the last of the honour guard, applause erupted from behind him. He continued to hold his head high as he walked out into the square.

As he reached the centre of the compound, he felt a pressure below his footstep, and heard a distinct click. He knew that sound very well, as he had armed dozens of these same devices when he served overseas. He brought his back foot forward next to the other and stood at attention. He felt he had served his country well and could move on with honour.

With one final salute to the flag above, he stepped off the pressure plate.

CHAPTER TWENTY-SIX

With the exception of a few key security personnel, all the inhabitants of the Farm had turned out to gather around the racetrack and watch the morning's spectacle. The crowd was abuzz with talk and speculation, as they waited for the big moment when Richards pushed the button and flames engulfed the building before them.

Among the congregation of facility staff, Catherine and Stephen stood together, off to one side, away from the crowd. They stood close, not quite touching, and they talked quietly between them. Catherine periodically stole glances around the crowd, curious if anyone could tell that the two of them had slept together. No one appeared to care.

Not too far away, Kevin Richards kept very much to himself. He had only recently joined the crowd since he came out from behind the trailer, after turning on his gas valves. He strategically placed himself in a location where he could clearly observe all the excitement. He wanted to be certain not to miss any of the action, as this was sure to be one for the record books.

A score of heads turned back to the roadway, at the sound of a bright red firetruck, which slowly approached their location. Three figures walked alongside the truck. Everyone immediately recognized Captain Hawkins and Dr. Lough, but the third person was unknown to most. Judging by his uniform however, he was certainly a representative of the Fire Department.

While Hawkins and the fire chief were deep in discussion, Dr. Lough walked quietly, her hands folded in front of her, cheeks flushed, and she clearly avoided eye contact with others. She obviously had something to hide, and it wouldn't take much for others to figure it out; but as the roaring firetruck was at the centre of attention at that moment, her relationship with Hawkins took a back seat.

The three continued walking toward the track, while the truck stopped in front of the water tower. Four firefighters leaped from the truck and began to unravel a hose, which they used to connect their pump to the valve at the base of the tower. They then rolled out two more hoses that they extended out from the truck toward the trailer. Despite the controlled burn, they would be at the ready for when the time came for their intervention.

A dull murmur of conversations washed over the crowd of onlookers, while the trailer sat peacefully in the distance. The general belief of those present was that Ian Montgomery remained sound asleep in the makeshift apartment, completely unaware that, at that moment, he sat above their heads atop the very water tower that cast a long shadow over the track. Only a few minutes remained.

Hawkins broke away from his group of three and strode to where Kevin Richards stood alone. He spoke quietly, issuing his final instructions, to ensure that the operation went off without a hitch. As Hawkins spoke, Richards nodded in agreement. He stepped away, scanned the crowd and glanced at his watch. He spoke out, loud enough for those around him to hear.

"Countdown in two."

**

"Good morning. This is Laura Bentley, reporting within the gates of the Farm, to witness firsthand an actual contract that is about to be completed under the supervision of the facility supervisor, Captain Travis Hawkins. Though I am unable to reveal the name of the client, it is my understanding that he has come here to seek end-of-life measures after a valiant battle against cancer.

Little has been shared publicly, about the nature of the contracts, or how they are carried out. We only know that they offer extraordinary options when it comes to the method of termination. In this case, the client in question has chosen to die in a fire, the same way his wife was killed in Fort McMurray only a few years ago.

The voice you may have heard a moment ago from behind me was none other than Captain Hawkins himself, who has given us a two-minute warning before they will begin. All eyes are now on the trailer to my left, where the client currently resides, and where his fiery death is about to take place.

I will continue to film the action throughout the event, to give you all a clear window into the Farm."

**

The suspense was killing him, and Ian Montgomery decided to chance a look. With his back flat against the wall of the tower, he carefully craned his neck to peer over the railing of the catwalk. From his perch, he could clearly make out the crowd that had gathered to watch his alleged demise. Though their backs were to him at that moment, he easily made out Dr. Lough, who stood with a member of the fire department, but he couldn't locate Hawkins. Several fire fighters worked to string out hoses to, what he assumed was their truck. He couldn't see it from this vantage point, but the rumbling of the engine was unmistakable.

Two men were talking off to the side. As one turned to walk back towards the others, Ian clearly identified Hawkins. The captain looked over the crowd. Shit! Did he just look up toward the tower? Ian plastered himself back against the wall of the tower, hoping Hawkins had not seen him. A voice called out, "Countdown in two." Even at that height, Ian could recognize Hawkins' distinctive voice. He was satisfied that no one was aware of his location.

Ian once again peered over the catwalk. Hawkins had moved over to stand with Dr. Lough and their guest. The personnel all talked between themselves, all but the one man that Hawkins had the conversation with: Kevin Richards, his would-be assassin. He stood alone, hands in his pockets, staring intently at the trailer as if determined to ignite it with the power of his mind.

Front and centre, with an unobstructed view of the trailer, his guest, Ms. Bentley spoke into a camera, which she had set up on a tripod. She was under the assumption that she was here to witness the contract on his behalf. Little did she know; he had invited her to broadcast his message to the world.

Hawkins raised his arm, once again to look at his watch. He turned to speak to his colleagues, glancing back at the time periodically. At last, it came.

"Ignition in three, two, one…"

**

At first, nothing appeared to have changed. Heads turned to look at Kevin Richards who held the small remote in his hand. Judging by the satisfied smile on his lips, he had already pushed the button, so attention returned to the trailer. There it was, the faint glow in the front window, gradually brightened and flickered under the shadow of the water tower. Conversations began to get louder, more excited. They could hear faint sounds of cracking and popping wood, but the fire remained contained in the outer apartment. The bedroom window remained dark.

Smoke started to escape the trailer through various cracks and holes around the structure. The area began to smell like a campfire. The crowd looked back and forth between themselves and the trailer, in anticipation of excitement to occur. Among all the confusion, Richards stood, watching the trailer, unwavering. He smiled like the cat that hunted his prey.

Soon the flicker of light began to dim as the fire consumed the oxygen in the tight quarters. The crowd watched, barely breathing, looking for the flash of light in the bedroom window to indicate that Mr. Montgomery had opened the door. Any sign that the inferno engulfed the small apartment. What was the hold up? Surely, he couldn't sleep through the fire. Had he silently passed away in his sleep? It had taken far too long; it had to have been nearly five minutes.

**

There was little concern about concealment any longer. No one would be looking up at that moment. All eyes were on the trailer, attentively waiting for an event that would never come, at least not from that direction. Ian knew better. He knew the excitement would happen in another few moments, behind them at the administration building.

230

He was too far away to hear the conversations below, but he didn't need to. He could see the confusion in the way the crowd looked from the trailer to Captain Hawkins, then back to the trailer. Feet began to fidget with impatience and some personnel had lost interest. Many were deep in conversation with others around them. In fact, the only two who appeared to remain transfixed on the target were Hawkins and Richards. Even Dr. Lough looked around for answers.

Ian looked at his watch. It read 8:04 and 18 seconds, 19, 20. The seconds counted off to the moment he waited for. He skulked around the catwalk to the eastern side of the tower. From there, he was unable to see the entire administration building, but he could see enough of it to witness its destruction. Besides, the explosion should be large enough to see over top of the nearest structures.

He looked at his watch. Thirteen seconds to go. This is it. Eight seconds. He gripped the railing tight in anticipation and squinted to help shield his eyes from the impending flash. Three seconds, two, one.

The compound was silent. There was no ear-shattering explosion, no flash of bright light, no secondary explosion at the fence line behind him. He stared with wonder at the front entrance of the administration building that clearly remained standing. Then he heard a sound he had not expected. It took him a moment to clue in, to what it was. It was the rush of water, followed by a hollow gurgle from the tower behind him. The firefighters had started to extinguish the fire.

Something had gone terribly wrong.

Soon, Hawkins would discover that he was never in the apartment, and he would send out a search party. How long would it be before they discovered his explosives? He was trapped, and he knew it. He had lost his escape route. His mind circled around the events. How could this have happened? His only hope was to hide the devices before anyone discovered them. Claim he reconsidered. They might even believe him.

He had to move quickly. Ian ran across the catwalk to where the ladder waited for him and looked down to the bottom before he descended. Shit! Three guards stood below him, arms extended, with their handguns trained on him. Immediately behind them stood Captain Hawkins, hands clasped behind his back, smiling up at him.

A flash of light caught his attention. He looked straight out over the trees to the other side of the fence, where two military vehicles, lights flashing, converged on an old pick-up that waited in the field. The truck took off and the police continued their pursuit. Ian lost sight of them as they rounded the facility, but he continued to hear the sirens trail off in the distance.

**

Ian Montgomery had barely stepped off the ladder before the guards wrenched his arms behind him and tightly clamped cuffs around his wrists. As Hawkins drew near, he spoke with clarity. "Mr. Ian Montgomery, I hereby charge you with an act of terrorism against the Government of Canada as per section eighty-three point zero one, of the Canadian Criminal Code. You have the right to retain and instruct counsel without delay. Anything you say can be used in court as evidence. Do you understand? Would you like to speak to a lawyer?"

Ian's mind however was not on legal representation at that moment. He was far too busy trying to work out where it all went wrong. What happened to his explosions, and why the hell was he in cuffs, face to face with his enemy? The plan was perfect; he should have been well on his way by then.

"But how...?" Was all he could manage to ask.

Hawkins explained with pride, "We can all thank Mr. Richards for stumbling on to your little scheme. Had he not seen you coming back to the apartments during the protest rally with a brand-new bag, we would not have had a reason to look back on the security tapes. You might be interested to know that less than a third of our cameras are clearly visible from the ground. We recorded every step you took last night, and then we followed behind you, disabling your devices while you napped in the woods."

"But the guard." Ian could not believe how much he took for granted. "He told dispatch everything checked out."

Hawkins couldn't help but laugh, "Wow, you truly are a gullible one, aren't you? I was quite surprised how well that turned out. I had expected you to panic and run. Your evasion tactics made the tapes far more entertaining to watch though."

Ian remained confused, "I don't understand. If you knew what I was planning, why didn't you just arrest me sooner? Why did you allow this to continue?"

"We wanted to see if you were determined enough to follow through on your attack. However, more than that, I wanted to make certain I was able to take down your organization permanently. Besides, I had promised Mr. Richards a fire, and since he was paramount in uncovering your plan, I was happy to oblige."

Ian looked away from Hawkins to find Kevin Richards, who stood just a few metres away, holding the small electronic transmitter. Right next to him was the reporter, Laura Bentley, camera in hand, filming his arrest.

"You were in my room?" He directed the question to Richards.

The contractor smiled. "Housekeeping normally doesn't come until after the contract."

Hawkins continued, "You've been had, Mr. Montgomery, or should I say, Mr. Niomey, and now you will be going away for a very long time. Take him back to the holding cell please, Sargent."

As the guard escorted Ian Montgomery to the golf cart, he did not put up a fight, nor did he speak. He merely walked, head down, precisely where they led him. It wasn't until he was strapped into the seat and the cart jerked into motion that he finally looked back towards Hawkins and his entourage. His face was unreadable, but everyone knew exactly what ran through his mind. "What the hell just happened here?"

CHAPTER TWENTY-SEVEN

"And so, the question remains. Are Captain Hawkins and his associates a group of altruistic heroes, on a quest to rid our country of its pain and suffering, or are they a corrupt band of vigilantes, hell bent on protecting the world from the scum of the earth? Well, they won this time, and managed to keep their noses clean in the process, but rest assured, I will continue to report on the goings on here at the Farm as long as there are clients taking a one-way trip through these gates. This is Laura Bentley, in Penzance, Saskatchewan."

"I can't believe you didn't tell me." Dr. Lough berated Captain Hawkins, drawing his attention away from the closed captions that scrolled across the bottom of the atrium television. She scowled at him from across the lunch table.

The two of them had spent the previous three hours neck deep in paperwork and red tape, before he could hand custody of Ian Montgomery, and his accomplice Byron Daniels, over to the RCMP. Around the same time, Hawkins was mirandizing Montgomery; the second team of security personnel had caught up with Daniels and returned him to the compound. The two men shared the cramped holding cell in the back of the administration building until the transfer of custody was complete. The authorities had also requested an investigation against the Oncologist, Dr. Jason Simpson. Overall, it had been a busy morning. This was the first time since they arrested Ian Montgomery, that Valerie had the chance to tear into him.

"You let me believe that he was a legitimate client. What happened to full disclosure?"

"I'm sorry Val, but I couldn't ask you to lie for me again. I gave you the gift of plausible deniability. If he had discovered that we were on to him, he might have panicked and pulled the plug."

"But why allow him to make it that far? Why didn't you arrest him when you found the explosives in his room?"

"Once Mr. Richards figured out who he was, it wasn't a difficult guess as to what he was up to. We wanted to nail him to the wall. At that time, we only had him on possession, conspiracy if we were lucky. We wanted to get him on attempt. We needed him to believe without a doubt that he would get away with it. For that reason, we had to have as few people in the loop as possible. I'm sorry you weren't one of them."

Valerie set down her Reuben sandwich with a sigh, "I feel like the worst psychologist in the world right now. I honestly believed his story. I really thought he was a good man. I hate that I didn't see it."

Travis grabbed hold of her hand, "Don't beat yourself up over it; you're a very compassionate woman. He's a con artist, and had us all fooled, until Kevin found him sneaking around. He certainly has given me reason to doubt our screening process."

"I will have to talk to Mr. Richards this afternoon. I'm sure he is holding back some resentment over his inability to complete the contract."

"I wouldn't be so sure about that. I spoke to him briefly. He doesn't seem to care about the contract. We let him start a fire, and he thoroughly enjoyed taking Montgomery down. He said he felt like one of those crime-scene investigators from TV." Hawkins chuckled at the thought.

Valerie laughed along with him. "Oh, my gawd, could you imagine? I'm not sure that CSI Saskatchewan would necessarily fly with the critics."

"Excuse me, I'm so sorry to interrupt." a soft-spoken voice barely cut through their laughter.

Travis and Valerie looked over to see that Catherine Dean stood next to their table. She was so quiet; they hadn't even noticed her approach.

"Good afternoon, Catherine." Valerie greeted her like an old friend. "How are you today?"

"I'm good." Catherine smiled, "I was wondering if I could speak with you for a moment."

"Certainly." Valerie dabbed her mouth with a napkin, "Why don't we go back to my office?"

"To be honest, I would like to speak to both of you, if you don't mind."

"No, not at all." Travis chimed in, "Please join us."

He stood and pulled over a chair for Catherine, which she gladly accepted. Valerie waited until he was seated again before she continued.

"So, what can we do for you? Is something bothering you?"

"Uhm." Catherine fidgeted with her hands while she carefully chose her words. "I'm not quite sure how to say this without sounding like a flake, so I'm just going to come right out with it." She hesitated to say any more, but a comforting smile from Dr. Lough gave her the courage to continue, "I think I'm ready to go home."

Valerie fought the urge to jump out of her chair and cheer. Instead, she kept her composure. "Are you certain this is what you want? Are you prepared to seek help outside of this facility?"

Catherine folded her hands meekly in her lap. "Yes, I'm sure. If possible, I was hoping you could recommend a counsellor for me."

"Absolutely, I can most certainly do that for you." She found it difficult to hide her enthusiasm. "I have the number for several in the Toronto area."

"Do you have any in Mississauga? I'm going to stay with my parents for a while. At least until I get back on my feet."

Dr. Lough could no longer hide her delight, "I can't begin to tell you how happy that makes me Catherine. I wish you all the best. And yes, I know a very good lady in Mississauga. I will tell her to expect your call."

Throughout the entire exchange, Captain Hawkins found himself unable to do anything but sit and listen with an ear-to-ear smile on his face. When he did take the opportunity to speak, he leaned forward and put a reassuring hand on Catherine's shoulder. "Please allow me to congratulate you on your decision Ms. Dean. If you should require anything, anything at all, please don't hesitate to call us. We have contacts in just about any field from jobs to affordable housing all over the country."

"Thank you, Captain Hawkins."

"In the meantime," he continued, "why don't you follow me back to my office and we'll get the paperwork started. We should be able to get you on your way first thing in the morning."

"Looks like I have some paperwork to do myself." Valerie added joyfully. "I'll walk back with you."

While Hawkins gulped back the last of his coffee, the women stood and began to make their way to the exit. As they all left the atrium, it became obvious to everyone around them that their collective mood had definitely changed for the better.

**

Stephen wasn't entirely certain why he had bothered to keep her account active all these years, but he could never bring himself to delete it. Lisa's profile page was a complete record of her adult life, which covered some of her childhood as well. Stephen's eyes began to water as he reminisced through her pages.

Lisa was born in Vancouver, where she lived her entire life, up until her premature demise. She grew up in the catholic school system before she received a scholarship in photography at the Emily Carr University of Art and Design. During her third year, she went to a party where Stephen, also in attendance, caught her eye. The attraction was immediate, and the rest was history. They were married a year and a half later in Stanley Park, unaware that they would have only fourteen months to enjoy each-other's company.

Lisa's favorite music was jazz and swing, her favorite movies were Immortal Beloved and Singin' in the Rain, and her quote of choice was, "A mind is like a parachute, it doesn't work unless it is open."

He continued to navigate through her page, reading the tributes posted by her friends and family, delighted to see that some of them were recent. It was nice to know that so many still remembered her fondly. The posts contained fond memories and inspirational quotes that gave the reader an open window into her extraordinary life. He was quite certain that if he had returned to his own page, that he had not opened since that day, he would see the very same people had posted venomous threats and degrading insults laced with colourful metaphors.

Next, he opened the tab, marked *photographs*, and started with a folder entitled *A Look Through My Eyes*. This page contained hundreds of photographs of people and nature she had taken herself. Lisa had a real eye for beauty, and an uncanny ability to make even the mundane come alive. He recognized many of the locations from vacation spots and parties they had both attended, along with the seemingly random yet remarkably beautiful shots around the city.

He paused on a photo that immediately caught his attention. It was a shot of him posed before the Haida killer whale sculpture, which stood in front of the Vancouver Aquarium. He remembered that day clearly. It was, not only the first time the two of them had gone to the aquarium together, but also the day he had proposed to her. Stephen looked so happy in the photograph, a face he had not seen in the mirror for a very long time.

He navigated back to the previous menu and selected the folder labelled *Photos of Lisa*. A list of thumbnails loaded up on the screen. Countless photographs involving Lisa in some form. By herself or with friends, graduation photos, wedding photos and vacation photos. At the top of the list, the photo presented as her profile pic, was a headshot she had used for her personal biography on her studio's website. It was a stunningly beautiful image. It highlighted Lisa's best features, her eyes. The most remarkable aspect of the photograph, however, was not as much the beauty of the subject as her amazing resemblance to the woman who had just left the apartment only a half hour earlier. The differences were obvious, but the two of them most certainly could have been relatives.

So many questions haunted his thoughts. Was Catherine nothing more than a painful reminder of the past, destined to torture him for his indiscretions? Did he dishonour Lisa's memory by pursuing a relationship with her? On the other hand, was she legitimately another chance to find happiness once again? An opportunity to do things right the second time around. It was clear that Stephen was the primary catalyst for her change of heart, and he wondered if she, in turn, could do the same for him. Could she fill that emptiness he had fought against all that time?

He needed that answer, and there was only one sure way to find out. He would have to try.

**

With no clients, remaining to meet with, Valerie and Travis decided to take the afternoon off and spend it together back in his apartment. Most of the afternoon, and part of the evening was spent in the bedroom in determined exploration each-other's bodies, but at that moment, they enjoyed a soak in the bathtub, stretched out with her lying back on top of him.

Travis gently kissed the top of her head, "You know, I think we can honestly say that this has been the most successful week we have ever had here."

Valerie turned her head to look up at him with a seductive smile, "I assume you aren't just talking about the last few hours here."

"Believe me, that's a huge part of it." He leaned down to kiss her sweet lips. "But I was also referring to the clients. One is on his way to prison; the other will soon be on her way home. No one died. It doesn't get much better than that. All we need now is to have Mr. Carlisle apply for early parole."

"Wouldn't that be nice? He seems to like her, so I suppose stranger things have happened."

Valerie adjusted her position slightly to prevent her leg from cramping, and as she did, she felt something hard poke into the small of her back. "Oh my," she purred, "are you ready to go again?"

"Are you kidding? I could do this all night."

Valerie turned around to lie on top of him chest to chest. "Whatever will the neighbours think?" she teased.

From that position, it was only a minor adjustment before he was inside her again. Water splashed around them as their synchronized movements created swirling waves in the crowded tub. When they finished together, she collapsed back down on top of him contently.

"I want to ask you something." Travis said, while he caressed her soft naked back."

"Mmm hmm," she moaned, "go ahead. You have me at your mercy."

"You start your week off on Tuesday, and I've been approved to take my flex week as we have no new clients. Darren has agreed to cover the desk. I want you to spend the week with me."

She propped herself up to look him in the eyes, "Was that a question?"

"Will you?"

"Did you plan to come to Saskatoon with me?"

"Not exactly, I kind of thought, perhaps something a little more romantic. There is a nice little Bed and Breakfast in Tofino, right on the ocean.

Valerie sat up and stared at him with a shocked expression. "I can't go to Tofino."

"Why not? How else did you plan to spend your week off?"

"I have been here for the last three weeks, so there is plenty I should be doing, but that's not the point. This isn't like driving into the city for dinner. There would be arrangements to make, flights, reservations, transportation."

"It has been arranged. The flight leaves Saskatoon Wednesday morning at nine fifteen and the room is booked for four nights. We can rent a car in Comox once we land. I even reserved a spot on the whale watching tour Friday night."

She was stunned silent.

Travis leaned forward to wrap his arms around her. "Come on. What do you say? Come with me. Everything is set."

"You bought plane tickets and booked room. What if I said no?"

"Are you saying no?"

She embraced him tightly and kissed him passionately before she responded. "You are seriously out of your mind. Thank you for the lovely invitation. Yes, I will go with you."

They continued their heated embrace until Valerie stopped him once again to stipulate, "But I'm buying dinners."

"We'll see."

That was the last they spoke of the subject that evening as their minds and bodies were otherwise preoccupied.

CHAPTER TWENTY-EIGHT

A cool breeze drifted across the compound and caught the flags high above on their poles. The afternoon heat had been unbearable, pushing the mid-thirties with no cloud cover to give relief from the sweltering, summer sun.

Fortunately, for Catherine and Stephen the evening wind cooled the air enough to allow them to escape the confined walls of the air-conditioned atrium and enjoy a quiet walk together under the stars. Their conversations inside the atrium had been casual to say the least, neither of them eager to delve too deeply into topics that were more personal. The sort of topics best kept out of earshot of so many others, who also sheltered from the heat.

The main topic of conversation was the surprise exposure of Ian Montgomery. The revelation took them both completely off guard. They never suspected that the seemingly sincere man secretly plotted to take down the entire operation. The authorities up to that point had kept the details to themselves, but according to the rumour-mill, Montgomery was apparently the founder of the PALM organization, and had spent the past two years planning the entire stratagem. The cloak and dagger charade monopolized the conversations, overshadowing the disappointment in their execution of the backdraft.

As the two of them walked hand in hand through the quiet compound, however, their conversations began to gravitate towards a more personal nature.

"So, I took your suggestion."

"Which one? There have been so many." Stephen replied sarcastically.

"I called my mother. Surprisingly enough, she was incredibly happy to hear from me."

"Why is that so surprising? No matter what, she is your mother."

"I don't know." Catherine felt a bit ashamed. "The last time we spoke was less than cordial."

"So, what did she say?"

"She wishes I had come to her sooner. She said that I could always come to her for anything."

"Funny, I'm quite sure I heard someone say something like that once. Fairly recently I think."

Catherine ignored his sarcasm, "Anyway, they invited me stay with them until I can get back on my feet. They want me to get my High School equivalency, but I don't know, maybe I will. After all, it's not like I have a tremendous number of options right now."

"After all the shit you have put yourself through over the past few years, I think it's time for you to do something that will make you happy. Forget about what will make your parents happy. Hell, go find yourself an agent and cut a CD. You certainly have the voice for it."

"Oh, wouldn't that be something." Catherine mused, "But unfortunately it would never happen."

"Why the hell not? You are extremely talented."

She squeezed his hand gratefully, "Thank you for the compliment, but even if that is so, the music industry rarely looks at talent per se. They only seem to care about marketability. I'm not an eighteen-year-old bombshell."

"You'll never know unless you try."

"I agree. You are right about that. But you have to look at what the kids listen to these days, you don't have to be able to sing, you have to look good on the stage."

"Damn; and they call me a cynic. Look, it doesn't make one difference what societies norm is, or what everyone else is doing. You assume it's a foregone conclusion before you have even tried. If you believe you will fail and never attempt anything, there is no possibility of success. You have eliminated the option yourself. Don't make the decision for them, get right in their faces and force them to make their own decisions."

"And if their decision is, no?"

"Then you go to the next one, and the one after that. Set a goal and stick to it."

"But what if they all say no."

Stephen placed his hands on her shoulders, so they were face to face. "See that? You have defeated yourself before you've started. Treat each audition as the one that will say yes. Just because Joe Blow doesn't like your style doesn't mean Cindy Lou won't. The twenty-three who say no will be nothing more than a distant memory when you find that one yes."

"Twenty-three?" She choked on the question.

"I was trying to make a point. It could be twenty-three, or it could be three. You could be lucky enough to find it on your first shot. The point is, if you don't even bother, you have already lost."

Catherine pulled him close into a tight embrace, "You should have been a motivational speaker instead of a contract killer. You could have helped better people's lives instead of ending them."

"Could you imagine me as a motivational speaker?" he laughed.

"You motivated me."

After a gentle kiss, they turned and began to walk hand in hand back toward the residence. They walked in silence for a short while as they breathed in the cool night air and listened to the croak of the frogs in the distance. It had become a perfect evening that neither of them wanted to end.

Catherine broke the silence with a question of her own, "What do you plan to do? When you get out, I mean."

"I don't know. There are only two things that I'm any good at, construction and contract killing. I'm rather certain that my parole officer would frown upon me pursuing contracts outside the Farm, which seems to leave me only one option."

"Well, what about the piano?"

Stephen laughed, "Oh sure, that's a great idea. I'll just hang a shingle outside the halfway house and offer lessons to children."

"You're the one who said I should follow my dream, so come with me. You play, I'll sing. We can cut a CD together."

"You're serious."

"Why not?" Catherine began to get excited the more she thought about it. "We could be a duet, Carlisle and Dean."

The two of them had stopped walking and now stood face to face, eyes locked in each other's gaze. As Stephen stared, he couldn't help but see the pure honesty in her expression. This wasn't just a simple idea; this was something she truly desired. A dream she wanted to share with him.

"You know," He finally responded, "Carlisle and Dean doesn't seem to have all that nice of a ring to it. What do you think of The Carlisles instead?"

Stephen watched her expression morph before him. It began with a perplexed look as she tried to wrap her head around what he had just asked. Once it started to sink in, Catherine's eyes suddenly grew wide, and her cheeks began to flush. She tried to speak, but nothing seemed to come out of her mouth. "I...I..."

He took both of her hands in his own, "I'm sorry, I think I may have taken you a bit off guard." he chuckled nervously, "You don't need to answer right now, just take some time to think about it. Okay?"

Again, all she could manage was a subtle nod of her head. This time however, Stephen noticed another change in her expression. Although her eyes showed a state of shock, her lips revealed something entirely different as she held just a hint of a smile.

He dropped Catherine's right hand and moved next to her, to continue their stroll side by side. "Why don't we change the subject for now?" With that simple statement, Stephen felt her grip on his hand relax slightly.

"I spoke to Captain Hawkins yesterday." Stephen digressed, "Apparently, if I were to decide to cancel my contract, and pursue early parole, I would have to move back into the prison system. So, that would mean, if I managed to-"

Catherine stopped in her tracks, jarring Stephen into a sudden halt. She looked as though she had something she desperately wanted to say, but she couldn't find the right words to express her thoughts.

"What is it?" Stephen urged, "You can tell me anything."

Catherine struggled to speak, but managed the best she could, "I- I hope you don't think that I am hesitating because I don't want to. I mean I do want to; it's just that it's so soon. I mean we just met, and sure we have spent a lot of time together the last few days, and most of it has been wonderful, except for the killing part of course, and I think, I love you, but if you think about it, how am I supposed to know if it's really-"

Stephen quickly put a stop to her erratic rant before it became completely indiscernible. "Wait, please. You are speaking in circles. It's okay. I told you that I don't need an answer right now. I completely understand."

"I know," she tried to continue, "It's just that-"

Stephen stopped her again, this time with a passionate kiss. Catherine melted into his embrace and could finally relax for the first time since he took her off guard. Stephen himself, was the one to cut the kiss short however, suddenly very conscious of their terribly public display of affection.

"What do you say we continue this conversation somewhere a little more private?"

Catherine looked around to find that they stood in the middle of the open square, and she suddenly felt very exposed. "I think that might be a better idea." she blushed.

Their pace quickened slightly as they made their way back to the apartments, desperately wanting to segregate themselves from the rest of the Farm's personnel. The walk back was in relative silence, which allowed Catherine's mind to race, attempting to make sense of Stephen's question. Once they had entered the residence, they swiftly made their way up to Stephen's apartment, with no desire to linger out in the open any longer than they absolutely had to.

"Can I offer you a drink?" Stephen asked while Catherine made herself comfortable in the sitting room.

"Water will be fine." Catherine began to feel a bit awkward, as she thought about the bumbling reply she gave to Stephen's question. She couldn't even remember exactly what she said; only that it came out sounding very foolish.

"If you'll indulge me, I can do a bit better than water." He announced. He returned with a bottle of wine and two glasses.

"I thought alcohol wasn't allowed."

"In light of our newly found relationship, I called in a favour with one of the guards. It's not exactly Dom Perignon, but it should suffice."

He sat on the sofa next to Catherine and filled the two glasses, starting with hers, then set the bottle down on the coffee table. With a gentle clink, Stephen proposed a toast, "To us."

"To us." she echoed with a smile.

They clinked classes and each took a sip of the sweet wine. The Riesling was a little too sweet for his liking, as he usually preferred a dry red Merlot or a Cabernet Sauvignon, but not knowing what Catherine liked, he decided to play it safe and go with the sweeter white. Still, it served its purpose and helped bring the evening to a romantic climax.

Stephen raised his arm as she snuggled in, laying her head upon his chest with a contended sigh. He placed a gentle kiss on the top of her head before he decided to speak.

"May I ask you a question?"

"Another one?" she teased.

"No, that's not what I'm talking about right now. Well, not exactly anyway. I was wondering about your response."

"Oh gawd." she laughed at herself, "I'm so sorry, I was such a blabbering idiot."

"There is no need to apologize; I kinda threw you for a loop. But you did say something amongst all the gibberish that caught my attention and I wondered if you truly meant it."

"Which part, the horrible grammar or the disconnected sentence structure?" Catherine attempted to make light of the subject.

Stephen however, adamantly continued, "No, I was referring to the part in the middle. Is it true?"

Her eyes circled the room as she tried to recall what she said. "Oh, that." She took a breath and suddenly became very serious, "I don't know, I mean we've only known each other a short time, but I feel like-" Catherine took a moment to set her glass down and look him in the eyes, "I think I do."

That was all Stephen needed to hear. With one swift movement, he scooped Catherine up in his arms and was on his feet. The wine glass fell by the wayside. He stumbled his way back to the bedroom with her cradled in his arms, never once tearing his lips from her own.

**

Catherine lay naked on her side, with Stephen spooned tight behind her. His body radiated heat like a furnace, but she didn't mind. She wasn't about to move out from the embrace of his strong arms. Besides, the conditioned air that circulated through the apartment was sufficient to keep her comfortable. She thought life could not get better than that.

Stephen raised his body, propping himself on his arm, and gently kissed the nape of her neck. He waited for her contented sigh to subside before he spoke. "You know, I've been thinking."

"That's impressive, if you consider all the blood loss from your brain to other significant areas." Catherine teased.

He laughed at her quick comeback before he continued, "I was thinking about our situation. Not just the two of us here and now, but also the circumstances that brought us together, and I came to realize a couple of things."

Catherine turned to face him and wrapped her arm around his waist. "And what conclusions did you come to?"

"Well, first of all, I think I found the hole in Captain Hawkins' no-lose situation and how to exploit it."

She playfully pulled him closer, not certain how any of this managed to come up as pillow talk. "That's wonderful Honey, and how do you plan to do that?"

"It's going to take both of us, but I'll come back to that in a second, because I also found a flaw in something you said a couple days ago."

"Why are we talking about this now?" She tried to draw him in to another kiss.

Stephen didn't falter. "You had said the other day that the reason Lisa's death was so much different than the others was because we loved each other."

"Okay?" She leaned back on her elbows, as her mood was definitely spoiled.

He continued his momentum, "I believe that is only partially correct. I am certain that love had something to do with it, but there was another far more significant detail."

"Which is?"

Stephen leaned over her and planted a gentle and loving kiss on Catherine's awaiting lips. When he was finished, he spoke softly, and stared into her beautiful blue eyes. "With the sole exception of Lisa, every one of my previous victims wanted to die."

CHAPTER TWENTY-NINE

Day Seven

Things could not possibly be better than they were right at that moment. The stars must have been aligned just right, because all the events came together perfectly in the end. The leader of the PALM organization, Ian Montgomery was safely locked away in prison and no one remained who was willing to keep the group in operation. Catherine Dean's release papers were signed, sealed, and delivered; and she would be happily on her way within a couple of hours. Stephen Carlisle got the girl, so who knows, there's a good chance he might apply for early parole.

Most importantly however, not only had his relationship with Valerie finally blossomed, they would soon spend a romantic week together on the island. They might even leave the hotel room long enough to see some of the sights. All the arrangements were made. Everyone got exactly what he or she deserved.

With a respectful smile on her face, Amanda, the server currently on shift, set a plate of blueberry pancakes in front of Valerie, and eggs benedict before Travis. She then placed a small pitcher of syrup between them.

"Would either of you like a top up on your coffee?" Amanda asked, retrieving the hot coffee pot from her tray.

"I would love some more thank you." Travis slid his cup closer to the edge of the table.

"Just a glass of ice water for me please Amanda." Valerie requested.

"I'll be right back with your water." Amanda said once she had filled Travis' cup.

"As I was saying," Travis continued the conversation they had been immersed in before their breakfast had arrived, "It turns out that, except for his second, Byron Daniels, not a single other person in the organization had any clue about who Ian Montgomery was. They all knew the founder as Grant Niomey, so as far as they were concerned, Ian Montgomery didn't exist."

"And Daniels?"

"Just an idiot follower who blindly jumped at Montgomery's every whim. He had a loud voice, but his boss was clearly the brains of the operation."

Valerie paused a moment in quiet thought. Curious as to where her mind was, Travis reached out to hold her hand.

"What's troubling you?"

"Do you think he's right?" She asked, after a moment's consideration.

"Do I think who's right? Montgomery?" he was rather surprised by the question.

"Yes, is Mr. Montgomery right? Are we defying God's will by taking another's life before their time?"

"Wow." Travis sat back a moment and took advantage of Amanda's return with a glass of water to come up with a sufficient answer.

"I hadn't expected that question from you," he continued after she left. "Basically, you are asking me my beliefs on God's role in our lives, or rather in our deaths. The truth is, I'm an agnostic, I neither believe nor disbelieve. I think that we will never know with absolute certainty until it is too late to prove it one way or another. What I do believe, however, is if there truly were a compassionate God, would he prefer to see his children suffer in agony, or die at peace? I'm certain I would choose the latter, and if I were created in God's image, wouldn't it make sense that he would also? Makes sense to me."

"But what if you're wrong?"

"Then heaven is going to be pretty darn empty."

"Why would you say that?"

Another voice chimed in, "Because if he is not a compassionate God, then all the repentance in the world won't make a lick of difference. I challenge you to find anyone in this world who has lived their life free of sin."

Hawkins looked up to find Stephen on the balcony above, "Those were my thoughts exactly. How long have you been listening?"

"Only a moment, but I thoroughly enjoyed your argument supporting agnosticism."

Stephen turned and made his way down the stairs. He appeared, to Dr. Lough to have a little more bounce in his step than usual. It was easy to tell that he was in a delightful mood.

"You seem to be in good spirits this morning Mr. Carlisle. I trust you had a great evening."

"I couldn't be happier, my good doctor. Everything seemed to just come together last night."

Valerie was ecstatic, "I gather then, all went well between you and Catherine?"

"Better than I ever could have expected. I finally found what I have been searching for all of these years."

"That's wonderful Mr. Carlisle. I'm so glad-"

"Wait!" Hawkins interrupted abruptly, "What exactly do you mean by, *found what you've been searching for*?"

"Precisely what I said Captain." Stephen said smugly, "*Exactly* what I've been searching for."

"Oh gawd." Dr. Lough began to clue in.

"Mr. Carlisle," Hawkins spoke clearly and concise, "where is Ms. Dean?"

"She is currently upstairs in my apartment."

Hawkins was on his feet. "And will she be joining us this morning?"

"I rather doubt it. She is dead tired."

Dr. Lough became white as a sheet, "My gawd Stephen, what have you done?"

Hawkins pulled his cell phone from its holster and quickly dialed a number. He never gave the voice on the other end a chance to speak before he jumped in. "Hawkins here. I need a full security team to the atrium immediately. Get an ambulance here too ASAP. And that means now."

He snapped the phone closed and turned back to Carlisle, "Make no sudden moves Mr. Carlisle; security will be here right away."

"Fear not Captain Hawkins," Stephen said, as he sat in the closest chair, "I have no intention of putting up a fight. I await your team with bated breath."

Dr. Lough ran towards the stairs, but Hawkins quickly stopped her, "Please Valerie, wait for security. I don't know what's up there."

Stephen continued, with calm smugness, "You have nothing to worry about Valerie. Nothing up there will harm you. I assure you it is quite safe."

"How could you?" Valerie turned on him with venom, "She loved you."

"I'm quite aware of that Doctor. That's what made it all the more exciting."

At that moment the security team burst through the door, and under Captain Hawkins' orders, immediately took Stephen Carlisle into custody. He then selected two guards and indicated the stairwell. "Come with me. Room 203. Quickly now."

With the guards in tow, Hawkins ran up the stairs, taking two at a time, then cautiously approached Mr. Carlisle's apartment.

**

"Liver temp is eighty-five degrees Fahrenheit, which puts the time of death right around midnight." Dr. Wall announced, as she removed the temperature probe from Catherine Dean's abdomen. Carlisle had laid her body upon the bed, fully dressed, with her hands folded together upon her belly. This is where Captain Hawkins and Dr. Lough had found her when they entered Stephen Carlisle's apartment just twenty minutes earlier. Upon seeing the scene, Dr. Lough had run back to her office to give General McGovern a heads up, leaving Hawkins to deal with the investigators.

"Cause of death?" Hawkins asked.

The Medical Examiner continued her report as she further examined the body, "Signs of petechial hemorrhaging suggests asphyxiation, and traces of fiber in her nostrils support the theory." She indicated a pillow on the floor, "that's likely the culprit. There is some skin under her fingernails, she fought back, quite fiercely I would guess. I will do a rape kit once I get her back on the table."

"Unfortunately, I believe that he was having sex with her while he smothered her." Hawkins explained what Carlisle had told him. "He was trying to recreate his wife's death."

"My gawd. Why the hell would anyone want to do that?"

"I'm not sure I want to know what goes through the mind of a man like that."

"Excuse me Captain. I'm sorry to interrupt."

Hawkins turned to find a young officer patiently waiting to speak. "Yes Lieutenant, what can I do for you?"

"Captain Hawkins, the Sheriff has arrived for the prisoner transfer. He needs a signature on the custody documents."

"Thank you, Lieutenant, please inform him that I will be there presently."

Travis' heart sank as he scanned the apartment. An opened bottle of wine sat on the coffee table next to a wine glass that was half-full. A second glass lay empty on the floor. The evening had obviously begun with a romantic tone, he wondered at what point it had turned so violent.

The situation had also undoubtedly put an end to his romantic plans with Valerie. There would certainly be an investigation, where they would scrutinize over all his actions, and of course, they would drag Valerie into the mess as well.

"Captain." The doctor called from the bedroom.

"Yes Doctor." Hawkins joined the investigative team.

"U.V. has confirmed traces of seminal fluids. She has had sex within the last twelve hours, most likely right around the time of death."

"Yes, that is exactly as I had assumed. Carry on with the investigation; I have to go meet with the Sheriff."

"Yes sir."

As Captain Hawkins made his way to the front door of the apartment, he took one final look back towards the seating area. He had been so proud of himself for, not only bringing the two of them together, but also because he had brought down Ian Montgomery's plans. Now, he could see his own plans crumble down around him. He knew there would no longer be a trip to the island, before nor after the investigation; he wasn't even sure if there would be a relationship. He wondered how easily Valerie could get past this incident. She had warned him against the contract, and he ended up with mud on his face. A lot of mud.

With a deep sigh, Captain Hawkins exited the apartment to meet with the Sheriff, and for the first time that week, face uncertainty.

EPILOGUE

This is the CBC Evening News in Regina, with news anchor Bill Lancaster, Mark Kingsley on sports, and Beverly DeSala with the weather on this Wednesday, July twenty-fifth.

"Good evening, I'm Bill Lancaster and these are the top stories. Three were killed and another twelve injured in a suicide bombing during a protest rally in Afghanistan. Relief continues in Florida for the victims of Hurricane Penelope. And, in sports, our own Saskatchewan Roughriders trounced the Edmonton Eskimos with an impressive score of thirty-four to eight. But first:"

Many have asked over the years, *has Prime Minister Ron Alexander gone too far?* And now, once again his policies are under scrutiny. Laura Bentley is live on location with the story. Laura?"

"Thank you, Bill. For the second time in as many days, I stand before the front gates of the Government compound, commonly known as the Farm, a federally operated facility used to support and carry out acts of compassionate euthanasia. Little has been known to the public up to this point about what secretly goes on behind these twenty-foot-tall fences, but things are soon to become abundantly clear."

A lengthy letter was sent to my personal email account last evening that shed some light on the daily occurrences here on the Farm, with some shocking ramifications. The letter was written by one Stephen Carlisle, a resident of the Farm, who spoke of convicted felons carrying out contract killings in the name of euthanasia. Mr. Carlisle referred to it as a third-party transaction, where, and I quote, *the client puts in the request, the administrator accepts it, and an impartial contractor carries it out."*

"Have you been able to get comments from any other member of the Farm?"

"No Bill, I have not. The only person I have been able to get close enough to, was the guard at the front gate, and he refuses to comment on anything that has ever occurred beyond the fence line. There has also been no traffic going in or out of the compound."

"And have you heard any more from this Stephen Carlisle since?"

"I haven't, and I don't imagine I will. According to his letter, he is also a contractor for the Farm, and a convicted killer. If what he said is true, he may have just murdered another young woman outside his contract. He said, and I quote, *I have a lovely young lady awaiting me. She truly has no idea of the fate that awaits her. I will be sad once she is gone, but I simply can't help myself.* I won't mention her name, as her status is not yet confirmed, but he did say in the letter that he was in love with her."

"Have there been any comments from the local authorities?"

Sources in the RCMP have confirmed that the Farm is currently under investigation, but they refuse to comment further as to what exactly they are investigating. It is this reporter's belief, based on the letter, that there is corruption at every level right from the administrator Captain Travis Hawkins, all the way up as high as the Prime Minister's office."

"Thank you, Laura. We shall keep our viewers appraised as the story develops."

"Yes, we will. Thank you, Bill. This is Laura Bentley in Penzance, Saskatchewan."

**

To the lovely and talented Ms. Bentley,

I thoroughly enjoyed your report this evening on the earlier events at the Farm, and therefore being familiar with the area, I thought you would be the ideal candidate to receive first-hand knowledge of the inner workings of the facility.

First off, you should know the identity of the man who they arrested in front of you and your viewers this morning. A gentleman by the name of Ian Montgomery, who was a client here under false pretenses, was originally the intended occupant of the apartment, which was, only partially, burned down. This changed when it was discovered that he was the leader of a religious extremist group with plans to destroy the Farm from the inside out. He is currently in federal custody facing charges of terrorism. The man who discovered his deceit was in fact the contractor assigned to him and is currently carrying out his sentence at the Farm for setting fire to his commanding officer. It was always clear that he has a rather unnatural affinity towards fire.

There are several other persons of interest here in this extraordinary facility. We have a contractor on staff who used to spend his weekends at the local brothel carrying out his fantasies of autoerotic asphyxiation. He ended up killing one of the whores in the process and was here on a ten-year sentence for manslaughter. He has recently been moved to a federal prison, and issued a harsher sentence, for killing outside of a contract. Another contractor came here after dissecting his father-in-law while under the influence, after a party at one of Canada's many legalized hash bars. I gather you are beginning to see a trend but wait there is more.

You may at this point be wondering what exactly these contractors were hired to do. Well, I shall now reveal that secret. They are hired to carry out the actual deed of euthanasia, a loophole created to prevent the bureaucrats from getting their hands dirty. It is considered a third-party transaction. The client puts in the request, the administrator accepts it, and an impartial contractor carries it out.

Jay Newman

I gather by now you are confused as to why you have never heard of these horrible crimes. The reason for this my dear, is they were handled internally, specifically to keep the honourable Ron Alexander's nose clean. Had the public ever found out what was really happening behind those closed doors, the backlash would be catastrophic.

Of course, one more detail still remains. Where do I fit in to all of this? I am also a contractor at the Farm, but my contract will end tonight. You see, I am here because I murdered my wife nearly ten years ago, during an extreme high. It was brought on by a combination of controlled substances that I had consumed at Alexander's inaugural hash bar. I was immediately addicted to the thrill of the kill and have spent the last two years here trying to recreate the rush.

My most recent client, a Ms. Catherine Dean, came here for relief from her crippling depression. Yes, we occasionally treat that here too. It just so happened however, that Ms. Dean has several features that mirror those of my former wife, and our administrators found it in their best interest to exploit these similarities, to try to bring the two of us together. Though they appear to believe it to be a complete success, I am about to reveal to them that they are only partially correct.

It is true that we have fallen in love with each other, a feeling that neither of us have had in a very long time. It is also true that Catherine has cancelled her contract with the hopes that we can spend the rest of our lives together after my release. This is where everyone is terribly wrong. You see, it has recently occurred to me that the reason I have been unable to recreate the thrill of the kill is that all my clients have wanted to die. I have found that this

260

*is no longer the case. As previously mentioned, Ms. Dean
has cancelled her contract, and wishes to continue her
life. I shall now have the opportunity to, not only achieve
my ultimate goal, but also to exact my revenge upon the
illustrious Captain Hawkins.*

*So, if you will excuse me, my dear Laura, I'm afraid I
mustn't dwell any longer on this wretched computer as I
have a lovely young lady awaiting me. She truly has no
idea of the fate that awaits her. I will be sad once she is
gone, but I simply can't help myself. In the immortal words
of Aloysius XL Pendergast, "It's a very bad habit, but one I
find hard to break."*

*Sincerely,
Stephen Carlisle.*

CPSIA information can be obtained
at www.ICGtesting.com
Printed in the USA
BVHW051152271122
651727BV00012B/14/J